CHURCH OF THIEVES

CHURCH OF THIEVES TRILOGY: BOOK 1

IQ MALCOLM

To ~~Mikayla~~ Kat,
Welcome to the pinky

Church of Thieves

Cover by Rachel George Illustration

Published by Lost Umbrella Publishing

Platteville, WI, USA

www.iqmalcolm.com

ISBN: 978-1-7326223-9-5

Created with Vellum

For the Tuna Fish Casserole Fairy,

Thank you for making me feel welcomed, and showing me what it means to be a teacher. Although I only had the honor of knowing you for a couple of years, it was enough to change my life. I would say rest in peace, but I know you're having a blast fixing everything with duct tape up there.

NOTE TO READER

Content Warning: This story contains content that may be troubling to some readers. This includes, but is not limited to, depictions of and references to violence, torture, death, sex, and adult language. Please be mindful of these and other possible triggers, and seek assistance if needed.

PROLOGUE: ORA

Mother Sienna was right. Picking someone to rob wasn't as straightforward as it appeared. Well, not for us anyway.

Sometimes I envied the simplicity of the common street thief or San Fernando pickpocket. All they had to do was wander around Arremendia, searching for an opportunity. Our games hadn't been that easy since we were baby-faced acolytes getting trained in the art of thievery.

Simple scores coincide with simple rewards, and our Lord asks for far more than that. Father Ignacio's wine-laden words rattled around my head.

Our legless father was correct. Cuvar's temple and the charity work we provided could not be sustained by robbing the masses. He was the Lord of the Misfortunate after all, and stealing from them would be counterintuitive, to say the least. Instead, we robbed the wealthy, and that took far, far more planning.

A shadow flew across my desk, momentarily shading the scroll I'd been staring at. It had probably been nothing more than a bird flying past my arched stone window, but it still caused me to look up.

From the vantage point of my third-story room, I could see it was the perfect Arremendian late summer day. Blue skies and a smattering of clouds added an extra layer of beauty to our city. Not that it needed the cosmic equivalent of face paint to be beautiful, but I had to appreciate it with the thought of the rainy season only being a few months away.

Ding... dong... ding... dong...

Our temple's bells, and the bells of Arremendia's two other temples, rang to welcome the thirteenth hour of the day. More importantly, it signified the start of our Pozuelo game.

At this very moment, Tallis and the others would be in position near the banks of the Beltza River in the stadium district. Months of planning had revealed that Ianista Pozuelo made an offering to Potami, the river goddess, after every meeting he had at the stadium. Better yet, he took the same back road from the stadium to the temple each time. The poor bastard thought the offerings would make his gladiators perform better in their fights. Little did he know it would actually be the seed of his own undoing.

The tiles had been set. All we had to do now was let Pozuelo knock the first one over and watch the others fall into place. While Tallis, Damiana, and my older brother, Omar, set the game in motion, Mother Sienna assigned me a special task: selecting our next target.

It was an honor for many reasons. The chief among them being that it signified that she was grooming me to become a priestess. Ever since I was ten years old, I wanted to run my own finger because of her. She might have been slight and quiet, but she knew how to dominate a room and command respect with such a level of sophistication that I wouldn't be surprised if she was a deity walking among us.

Now she was training me—me of all people—to replace her. The thought alone made me smile wide enough that it threatened to split my face in two.

Everyone at the temple had expected her to select Tallis as her successor. After all, he was the greatest thief to ooze out of Cuvar's cock in the last thirty years. However, not all great thieves made great fathers, and my friend had his eyes on another position anyway. Although no one outside of our finger knew of his goal to be the next living saint, I was confident Mother Sienna was one of them.

In the end, his wants and my wants didn't matter. Every position within Cuvar's temple, especially positions of power, had to be earned. Mother Sienna had chosen me because of what I had done during my twelve years in the church, and it was time to prove her correct once more.

I brought my focus back to the scrolls in front of me. Over the course of the past week, I had gone from the ten options the priestess gave me down to the final three. Although decisions like this shouldn't be rushed, my gut screamed that I couldn't wait much longer. Making a decision too quickly might have come off as ill-conceived, but taking too long would be equally criticized as it might suggest indecisiveness. I needed to play my hand right. One way or another, I would make my decision today.

Despite having the remaining scrolls nearly memorized, I still opened them.

Option one, Romain Ibarra. Pro, he had acquired a ridiculous amount of money from securing hard-to-find items for his even more obscenely wealthy clients. Con, one of those wealthy clients was the royal family, and robbing the royals was strictly off-limits. Although Ibarra wasn't a noble himself, would his close connection to them cause us more harm than good?

"Ibarra was caught in bed last month with the prince's mistress..." My voice drifted off as I reread the sentence.

That one line added two more pros and one con in my eyes. The obvious negative was that it would be difficult to rob someone if they'd been run out of town. However, that didn't seem likely, as a month had already passed since the incident. The positives were that it gave us an in and also revealed a weakness. Losing a major customer would make him more open to taking on new ones, and sleeping with the prince's mistress was practically the definition of someone who took high risks without thinking them through.

Our second option was Zara Suarez. The recently widowed mark was now the key to the Suarez Shipwright business and their well-known fortune. Pro, there had been multiple reports that Zara and her sons had had many disputes over who should run the family business. A house divided was easier to separate from their funds than a unified front. However, there were two cons in my eyes.

Number one, could I really support the idea of stealing from a woman who was trying to stand up against the patriarchy? Despite our kingdom's advancements, there was no denying we still lived in a man's world. She had helped to build the family business and was now in a position to lead it. Could I really bring myself to ruin that for her?

Con number two, the Suarez shipyard had been influential in setting up Arremendia as a naval and trading powerhouse, which in turn led to a boom in the city's economy. Would robbing this family destroy the company and, in turn, hurt the city as a whole?

I brushed the fly away from the third scroll, causing the

little nuisance to buzz around my head for a moment before flying out the window.

Option three, Hans Becker, a representative of the Havertzian Brewing Company. He had been traveling to Arremendia sporadically over the past few months, looking for a way to bring the company into our empire to expand their market.

Pro, no one would bat an eye at us stealing from the foreign brewers. Con, his travels to the city hadn't been on a set schedule and would make planning difficult. Pro, all the members of our finger would enjoy the opportunity to savor fancy foreign beer. Con, we would need to forge a lot of paperwork to make it appear as though we had real estate options for them to build their brewery. Pro, stealing from them might persuade the Havertzians to not try to enter our marketplace, and that would be to the benefit of all our local breweries and spirit providers.

Out of my three remaining choices, there was really only one that I didn't like. I placed the Suarez scroll with the other discarded options. It looked as though our widow wouldn't have to add us to the list of her growing problems.

As my brother would say, the time had come to either shit or get off the pot. It wasn't one of his more elegant colloquialisms—to be fair, nothing he said could truly be described as elegant—but it did ring true for my circumstance. I slipped the Ibarra scroll into the hidden pocket inside my hideous white acolyte's robe.

Okay, maybe hideous was the wrong word for it. The thick, coarse robes were unflattering, to say the least. Not only did they manage to hide every curve, but the material also retained so much heat in the summer that it felt as though you were walking around in your own Balish sauna.

"They're not supposed to be pretty," Mother Sienna had

told me time and time again growing up. "We need you to look ordinary in those robes so that the whole world looks past you. If we made ourselves appear desirable, then people would pay us too much attention to complete our Lord's work."

She had a point, and like most of her points, this one still rang true. Hopefully, the scroll in my pockets would take me one step closer to the more flattering, breathable, crimson robes of motherhood.

I left my chambers and made my way to our temple's adjoining school. Mother Sienna's lessons on false facing always took place after lunch and should have been on the verge of ending. Her classroom seemed far too quiet as I approached its door, and the reason for the silence became apparent the second it swung inward.

"Oh, Ora," said Father Roberto in his standard drawn-out, righteous tone. "I know you could use some more arithmetic lessons, but I take it that is not the reason why you have interrupted my students' test."

I peered past him to find three prepubescent acolytes staring down helplessly at their papyrus scrolls. A shiver went down my spine at the memory of his horrid exams.

"Apologies, Father," I said, swallowing the thousands of insults that balanced on the tip of my tongue. As much as I wanted to unleash them upon him, I restrained myself. If I wanted to be a mother, then I had to prove to all of them that I was capable of playing the game. "I had no intention of interrupting your test. In fact, I was trying to catch Mother Sienna. This is usually the end of her class time. You wouldn't happen to know where she is?"

The raised bushy eyebrow and the wry grin he offered only served to confuse me further.

"Haven't you heard?" he asked in a hushed tone as he

leaned forward. The scent of sausages and apples clung to his breath.

"Heard what?"

"Your dearest mother canceled her class because of a surprise visit from one of our royal patrons who wanted an audience with her."

I gulped. Why would a member of the royal family wish to meet with her? It appeared as though we would have more to talk about than my simple selection.

"Thank you, Father Roberto," I said and turned to leave.

He started to speak but stopped himself before it formed any recognizable word.

I paused and shifted my posture in an attempt to make it scream *what is it?*

"If your matter with her is urgent," the aging priest said, "then you can always wait for her at her chambers. Royal visits, although rare outside of official ceremonies, seldom take longer than our classes."

After thanking the father once more, I made my way back to our quarters through the courtyard. Although I should have continued prepping my presentation, the only thing my mind wanted to focus on was why a member of the royal family wanted to see her. However, none of the scenarios I imagined felt right.

Instead of taking the stairs up to my third-story room, I headed toward the priestess's chamber, which was on the main level.

My hidden scroll brushed against my side, prompting a thought that brought a smile to my face. *One day, I'll live in one of these luxury downstairs chambers, and I'll never have to climb those dastardly stairs ever again.*

Was it the best motivation for motherhood? No. But

anything that pushed you farther along the right path was a good thing, right?

I felt my smile grow wider as I reached out to knock on the priestess's door.

Crash!

The sound of shattering glass made me freeze in place. For a split second, I doubted whether the noise had been real. I snuck a glance over my shoulder to find... nothing. The floor seemed eerily quiet. *Where is everyone?*

The question snapped me back to my senses. If something had gone wrong, then I was the only one who would be able to do something about it.

"Is everything all right?" I asked after knocking on the door.

No one replied.

I took a steadying breath and opened it. "Mother Si—"

Her name snagged in my throat.

The priestess lay face-first on the ground in a rapidly growing pool of her own blood.

I cried her name once more and sprinted toward her. A curse escaped my lips as I dropped to my knees. The floor surrounding her was littered with shards of glass from her now broken tea table, and some of them pierced my shins.

"This can't be happening. This can't be happening," I said over and over again as my mind struggled to block the pain radiating up from my legs.

My wounds could be licked later. The only thing that mattered at that moment was preventing Mother Sienna from dying. I needed to stop the bleeding. She had saved my brother and me from slavery, raised us as her own, and given me purpose. I would be damned to see the gods try to take her from me.

In dire need of cloth, I tore a strip out of the priestess's silk night-robe. Despite my confusion as to why she wore it, the material was far easier to rip than her standard temple robe.

"Please!" I yelled as I rolled my teacher, my savior, my chosen mother, onto her back. "Someone he—"

For the second time, my voice failed me.

My blood-soaked hands flew to my mouth, enveloping it in the taste of copper. I knew the wound had to be bad for her to bleed this profusely, but my mind couldn't grasp the sight before me. Someone had slit the priestess's throat from ear to ear.

Tears burst from me like a breached dam as I sank my face into her bloodied chest. "No no no."

Footsteps thudded against the stone behind me. Someone must have heard my cries and came to help.

I couldn't have been more wrong.

Before I could brush my blood-coated hair that blocked part of my vision, something struck me in the head.

Don't worry, Mother, I thought as the blow knocked me onto my back. *I'll see you soon.*

1

TALLIS

My lungs screamed for air as the man I called my brother sank his fingers deeper into my neck. A hint of malice gleamed in his brown eyes as the rough stone of the alley wall tore into my back.

The moment spots of black began to seep into my vision, I tapped him on the arm.

Omar dropped me like a sack of spoiled vegetables. "How was that? Do you think Pozuelo will buy it?"

"You are being far too delicate," I wheezed as I pushed myself back onto my feet. "I've had barmaids choke me harder than that."

My friend's laugh chimed with the temple bells in the distance. The thirteenth hour was upon us.

"And people say I'm the sick one," Omar said.

My heart rate began to slow once more as I sucked in a few deep breaths. "I think that has to do with the quantity of lovers you take, not what you do with them."

"They should blame the gods then for bestowing me with such looks and the charm to match."

It might have been hard for a passerby to believe him

given his disguise at that moment, but there was some truth to his words. Underneath that bulbous prosthetic nose and heinous face paint hid an attractive man. In fact, both of the Sandoval siblings could be described as being too beautiful for their own good.

"Aye," I said. "Don't forget about the dose of humility they blessed you with as well."

"But of course," he said, patting me on the back. "On a serious note, though. How was that performance? I don't want to rough you up too much, but I also need Pozuelo to believe it."

"Honestly, feel free to go harder."

His falsely thickened eyebrows nearly arched off his brow.

"Seriously," I continued, "as long as you don't break anything, we should be fine. Just aim for my softer sections. You said it yourself, we need to make this believable."

"But—"

"No buts. We could easily take 100,000 crowns off this bowlegged fool. Let's leave nothing to chance."

He flashed me a devilish grin. "If you insist. Just remember that you asked for this, so don't go crying to Mother Sienna after I beat your ass."

That only happened one time, and we were eleven. As much as I wanted to tell him where he should shove his remark, we needed to focus on the task at hand. The Ianista and his doctore, Basilius, would be walking past our alley at any moment. We needed to be ready.

A stone clattered to the ground only a few feet from where we stood.

Was that the signal?

I looked up to find Damiana's cloaked head peering over the side of the rooftop above.

They're coming, she signed before disappearing from sight. Pozuelo and his dutiful servant had entered the side street. Our game would begin in less than a minute.

"You ready?" whispered Omar.

I nodded. "Do your best to choke me harder than your sister does."

It was a low blow for many reasons. For starters, it was a blatant falsehood as Ora and I had never been together, and we never would be. Although the feelings she had for me since childhood had never been much of a secret, a plethora of things made sure it never grew from there.

Based on the fury that flickered in his eyes, my cheap shot prompted the response I desired. He was a good student of all our trades but a master of none. I needed him to be better than good today, and if that took some provocation, then so be it.

His fist flew into my gut, robbing me of all my breath.

"Listen here, you Gregusian piece of shit," Omar said, slamming me against the alley wall. "I'm not going to ask again. Where the fuck is the rest of your money?"

"I don't know what you mean," I said. The words came out fragile and wobbled like a Destian dancer.

His backhand landed hard and true. "Don't lie to me. I'm only going to ask you one more time before the real fun begins."

He unsheathed his knife. The sharpness of the sound sliced the alley.

"What in Potami's name is going on down there?" boomed a new voice.

About time, I thought as I cracked the blood capsule in my mouth with my molars. The taste of copper didn't last long as Omar kneed me in the balls with such ferocity that I felt our new onlookers flinch.

I spat out the contents as I collapsed to the cobblestone.

"It's none of your bloody business," Omar said, turning his blade toward them. "That's what it is."

As I writhed in pain, I caught a glimpse of the two men who walked toward us slowly. Pozuelo's silver silk tunic fell past his disfigured knees and was embroidered with enough gold to catch a dragon's attention. Basilius, on the other hand, wore much simpler garb than his master. The cloth barely covered the boulder-esque physique that propelled him to victory upon victory on the gladiatorial sands.

"Basilius, do my eyes deceive me, or is that man threatening my life with his sad excuse for a dagger?"

The former champion nodded. "Aye, master, I believe he has." His voice sounded like it had been cut from the same stone as the rest of his body.

"Come any closer, and I'll make good on that threat," said Omar.

Basilius cracked a smile. "I'd like to see you try."

As soon as the last word left the doctore's lips, his sword had been drawn. The long, curved blade had ended more than its fair share of lives, and I swore I heard it thirst for another soul as he spun it in his hands.

I was not sure if Omar actually shit his pants. However, the alley had smelled far cleaner a moment ago.

Without saying a word, my brother turned and sprinted toward the wall at the back of the alley. The former gladiator flew after him.

Pozuelo crouched down beside me. "Are you all right, good sir?"

I groaned as I tried to push myself back onto my feet. "I have been better, but I would be far worse if not for you. Who do I have the honor of thanking?"

The Ianista pursed his lips. Although he did not utter his question, it was written on his forehead for all to see. *What is a Gregusian doing in an Arremendian alley?* It looked as though my years of perfecting the accent were about to pay off.

"Apologies, master," said the doctore. "The bastard got away."

"Got away?" asked Pozuelo.

Basilius held up a section of severed rope before tossing it aside. "It looks as though the mouthy shit either lures people here regularly or has been targeting this one for quite some time."

Both of their eyes fell upon me as they weighed their odds.

"Well, we can rule out the latter," I said with the softened consonants of the Gregusian accent. "No one knows I am here except for my master, and he would not jeopardize his own cause as this business venture is as secret as it is urgent."

My words lay before him like a snare. All I needed him to do was nibble at the bait.

"I owe you more than you could imagine," I continued. "For you saved my master both his reputation and his chance to maintain his fortune. I don't know how we can begin to repay you."

The Ianista's lips curled into a smile. Apparently, he could think of a multitude of ways I could repay him.

"Tell me, Master..." Basilius's words hung in the air as he awaited my answer.

"Master Pierre LeBlanc," I said, removing my beret to enhance my grand, sweeping bow. "At your service."

The Ianista seemed satisfied with my answer, but his doctore plowed ahead. "Master LeBlanc, what is a Gregusian servant on an urgent business venture doing in the back alley of our city?"

His sudden ownership of the city was interesting to say the least as the former champion was originally a slave taken from a nomadic tribe on the Samda Peninsula half a world away. Nonetheless, it was a fair question.

Pain in my lower abdomen prevented me from standing completely upright. I would have crumpled back to the ground if not for the grip of my left hand against the alley wall. Maybe next time I would think twice before aggravating Omar.

"I can assure you that I had no intentions of being in this alley," I said. "But life seldom works as we intend, does it not?"

"Your words certainly ring true," said Pozuelo.

It was no surprise that he echoed my sentiments. Life had thwarted his intentions time and time again. Whether it was the gods who disfigured him, the father who wanted to kill him, or his dream of running the greatest gladiatorial house in all of Yenra but constantly falling agonizingly short, the man knew what it meant to scratch and claw for everything in this world. He also understood what it felt like for life to take it away. Unfortunately for him, we represented life, and it would bend him over the table once more.

"However," Pozuelo continued, "my doctore raises a valid point. If I allowed any of my servants to do business on my behalf, then I wouldn't send them to the other side of the continent without any belongings or proof of my desires."

I smiled through the pain. "Clearly, like my master, you are also no fool as he sent me with even more than what you listed."

The Ianista nodded his agreement.

"The belongings I've been granted for this matter are being brought to the Vesga as we speak," I continued. "Evidence supporting his business can not only be found in those belongings but on me as well. Lastly, my master secured a guard for my safe passage to the stadium."

Basilius loosed a deep laugh. "Not to speak ill of your master, but he must have hired poorly if your guard abandoned you here."

My shoulders slumped. "That is my fault, not his. Everything else has gone according to plan except for the guard. When he didn't show, I hired the man you chased away to bring me to the stadium. Fortunately, he didn't find the only thing of value on me."

I reached inside my tunic and pulled out a small black velvet pouch. A gold cursive "M" had been embroidered into the bag, and the letter was partially encircled by a bright-green line.

Pozuelo gasped as the bag wriggled in my hand. "That's... you serve the Magnificent Master Mosley?"

"The one and only," I said while I opened the bag and tilted it toward my palm.

A clear glass hoof stepped onto my palm, and a second later, the rest of the creature revealed itself. The trinket of the funny-shaped horse with its two spiraling horns was no bigger than two inches. While part of its body had been made from clear glass, the rest of it was covered in swirls of blue and yellow glass with the occasional blot of milky white.

"My master told me they call this creature an antelope in his world," I said as the trinket trotted cautiously around my palm before sitting at its center.

It had been the only true thing I had told him at that point. The Magnificent Master Mosley—a rather cocksure name to give oneself in my humble opinion—told me the story minutes before I stole the piece from his shop. Out of all the pieces I had stolen from my six-month training in Molino, it had been my favorite.

"What is this darkness?" asked Basilius.

I fought to keep the smile off my face. In a world that had been devoid of magic since the end of the Age of the Gods, "darkness" was one of many words to describe both the glassblower's mysterious arrival on our planet and his creations.

"Hold your tongue," the Ianista said. His words were sharper than his doctore's sword. "This is a living art."

The tension etched into the former gladiator's brow reduced into mere concern. However, the man was too well trained to voice it.

"May I?" asked Pozuelo, cupping his hands and raising them to my own.

With the slightest tilt of my hand, the miniature glass beast trotted down my fingers and into his waiting hands. "But of course."

Joy rippled across his face like a child on San Giovanni's Day. With all the bursts of nervous excitement that escaped his lips, one would have thought that I cured his leg instead of letting him hold an expensive trinket.

"We ought to rescue foreigners more often," the Ianista said as he spared a glance toward his servant. "Who would have ever thought a dream of mine could come true in an alleyway? I can't believe this is happening."

Basilius grunted. "That is the nature of miracles, Master. They tend to happen when we least expect them."

It was difficult to tell if he was being facetious or genuine, but I wasn't about to stab myself in the foot in an attempt to find out.

"That's it," I said, excitedly shaking my right hand with its thumb and pinky extended. It was a common gesture in the Gregusian Empire for having an idea. "I don't have much that I can repay you with for saving my life, but you can keep Nia once I am done meeting with Ianista Gutierrez. She was part of the proof I was telling you about, and she can remain your miracle afterwards."

The delight which radiated from Pozuelo's body vanished in a heartbeat. A single mention of Gael Gutierrez's name was all it took for our mark to look physically sick.

"My apologies," I stammered with all the sincerity I could muster. "I thought the gesture would please you, but I have clearly erred and made some offense."

"Fear not, Master LeBlanc, your thoughtful gesture was more than courteous," said the doctore while his master dropped Nia back into my waiting hands with all the coldness of a lover scorned. "It is the man you seek to do business with that displeases him."

I furrowed my brow and cocked my head ever so slightly. "Ianista Gutierrez?"

"Yes," Pozuelo seethed. "The bastard has cheated me on the sands and off them as well. When his life is snuffed out, not even Potami will be willing to carry that vermin's soul down the Beltza River. He'll be cursed to walk the world for all eternity. What in all that is holy would your master want to work with him for?"

There was no need to feign the shock that rolled across my face. I knew that he and Gutierrez were more than bitter rivals, but I had not expected him to react this harshly to the idea of Mosley doing business with him.

I held up my hands to declare my innocence. "Forgive me, Master..."

It was now my turn to wait for his name. However, it ended up being his doctore who gave it to me. “You have the honor of addressing Ianista Hector Pozuelo, the Defier of Blood and Forger of Panthers.”

Ah yes, his self-appointed title. The panther part didn’t bug me as his gladiators were known as the Panthers of Pozuelo. The “Defier” bit, however, felt a bit over the top.

“My apologies, Ianista Pozuelo,” I said. “I mean no offense, but my master's business is a private matter. As such, I cannot go into great detail at this time.”

A bead of sweat rolled down my back. The game teetered on the edge of oblivion, and I had to play this just right.

“My master is unaware that Gutierrez is a man of iniquitous character,” I continued. “His interest in him as a partner was one of practicality. Again, for reasons I can't go into, he is seeking a partner in Arremendia of great means and possesses property that can be guarded by highly trained, loyal men.”

I paused before casting my next line of bait. “If you know of any such men, then please usher me to them. Time is of the essence.”

My breath caught in my throat. This was the moment everything hinged on. If Mother Sienna’s birds were correct, we could take this man for around 100,000 crowns, bringing me 100,000 crowns closer to my freedom. The thought alone was enough to send a shiver down my spine.

A light twinkled behind Pozuelo's eyes, and I knew we had him.

“I know just the man,” he declared with all the excitement of a man who mistook the noose around his throat for a necklace. “I will need a day to get everything in order.”

"Are you sure?" I asked. "I don't want you to feel obligated—"

The Ianista cut me off with a wave of his hand. "Nonsense, I do not see obligation. I see an opportunity to both enrich myself and foil my rival. Come." He wrapped his arm around me and led me out of the alley. "Our business shouldn't take place here. Join me for lunch tomorrow at my villa, and we shall discuss our future endeavors."

Pozuelo played tour guide as he, and his doctore, guided me across my city to "Pierre's" hotel. Our mark showered me with facts I had already learned a thousand times over until we finally reached the Vesga's lift.

Mother Sienna had selected the mountainside hotel as my character's temporary residence.

Between its location being a few hundred feet above the rest of the city and its exclusivity, it made it difficult for anyone to spy on us. If anyone were to try it, then they'd most likely keep an eye on the hotel's three lifts. They were the only entry and exit points that the public was aware of, after all.

"Until tomorrow, Master LeBlanc," Pozuelo called as my lift began its slow ascent.

As I echoed his farewell, it should have been a moment to celebrate. However, my evening was only about to begin. Mother Sienna had an important recruiting mission that she could no longer make due to an unexpected royal visit, and she entrusted me to meet the potential new acolyte.

The work of a holy thief is never finished, I thought as Arremendia shrank beneath my feet.

2

NEREA

Wait for my line. Pull the lever.

They were the only jobs I had remaining in tonight's rendition of *The Tragedy of Leojung*. Although I wasn't usually tasked with making sure my props worked during the play, with Raul being too drunk to pitch in, I got the honor of pulling double duty.

I didn't know what gave away my boss's presence first: the stench of tobacco or the weight of his eyes as they fixated on my backside.

Because he couldn't see my face, I loosed an eye roll. "Yes, Julio?"

My whisper cut through the air. Hopefully, I laced it with enough bite for him to register my displeasure at his presence. Telling a man off, especially the man in control of your livelihood, was a balancing act. As sad as it was to admit, history proved that the greatest danger women faced were men who felt wronged.

Applause erupted from the audience as the scene ended and the crew rushed to change the scenery. Ivan, the actor playing Leojung, flashed me a thumbs-up to symbolize the cord was set.

Once I pulled the lever, the cord would send the table it was attached to flying toward us. This retractable pulley system was only one of my many inventions that revolutionized the effects used in the De La Fuentes Theater Company's productions.

"I wanted to make sure you are ready and know your cue," he said as he placed his hand on the small of my back.

My skin crawled at his touch. He wasn't here for that, and we both knew it.

"It would be a lot easier for me to focus on my cue if my mind wasn't preoccupied with the thought of cutting off your hand and shoving it so far up your ass that you tickle the inside of your rib cage with every step you take."

There was that balancing act I was talking about. I think I nailed it, didn't I?

His hand left my back in an instant, and I turned around to find him slack-jawed.

"Now—"

"Nerea," Simone called before I could give Julio another piece of my mind. "The latch to my harness is missing! We need to fix it before my next scene."

"Duty calls," I said, turning my attention back to my boss. "Can you handle pulling this lever?"

For the first time in my two years of knowing him, Julio shut his mouth. He nodded.

"'I am the messenger of the gods. Who are you to question me?'" I said as I patted his bony chest. "It's your cue. I just want to make sure you're ready."

With those parting words, I followed the panicking actress away from the stage and into the bowels of the Maternity Theater.

Although its true name was the Penelope Theater, no one, including the queen it was named after, called it that. The former temple-turned-theater's nickname was derived from the hundreds of sculptures of nude, pregnant women that were carved into the entirety of the upper portion of the building's exterior.

"All right," I said as we entered the closet they called my workshop. "Let's see how bad it is."

As I started to comb the mental list of tools I could use to fix the harness, Simone arched one of her painted-on eyebrows. "Wow, you fell for that?"

Fell for what? I thought.

"Well if I fooled you, then we don't have to worry about Julio realizing the truth," she continued. "Sorry, sometimes I forget how good at this acting thing I really am."

Before I could spit out my question, she spun around, sending her costume's blue skirt twirling in her wake. "See, the latch is still there."

"Why?" I asked as I ran my fingers over my shaved head.

It wasn't the most eloquent question I had ever asked, but it was all I could muster in the moment.

"I believe what you mean to say is 'Thank you for getting me away from Julio and saving my job at the same time.'" Simone winked. "And you're welcome, by the way."

I scoffed. "Please, I had it completely under control."

Disbelief was etched into her saucer-esque eyes.

"I'm serious," I continued. "Apparently, my rejection was too subtle for him last time, and because of that, he left me no other choice."

"Your only choice was to threaten him? That's insane. You need to be more careful than that."

Simone rattled off more sage advice, but I tuned out. All I wanted to do was ask why I had to be the careful one. Why couldn't it be that Julio should be careful around me? However, I knew the answer to those questions. Those who held power never had to heed the powerless. It was our duty to avoid being destroyed by their wake.

Between fleeing from a war-torn Binsoro, surviving in refugee camp after refugee camp before being allowed to live in San Fernando, and all the struggles that came with it, life had thoroughly taught me the consequences of power dynamics.

"I hate to say it," Simone said, "but it's the reality of our world. You're a woman, a person of color, and a foreigner. Regardless of your talents, there aren't many jobs available in this city for people like you, and the last thing I want to see is your pretty face on the street. You need to be more careful."

As much as she hated to say it, I equally hated having to acknowledge the truth of her words. My existence felt like it had been held together by a fraying thread. Losing this job could be the action that finally severed it. The last thing I needed my mother to witness, especially in her final days, was me having to scrape together a living from the street.

I took a deep breath before nodding. "You're right. I'll be sure to be caref—"

A shriek ripped through the air. Before I could fully register the noise, we were sprinting back toward the Maternity's stage.

My heart raced as memories of my village burning filled my mind. The screams from that night had formed the chorus of my nightmares, and this new howl of pain felt designed to join my haunting harmony.

We found the source of the commotion just offstage right next to my lever. A small crowd of stagehands and actors surrounded Luna. The chorus girl, who was also an understudy for a few characters, cradled her mangled leg as she cried.

"What happened?" I asked Ivan.

Someone burst up from the crowd around Luna. No, not someone, it was Julio. His normal olive complexion had morphed to a deep red, and his eyes bulged from their sockets. "I'll tell you what happened. Your machine broke. It launched the table early and nearly killed her!"

That wasn't possible. If it broke, then the table wouldn't have moved. It could only move if someone pulled the lever or physically removed the release.

"You're fired, Nerea," he said. Each of his words dripped with venom. "I can't risk your contraptions hurting anyone else."

Realization bit me like a viper. "You did this."

Julio had been walking away, but my words stopped him in his tracks. "What?" He slowly spun around to face me.

"That's not how this thing works," I said, pointing at the lever. "The cord can't recoil unless the lever is pulled."

Julio's eyes widened, and his nostrils flared. They were the only indications of guilt I needed to cement my theory in my head.

"Why did you pull the lever early?" I asked.

I felt the weight of everyone's eyes offstage as they shifted back and forth between the two of us.

"I, ugh," he stammered as his hands gesticulated wildly. "That is preposterous. What are you suggesting?"

My hand shook as I struggled to remain calm. "I'm not suggesting anything. You were clearly so hurt by yet another one of my rejections that you decided you needed a reason to fire me."

The accident's awe must have worn off because the murmuring of the crowd behind the curtain intensified.

"You saw that Luna was in the way and thought it would give you extra justification to let me go," I said, my voice rising with the crowd. "That's why you pulled the lever, you pathetic little shit of a man!"

Julio bared his stained yellow teeth. "I am going to settle down the audience. If you are not gone by the time I return, I'll have the blackcoats drag you out of my theater and have you arrested for trespassing." He chuckled to himself. "Who knows, they might be able to loosen you up a bit on your way to the dungeons."

I took a step toward him, but Ivan caught me by the shoulder. It was probably for the best as I was prepared to claw Julio's stupid smirk off his face.

"He's not worth it," Ivan whispered as Julio walked away. "I'll help you gather your stuff."

It was a kind gesture but a pointless one nonetheless. I had nothing to gather. Everything in my workshop belonged to Julio's theater company. The only thing left for me to do was to leave and figure out what in the world I could do next.

My mind rattled through different possibilities as I stepped out into the warm Arremendia summer night. Maybe I could make trinkets to peddle on the streets? It wouldn't make us that much money, but it would be better than selling my body or selling my inventions to one of my neighborhood's gangs.

My shoes clicked on the cobblestone as I hurried to the river walk. Our run-down apartment was about a fifteen-minute walk away, and the faster I got there, the better. I was beyond ready to put this day behind me.

"Excuse me, Ms. Zabala," a man called from behind.

It wasn't the silkiness of the stranger's voice that caused me to freeze but rather his use of my last name. My former colleagues had only known my first name, and I wasn't really on speaking terms with anyone in my building outside of my mother. For my family's name to stumble out of this man's lips was either a mistake or a mystery I needed to solve.

I cautiously peeked over my shoulder to see who was talking. My breath caught in my throat. Was the moonlight playing tricks on my eyes or was the most attractive priest I had ever seen in my life really trying to get my attention?

The question raised a swarm of red flags in my mind. This was most likely a trap. Trying not to give away my plan, I searched for anything in my possession that I could use as a potential weapon. I might not be able to do a lot of damage to him, but if I could mess up his perfectly squared jaw or one of his forest-green eyes in my escape, then that would make for a bit of consolation.

"Excuse me, Ms. Zabala," said the fake priest. He signaled for me to wait with his outstretched hand when he saw that I noticed him. "I'm sorry. I didn't mean to startle you. I come bearing urgent news regarding your mother."

The sincerity in his voice gave me a reason to pause my subtle search for a makeshift weapon. Could he have been a priest after all? I spun to face him.

My first instinct still stood firm. Religious leaders didn't look like him. Besides his chiseled jaw and stunning green eyes, he also had smooth olive skin and shiny black curls that refused to remain hidden under his flat white beret.

"And you are?" I asked.

He cracked a smile that would have broken hearts if he had chosen any other profession. "Apologies, my name is Brother Tallis, and I am an acolyte of the Lord Cuvar. You and your mother met with my priestess, Mother Sienna, a few weeks ago."

I let out a low "ah" as the puzzle began to sort itself out in my mind. How I hadn't registered the large, embroidered symbol on his robe was beyond me. One look at Cuvar's overlapping hands should have been enough to inform me of which church he served. Besides that, I should have also recognized he was far too young to be a priest. If he was older than me, then it could have only been by a year or two.

"She wanted to speak to you herself," the acolyte continued, "but she was called away on royal business. So she asked me to speak with you on her behalf."

My brow furrowed as I replayed my previous conversation with the priestess. I hadn't wanted to go to the temple in the first place, but like the stubborn lioness she was, Mother had insisted that I bring her.

"I've prayed to all our gods, and they have stopped answering," she had said. "Maybe a god from this land will hear me better."

As foolish as I found her belief in the gods, the truth was that I would do anything for that woman. She had carried me through more than any mother should, and what was her reward? To get sick and wither into a shell of herself? If asking a foreign god for a miracle eased her mind, then who was I to deny her?

"And how did you get so lucky?" I asked.

He smirked again, revealing a single dimple on his left cheek. "The Lord works in mysterious ways."

That he certainly does, I thought to myself as I turned and motioned him to walk with me. "What urgent news did Mother Sienna wish for me to pass on to my mother?"

Brother Tallis let out a soft laugh.

Heat rushed to my face. Whether it was out of embarrassment or anger, I wasn't entirely sure. "What?"

"Sorry," he said, recomposing himself. "The news isn't *for* your mother. Rather, it is *about* her."

My eyebrow arched. "There's no need to apologize. Just get on with it."

A nearby pigeon cooed its agreement.

The sound reminded me why this was one of my favorite places in the ancient city. Not only did it provide scenic views of our mountain-shrouded paradise, it also provided a sense of calm that the rest of the city sorely lacked. Even the pigeons, who would normally try to steal every unguarded scrap of food you possessed, merely offered you their opinions in this hallowed space.

"Of course, my apol—" The acolyte cut himself off before he could apologize again. "Mother Sienna promised you that if there was anything else we could do for your mother, then she would let you know. There's been a recent opening among Potami's healers, and she was able to secure the place for your mother."

An explosion of joy ripped through my chest. The Goddess of the River's temple had the best doctors in the city. Mother's recovery would still be a long shot, but at least they could make her final days more bearable.

The feeling dispersed as quickly as it had appeared. Miracles weren't real. Everything in life had a catch, especially when it felt too good to be true. So what was the catch here?

"And what will this cost me?" I asked. "Surely Arremendia's most prestigious doctors are not cheap."

Brother Tallis offered me his hand as we climbed the steps to one of the many bridges that crossed the Beltza River. I promptly turned it down.

"My priestess has become an admirer of your inventive mind, and she believes your creations could help secure funding for our temple and its endeavors," said the acolyte. "In exchange for securing your mother's medical needs, all she asked in return is that you work for the church as an inventor."

A smile crept across my face. Despite tonight's earlier disaster, it felt like things were looking up for me for the first time in years. I was on the verge of securing both the help that my mother desperately needed and a job that would allow me to do what I enjoyed the most in this life.

"To be clear," Brother Tallis said as the moonlight captured the entirety of his face, "in order to work at the temple, you would need to become an acolyte. It's honestly not that big of a deal. I just didn't want it to come as a shock to you later."

As much as I appreciated his honesty, it cast some doubt in my mind. "If that's the case, then you ought to know now that I don't believe in the gods. Is that a deal breaker?"

He flashed another of his single-dimpled grins. "Can I trust you with a secret?"

If he kept looking at me like that, then he could trust me with just about anything. "Of course."

"I don't believe in the gods either."

The surprise on my face must have been palpable as he immediately plowed forward.

"I know, I know, I know. How can one serve a god he doesn't believe in? How I came to work for Cuvar is a long story for another day, but I'll continue to serve him for the rest of my days because I get to do the thing I love the most for a living. Not many people get to say that."

We continued to talk about the church, my potential role, and life in general as we walked the rest of the way to my apartment.

"Well, this is me," I said once we finally reached my derelict building.

He halted alongside me. "Very well. Before I go, I want you to know that there's no need to rush your decision. Whenever you decide, come to the temple and let us know."

I thanked him for the opportunity and exchanged pleasantries before saying goodbye. However, as I went to unlock the front door, a thought struck me. I already knew my answer, so what was the point in waiting?

"Brother Tallis," I called out.

His moving outline froze on the street momentarily before walking back to my building. "Yes, Ms. Zabala?"

"Tell your priestess that I accept her offer and that I look forward to working with all of you."

The acolyte's eyes glimmered with the promise of what was to come. "We'll send for you on the morrow, then."

Without saying another word, he disappeared into the night.

3

TALLIS

I could practically taste the celebratory beers as I took the temple steps two at a time. Today went better than we expected. Not only did we have Pozuelo eating out of the palm of our hands, but the prospect Mother Sienna had been raving about agreed to join our order far sooner than any of us had anticipated. All that was left to do now was to celebrate our achievements accordingly.

"Don't give me a maiden, don't give me a maiden," I sang softly to myself as I reached the temple doors.

The ode to experienced lovers was one of Omar's favorite pub songs at the moment. We were only a few minutes away from the three of us slipping off to the bars to sing at the top of our lungs. Who knew, maybe even Ora would remove her self-imposed shackles and come have fun with us.

The tune died on my lips momentarily when I went to open the door only to find it locked. I shrugged and pulled the lockpicks from my sleeve. Although the doors were not usually locked at this hour, it wasn't entirely uncommon either.

I hummed the cheery melody as I went to work on the lock. The door unlocked as I reached the chorus. Naturally, I belted it out as I pulled the door open.

"I don't want a maiden. I don't want a maiden." I quickly spun around to close the door behind me and began to relock it. "I'm not here to teach. I want to be ladened with pleasures, with pleasures, with pleasures galore. To me they're all saints." The lock clicked back into place, and I began to turn around. "Don't you dare call them whor—"

The song caught in my throat at the sight of a sea of disgusted eyes staring at me. They belonged to almost the entirety of our church, and they were all dressed in black. A wave of heat flooded my cheeks as realization dawned on me.

Someone had died today, and this was the first night of their funeral rites.

"Shit," I murmured to myself before catching Father Roberto's eyes. "Sorry, terribly sorry. I'll stand over here and shut up."

Father Roberto stared at me with the same scorn he normally reserved for Ora after thwarting his attempts to make her fail his math exams. Was this how she felt in his class? Probably not. The disdain from the rest of our order seemed to intensify the feeling in a way the priest's bushy eyebrows couldn't convey by themselves.

"Thank you for honoring her with that moment of silence," Father Roberto said, shifting his gaze from me and continuing on with the ceremony. "Let us sing tonight's final hymn, *Blessed Be the Thief*."

The ethereal song rang out low and true as the scent of melting wax filled the air. A swift glance to my right confirmed that the first few candles had been lit, and soon, an acolyte from the other aisle would walk over to spread the flame to my nonexistent candle. The looping melody would continue until the flame reached Father Roberto's candle.

Cuvar's cock, I cursed internally. Given my previous gaffe, I couldn't afford to be the reason this procession halted again. Where in the world were the bloody candles?

"Ow." I bit my tongue to quiet the pain.

A sharp elbow had not-so-delicately nudged my rib cage. I looked down to discover its owner was a redheaded acolyte who couldn't have been more than eleven. Her face was smattered with freckles, and her features appeared to be as pointy as her elbows.

"You can have mine," she said as she raised her unlit candle. "It's only right, seeing as you knew her better than I did. I'll go find another."

Although my mouth thanked the young acolyte, my mind remained transfixed on her words. Who the fuck had died? My heart raced as I scanned the black-clad figures before me for anyone I recognized.

The most obvious absence was that of Mother Sienna. As one of the five priests and priestesses of Cuvar's temple, she should have been on the altar alongside Father Roberto, Father Ignacio, Father Sebastian, and Father David.

This realization caused my chest to seize. *This can't be happening. Please tell me this isn't happening.*

"Tallis," a boy whispered.

My head snapped to the right to find one of Father David's acolytes trying to get my attention. The pimple-faced boy had come over to light my candle.

"Apologies," I said, grateful for the distraction.

I dipped my candle toward his to accept the flame and proceeded to pass it on to the acolyte's candle to my left.

Even though the act was as simple as it was brief, it was enough to pull me from my panic.

I gave myself the updated task of spotting the rest of the members of our finger. If Mother Sienna had been the one to pass, then they would all be in attendance to honor her.

A smile stretched across my face as I spotted Damiana's hulking frame toward the front of the room. The smile was not for her alone but rather for the fact that she was alone. The Sandoval siblings should have been by her side, but they were nowhere to be seen. I peered around the room to make sure I hadn't missed either Ora or Omar in my haste.

"Praise be Cuvar," I said under my breath before rejoining the song. The Sandovals were not here.

The tension in my shoulders eased as relief coursed through my veins. A small part of me felt ashamed of my body's reaction. Although it wasn't Mother Sienna who had crossed to the other side, another member of our order had died. I needed to show my respect.

After two more rounds of the hymn, the flame finished its sinuous journey to the altar. With his candle lit, Father Roberto raised his flame to the first of the fourteen silver candles that now stood proudly at the temple's heart.

"May her soul's journey begin," the priest announced as the flame caught.

"May Cuvar show her the way," we replied in unison.

We would repeat this ritual every night for the next fourteen days. Assuming the candles were still lit come the fourteenth morning—which they almost always were—then her body would be allowed to float down the Beltza to meet Cuvar's embrace.

With the ritual's final words spoken for the night, the other acolytes began to file out of the sanctuary and toward the dorms.

I decided to hang back and wait for the place to clear out. The priests would most likely be the last to leave, and I wanted to speak with them. If not to find out who had passed then to at least apologize for my uncouth entrance.

A few solemn acolytes made eye contact with me and nodded as they passed. As much as I hoped their silent understanding was for my earlier embarrassment, I couldn't shake the notion that it wasn't the case. My shoulders tensed as Damiana joined the other priest on the altar.

Was it possible that all three of them had died today? It would explain why none of them were here for tonight's ceremony.

No, I thought as I took a step toward the altar, *that can't be possible. Their bodies can't be getting readied in the crypts right now.*

My thought process was shortly affirmed once I recalled Father Roberto's word choice during the ceremony. He had referred to the deceased as her. If I had lost nearly every member of our finger, then he would have used a plural pronoun, right?

"Tallis," Damiana said the moment she spotted me on my way to the altar.

She jogged toward me, and the priest strolled slowly behind her.

My heart sank once more, and I braced myself for the worst. The second I saw our giant's red and puffy eyes, I knew it had to be one of our own who had died.

We had known each other for over fifteen years now. In that time, I had only witnessed her cry once. Even those had been tears of rage as I had accidentally squashed her pet cricket Bartholomew, better known as Sir Barfie III. She had beaten me to a pulp that day. Let's just say that if it turned out that I'd be unable to have kids, my punishment for Sir Barfie III's death would be the reason for it.

“Damiana,” I gasped as she squeezed me into a bear hug. “What in Cuvar's name is going on?”

One of her warm tears fell on my neck as she pulled back slightly from our embrace. “Mother Sienna, she... she was murdered.”

Those three words flattened me like a landslide. They drove the air out of my lungs and robbed my knees of their stability. If Damiana hadn't been holding me, I would've fallen to the floor and remained there until it was time for my soul to travel down the Beltza.

Murdered? I couldn't wrap my mind around the word. All deaths were terrible and always came too soon, especially in the eyes of the deceased's loved ones. It was a reality everyone would have to face one day. But murder?

If death was but a common tax, an expected loss, then murder was a theft which robbed you of everything you held dear and basked in taunting your anguish.

More warm liquid streaked my face, but this time, the tears were my own. How could someone murder my mother? Although she was not the one who birthed me, she had granted me a new life when she’d saved me from the gallows. I might have been a mouthy little shit who had robbed Potami's temple, but I was only eight years old. She had risked everything to save me, and I was nowhere to be found when her life was at stake.

"I know, I know," Damiana said as she patted my back with one of her large, callused hands. "Hopefully, Omar will be back soon with some good news."

I pulled back and wiped my excess snot away with the sleeve of my robe. "Are Ora and him tracking her killer? I noticed neither of them were here tonight."

Our feared warrior sucked in air through her teeth. "No, Omar is watching over Ora's body at Potami's temple."

Just when I thought things couldn't get any worse, life managed to sneak in one more punch to the gut.

"The fathers think she walked in on the murder because she was found unconscious and bloodied in Mother Sienna's chambers," Damiana continued. "They said she still had a pulse when she left, but if she's half the warrior I know she is, then she'll be able to pull through and give us the lead on our mother's killer."

I felt my mouth move, but no words found their way out. What was I supposed to say to that? What was anyone supposed to say?

Although she had sprinkled her news with the thinnest layer of hope, like a poor disguise, it did nothing to cover the truth. This killer, whoever they were, had most likely also taken the life of our sister and left little to no evidence in their wake.

If Cuvar, or any of the other gods for that matter, were real, then this was the time to prove it. Two of his most devout followers—one of whom was a saint, if not by name then by deed alone—had been stolen from this realm. They deserved to be avenged, and I would get it one way or another.

Lord, if you're listening, I thought, praying for only the second time in my life. *Set their killer in my path, and I shall do the rest. I promise.*

"Ah, Tallis," Father Roberto said as he stopped before Damiana and me with Father David by his side.

Despite the somber occasion, I braced myself for his inevitable rebuke regarding my entrance. The curmudgeon had a knack for not letting people forget their mistakes.

"I'm terribly sorry for your loss," he continued. "I hope

you'll choose to honor her memory by working for my finger."

The room spun with his words. I expected his condolences, but it was the last part that was nonsensical. Although I grasped his meaning well enough, it seemed too idiotic to be true, especially given the circumstances.

"Do you mean to split us up?" I asked, shaking my head in disbelief. "Why in Cuvar's name would we do such a thing?"

Father David sent me a glare that made me want to tell him where he could shove our Lord's member.

"My apologies, young Tallis," said Father Roberto, raising his hands to protest his innocence. "Trust me when I tell you that I meant no offense with my remark."

Just like he meant no offense with his condescending young prefect to my name. I had to bite my tongue to keep my eyes from rolling.

"The reason why we think it makes the most sense to disband the remains of Mother Sienna's finger is because she left no successor in her wake," the thumb-shaped priest continued. "Furthermore, three of your four remaining members are only one copper away from moving on from our Lord's temple here in Arremendia. It is just the logical thing to do. Please forgive me for my brashness."

Father Sebastian sent Roberto a sideways glance as he and Father Ignacio joined us. The two of them had been farther back as our thieving master had chosen to accompany our legless priest at his pace.

The moment I registered the annoyance on Father Sebastian's face, everything else clicked into place. This had nothing to do with what made the most sense, just as the physical distance between our temple's priests had had nothing to do with pace. The priestess's death had not only torn my heart asunder, but it had also caused a rift in power.

My savior hadn't even been dead for half a day, and this weasel of a man was already trying to tip the scales in his favor. The realization caused my blood to boil.

"I am neither a child nor a fool, old Father," I said. My voice rasped as I gave up on masking my rage. "I will not stand idly by as you choose to overlook my mother's wishes simply because you wish to secure a majority in the council."

Embers burned in Father Roberto's eyes, but I didn't give a shit.

Father David tried to intervene, and I silenced him with a flick of the wrist.

"For starters, she had named a successor," I continued. "She's been grooming Ora for motherhood."

Father David failed to hide his clenched fists in the sleeves of his robe. "The child is dying. You can't seriously suggest replacing Sienna with someone who is on the verge of joining her on the river."

"That is Mother Sienna to you," I snapped. "Never forget to give her name the respect it deserves."

Damiana cleared her throat. "Speaking of respect, our Lord's laws state that a new leader of a finger is to be chosen by the members of that finger. He says nothing about the other members of his hand getting a say."

I looked at Fathers Ignacio and Sebastian. "Is this true?"

Father Sebastian's face twisted into a grin, revealing a set of ever-deepening smile lines. Out of all of our priests, our middle-aged thieving master was by far the youngest and most reasonable one.

He brushed aside one of his graying curls. "Damiana is correct for the most part, but there is one exception. If the members of a finger cannot come to a decision on who should lead them, then it would be up for the council to decide."

The words were as clinking silvers to my ears.

"Then that settles it," I said. "We will make Ora our new mother. What do we need to do to make this official?"

"This settles nothing," Father Roberto said, making the room shake. Not with his volume but with the malice that dripped off his words. "This bickering is futile. The nominated member of your finger must be physically capable of serving Cuvar in order to be accepted for priesthood. Given her current condition, I doubt she'll be able to meet the requirements in fourteen days' time."

My jaw dropped with such velocity that I was surprised it didn't ricochet off the floor.

"Sadly, there is truth to what he speaks," Father Ignacio said upon noticing my confusion. "The members of the finger have until the day after the deceased's funeral rites have ended to name their next leader."

A question balanced on the tip of my tongue, but Father Roberto jumped in before I could release it.

"You see, all you're doing is delaying the inevitable. Let us not shame Mother Sienna's memory by arguing about this further."

With that, Father Roberto patted me on the shoulder with his sausage fingers and started to walk away. Father David, like the obedient dog he was, followed closely behind him.

Red seeped into my vision as I listened to their footsteps plod farther away. How dare he suggest that *I* brought Mother Sienna's memory shame when he was already plotting how to benefit from her demise? How could he imply that *I* brought her any shame when he was the one who was now hoping her chosen successor would die as well?

Although I had never been fond of the priest, he had never truly disgusted me prior to that moment. If I didn't want to tarnish Mother Sienna's memory, then I had to ensure that he didn't get his way. Hopefully, Ora would not only survive her attack but be able to perform the duties of priesthood in fourteen days' time.

My face tightened into a smile as an idea crossed my mind. It turned out that I had at least one more trick up these overly large sleeves.

"Father Roberto," I called, turning to face him.

The pair of asshats were about twelve strides away from me. Fortunately, this idea had struck me in the nick of time. If it had come a second later, then they would have been out the door.

Our Master of Sums let out a long sigh. "The hour is getting late, Tallis."

"No need to fear, Father. Like your lovemaking in your prime, I promise to keep this quick."

Father Ignacio let out a bark of laughter, but stopped it as abruptly as its start.

"I know you're not a fan of surprises, so I thought I should tell you this now," I continued. "Even if the pinky has to face the devastation of losing two of its beloved members today, we will still not let you get your way."

Father Roberto arched an eyebrow.

"You better go pray for Ora's speedy recovery. Otherwise, you will need to get used to calling me Father Tallis."

Damiana gasped.

The gravity of my words was not lost on her. Priesthood was a position you held for life and one that kept you at the same temple. Since my indoctrination to the Lord, my dream had always been to become Cuvar's living saint, as it would allow me to travel the world stealing in his name. Filling Mother Sienna's shoes would mean giving up on that dream.

Father Roberto's nostrils flared ever so slightly before he bowed his head. "May Cuvar's will be done."

Trust me, I thought as I echoed his sentiments, *I'll make sure of it.*

Without saying another word, the pair of priests stormed out of the temple.

"Well," Damiana said as the doors clattered shut behind them. "That was only a little uncomfortable."

Father Ignacio rolled up to us, and the smell of fresh wine arrived with him. "So is every other conversation with that old tart."

I couldn't help but smile. Sure, Roberto was pushing seventy, but Ignacio was only two years his junior. It seemed a bit like the pan calling the cauldron black.

"Regardless of his unpleasantness," said Father Sebastian, "you would be wise to be cautious with your words around him. He is a dastardly opponent when he doesn't despise you. I can't imagine what lengths he'd be willing to go to to spite someone who embarrassed him."

My nose wrinkled as I tried to decipher his meaning. Was it supposed to be a warning for me, or... had he suggested something darker?

A shiver ran down my spine, and I shook it off. No, Father Roberto may have possessed the personality of a gaping asshole, but I highly doubted he was capable of having another member of this temple, let alone my priestess, assassinated.

"It will be nice to have his ire focused elsewhere," the priest continued. "I owe you a debt."

I leapt at the offer. "If you're serious, I could use four of your best blades to stand guard over Ora tomorrow. We have a game that we'll be wrapping up, and I need Omar's eyes."

"You don't trust me to look out for you now?" Damiana asked.

She tried to play her tone off as mock offense, but the hurt she felt was poorly disguised.

"I'm trusting you with a more important task," I said.

Our fearless warrior perked up at the mention of her touted role.

"We have a new member of the pinky joining us tomorrow, and she's pretty," I continued. "Nerea will need to be shown around and readied for what's to come. The last thing she needs during this transition is Omar drooling all over her."

Damiana nodded. "The poor bastard does drool a lot."

Father Sebastian cleared his throat. "I'm sorry to interrupt your discussion of Omar's medical problem, but how long would you need my blades to stand guard?"

All of tomorrow was the minimum I needed them for, but I wondered if I could milk a little more out of the deal.

"I'd like for them all to stand guard tomorrow from after breakfast until three bells, but we will be stretched thin until after Mother Sienna's funeral rites end. If we had one or two of your blades on call for guard duty through that point, then our finger would certainly remember your kindness when our new priestess is named."

My former thieving instructor stuck out his hand. "Or priest."

The words tied my stomach in knots, but I took his hand nonetheless. "Or priest."

4

NEREA

The world seemed to spin faster beneath my feet with each passing day. How was it possible that we had been in Arremendia for four years when I would have sworn I was only a goofy teen playing in the savanna just a few weeks ago? If I risked a blink in this moment, then where would I be the next time my eyelids opened?

No one ever told us how fast life would pass or how it only sped up with time. Maybe my grandma or one of our village elders had tried to convey it in one of their stories, but I wasn't the best listener as a kid. I was too caught up with creating contraptions to notice it back then. Now... now the passage of time and its changes screamed at me like a petulant child. If only this could be another puzzle capable of being solved.

"What are you thinking about, Rea?" Mother asked.

My shoulders jerked at the sound of her voice. How long had she been awake?

"Come now, child. I'm not so close to death that my presence should startle you like that."

I wished her words were true, but with each week that went by, it looked as though she'd taken another step toward death's door. Her dark skin that used to hold the vibrancy of rich soil had dulled, and every bit of flesh on her body appeared to have sunken into her bones. The only things about her that still felt like my mother were the shine in her brown eyes, the quickness of her mind, and the sharpness of her tongue. They were the only things that provided me with a sliver of hope that this could work. That it wasn't too late.

"You had a way of startling me even when you were the portrait of health," I said with a laugh as I sat beside her at the edge of her bed.

There was a knock on the door, and before I could respond, it squeaked open. One of Potami's acolytes serving as a nurse stepped into the room.

"I'm terribly sorry to intrude," she said, "but one of Cuvar's servants is here to escort you to your new temple."

I struggled not to laugh. Her wording had made it sound like our previous housing situation had been a temple as well. Then there was the other added layer of humor that I, a stout nonbeliever of the gods, was about to become an acolyte to one of them.

My mother took my hand and brought it to her lips. "I know this won't be easy for you, but I want you to know how proud I am of you."

A tear welled in the corner of my eye, and I dabbed it away with my free hand.

"One day you'll look back on this arrangement and realize it was an even bigger blessing for you than it was for me," she said.

I smiled down at her. "I think I'm closer to that realization than you think."

It was the truth. Although I would never be the easy believer she was, I'd have to be devoid of all my senses to not see what a blessing Mother Sienna and the temple had bestowed upon me. Not only were they gracing me with an honorable job, safety, and better living conditions, but they had given me the greatest gift of all: more time with my mother.

After hugging her goodbye, I followed the acolyte outside. Much to my surprise, she didn't lead me to Mother Sienna or Tallis but rather the largest woman I had seen in my entire life.

I had always thought I had been tall at 5'7", but she had a solid half foot on me and looked as sturdy as a toopla tree. The acolyte wore the same white robes as Tallis; however, instead of a beret, she wore crimson ribbons in her intricately braided hair. Well, what hair she had remaining as the sides of her head had been shaved clean.

A smile crossed her face when she caught me looking at her. "You must be Nerea, then. I'm Damiana. It's a pleasure to meet you."

Her voice caught me off guard. Given her size, I expected it to be deeper, almost manlike, but hers possessed the musical quality of a pure alto.

"It's nice to meet you as well," I replied after a pause that lasted a half beat too long. "I'm sorry, please don't take this the wrong way, but I was expecting Mother Sienna or Tallis."

Damiana's smile vanished for an instant before she opened the carriage door. "Things are usually busy whenever a new acolyte comes to the temple, but your decision to join us wasn't the only major occurrence yesterday..." She paused to squint up at the sky as if the right words were among the clouds. "It's something that's easier to talk about in private."

Her demeanor was difficult to read, and it piqued my curiosity. There was a puzzle here that was begging to be solved.

My chauffeur gestured to the open door with one of her large hands. "Shall we?"

There was no sense in delaying the journey any further. I stepped up into the carriage and immediately took the cushioned bench seat that faced forward. In all my life, I had never ridden on a horse—or anything pulled by one for that matter—but the thought of traveling backward sounded like a disaster waiting to happen.

The carriage shifted as Damiana entered but quickly righted itself. She took the seat across from me before knocking on the wall behind her.

My breath hitched as the vehicle lurched forward.

"Don't worry," my soon-to-be fellow acolyte said, smiling past her nose that had clearly been broken on more than one occasion. "You'll eventually get used to it."

The carriage shook slightly as the wheels carried us over the cobblestone streets. I tried to casually brace myself against my seat in an attempt to mask my discomfort.

"Now that we're in private," I said, intentionally changing the subject. "What happened yesterday?"

Damiana bit her thin bottom lip, her eyes glazed over for a moment. "I guess there's no sense in toeing the waters as you'd find out soon enough. Mother Sienna was murdered yesterday, and Ora—she's another acolyte in our group—well, she was badly hurt in the attack as well."

I shook my head as I struggled to process her words. Who in their right mind would kill a priestess? I had heard the rumblings of people upset over temples not having to pay taxes, but this? This seemed like too strong an act for such displeasure.

"Tallis would have come, but he had an important meeting he couldn't get out of," she continued. "Which means you lucked into having me give you the grand tour." Damiana cringed. Apparently, someone wasn't too happy with their choice of words.

"I'm sorry for your loss," I said, instinctively taking her hand. *What does she do at the temple to make them so calloused?* "I can't begin to imagine what you're going through."

She thanked me, giving my hand a light squeeze before letting go.

"If you don't mind me asking," I said, "do you know why she was killed or who did it? I never pictured temple life to be dangerous."

She started and stopped a few times before apologizing.

"There's no need to apologize," I said. "I shouldn't have pushed."

Damiana shrugged. "It's not that. I just didn't know where to begin."

I nodded my understanding.

"Tallis is the one who is good with words," she continued. "Omar can be a pretty good talker, too, when he's trying to get a barmaid's smallclothes off. Me, I'm blunt. So I might as well be blunt with you."

My lips rose to form an easy smile. Although this Omar fellow might not have enjoyed her assessment, I liked her bluntness. You never had to worry where you stood with people like her. They would let you know for themselves.

Damiana leaned forward in her seat. "The truth of the matter is we have no idea who killed Mother Sienna. Our only hope is that Ora wakes up and remembers who the killer was. As for your other question, it's not the temple life that's dangerous. It's what happens outside of it that can occasionally cause trouble."

The heaviness of her words sank into me, sucking me deeper into the conversation. What the fuck had happened to *I am the blunt one*? There was something strange going on with the temple, but I couldn't put my finger on it.

"Could you be a little more vague, or are you worried the walls have ears?"

She chuckled at that. "No, we're in here because the streets have ears, and you have an important choice to make before you leave this carriage."

A lump, heavy as a stone, formed in my throat, and I struggled to swallow it.

"However, it's hard to make a decision without knowing all the important information and getting your questions answered," she continued.

"Before you get any further," I said, raising my hands to help cut her off, "this isn't one of those if-you-don't-agree-to-this-offer-I-will-kill-you-before-you-leave-the-carriage sort of conversations, is it? My life may be less than ideal, but I am rather fond of it."

Damiana grimaced as she tilted her head side to side. "Not exactly."

My eyes widened as my eyebrows tried to arch themselves off the top of my head. What had I gotten myself into? Sweat formed on my palms, and the carriage suddenly felt ten times smaller.

"No matter what happens here today," the acolyte continued, "you'll leave this carriage alive. If you choose not to join the temple and start telling people the truth about us, then you would most likely come across an untimely accident."

Despite the potential threat she ended on, a sigh escaped my lips, and my heart rate began to slow again. "I guess that's fair."

"I like to believe so."

There was a lull in our conversation as I recomposed myself.

"So, if you're not a temple, what are you, then?" I finally asked.

A bump in the road sent the pair of us momentarily into the air. I couldn't tell if her laugh was for our brief flight or my question.

"We are most certainly a temple dedicated to the service of our Lord Cuvar, the God of the Misfortunate," she said. "It's how we raise our funds for the Lord's service that may disturb the public." She smiled at her own words. "Well, the wealthier members of the public at least."

To Damiana, the words were probably nothing more than an inside joke, but to me, they had been like cleaning off a looking glass; suddenly, everything had become clear.

"You're a church of thieves?"

Damiana's smile widened. "It was the wealthy bit that gave it away, wasn't it?"

Her admission rocked me harder than the carriage ride. I had often joked that organized religion stole more from the people than it gave to them, but I didn't realize that my assumption only scratched the surface.

"Believe it or not," Damiana continued, "this is almost as new for me as it is for you. It has been a long time since my finger took on a new acolyte, and most acolytes are brought on as children."

Questions swirled in my head like a whirlpool, overwhelming my senses. Either I hid my confusion better than

I thought possible, or she was willfully ignoring it as she powered through what was possibly a rehearsed speech.

"Because I haven't been tasked with bringing on a new acolyte before, I'm not entirely sure where to begin. So I am going to let you ask all the questions you want, and I will answer them all truthfully until we are both blue in the face. How does that sound?"

"How can you steal from the people you're supposed to be helping?" I asked, firing off a question instead of answering her own. "Isn't Cuvar supposed to be the God of the Misfortunate or something? How can you stomach this hypocrisy?"

Surprisingly, her smile never wavered. "I'll take that as this format works for you."

She laughed at herself again, and my knuckles tightened as I wrapped my fingers around the seat cushion.

"Right," she said, clapping her hands together. "To answer your first question, we don't steal from the people we help. We only steal from the rich, and we use those funds to pay for all the services that help the misfortunate, like your mother."

My stomach churned at the mention of her name. As grateful as I was for her to receive their medical support, another part of me despised her being used as an example and the insinuation that she was a misfortunate.

However, that was just my pride talking. How else would you describe a woman who had to watch her family destroyed due to a war? How else would you describe a woman who had to flee the land she loved for that same war? How else would you describe a woman who forged a home against all odds in a new land only to be struck down by illness?

Many words came to mind, but I couldn't deny that *misfortunate* belonged among them.

"Your second question is an easy one. Yes, Cuvar is the God of the Misfortunate. As for your last question, I find it all rather easy to stomach. I do my Lord's work by taking from those who have far too much and use our gifts to give to people who have suffered far too much."

Almost every fiber of my being wanted to disagree with her sentiment. However, I couldn't entirely disagree with her logic. Part of me even found it more than palatable. If what she said was true, they weren't hoarding it for themselves nor were they taking advantage of the same people they were supposed to be helping.

"Aren't you worried about getting caught?" I asked. "It doesn't take a scholar to realize that the wealthy are more connected to power than the masses. What's keeping your victims from going to the king? Surely if he found out, then this whole scheme of yours would crumble on top of you."

"King Kepa is not a problem at all," Damiana said, brushing off my question with a lazy wave of her hand. "As for our targets, we make sure they have no idea what hit them. This is done through several months of careful scouting, selecting, planning, and finally executing our mission."

I scoffed. "I don't give a damn about how much planning you do. How can you look me in the eye and tell me that the king is not a problem when you are robbing from the most powerful men and women in Arremendia?"

"Not only is the king aware of what we do, but he, and every ruler before him for the past three centuries, has been in on it as well," she said with an air of nonchalance.

My jaw sank to the floor.

"Just for the record," she added while I struggled to process her previous statement, "we also steal from our city's many wealthy visitors. I know you didn't technically ask about it, but I feel as though I needed to correct your earlier statement in the name of being completely honest."

Was she insane? How could she be worried about the small detail after she dropped the revelation of a lifetime on me?

"What do you mean the king is in on it? Why would he allow you to steal from his people?"

Damiana pulled open a slot inside of the carriage and peeked outside before closing it shut again. "That is a good question with many answers. Would you prefer to hear the kinder or more devious reasons first?"

"Does it matter?"

"Not really," she said with a shrug. "I'd just like to take your preferences into consideration. After all, we may be working together for a long time if you still choose to go through with this."

Although she struck me as the kind of person who couldn't get through three sentences without making a joke, something about the way she said it made me believe she was being sincere.

"I guess you can give me the good news first."

"You got it," she said, joy flickering in her eyes. "One of the many ways our Lord's temple benefits His Majesty is that we handle many charitable services that he then doesn't have to worry about or pay for. We heal the sick, we feed the hungry, we house the homeless, and we provide hope to those that have lost it."

It all sounded good in theory, but even a fool knew that the brightest lights cast the darkest shadows.

"And what are his more devious reasons?"

"He sometimes uses our skills to his advantage by selecting targets for us," she said, not missing a beat. "I guess it's not *really* devious in the grand scheme of things..."

Damiana kept talking, but I had tuned out. Her answer had been so obvious that I was a bit annoyed I hadn't realized it sooner.

Since the dawn of time, those who held power wanted one of two things. The ambitious among them sought to acquire more of it, but even the laziest would go to great lengths to retain their power.

"You know how it is," the thieving acolyte continued. "If someone in the city is amassing too much wealth, and His Majesty sees this person as a threat to his rule, then he will task us with alleviating the problem by separating them from their fortunes."

Their symbiotic relationship was ingenious, albeit disturbing. It was like witnessing a little bird feast on the flesh stuck between a lion's teeth. The bird got what it needed to sustain itself and its children, while the lion was able to maintain its health, helping it stay in control of its surroundings.

The image caused a new question to bubble up in my mind. How did I fit into this pecking order?

"Tallis told me that I would be working as an inventor," I said. "Is that all I would be doing, or would I take part in your robberies?"

Damiana let out a boisterous laugh. "No, no, no." She wiped a tear away from her eye. "No offense, but you would make a shit thief."

"Thank you?"

I wasn't sure how her words were supposed to be offensive. Almost every other person outside of Cuvar's service would view those words as a compliment.

"Not all of our acolytes serve Cuvar through robbery," she said as she struggled to recompose herself. "Every member of the temple has their strengths and weaknesses, and our Lord is served better when we utilize our strengths. Mother Sienna raved about your ability to solve problems through your creations. She saw how they could potentially help in our schemes, and that is what you were brought here to do."

As flattering as it was to me that the priestess had been fond of my work, it was equally as odd. How had a woman I had met once two weeks ago been familiar enough with my past to rave about it? Either she was crazy, had a gut feeling about me, or their scouting network was more thorough than I could imagine.

"Do you serve your Lord through theft, or were you brought in for your gift for explaining things in carriages?" I asked.

Although she didn't laugh, her smile shone in her eyes. "I've done my fair share of thievery, but my primary role is as our group's combat specialist and insect aficionado."

"Wait, Cuvar requires you to use insects?"

She shrugged. "Not yet, I just love the little buggers. You'll have to come to my room to see my collection sometime."

An image of a room filled floor to ceiling with jars of bugs filled my mind. For a split second, I thought I felt something crawl up my leg, causing me to cringe.

"I have one more question," I said, changing the subject with all the grace of a fatally wounded beast.

Damiana gestured for me to continue.

"If I decide to join your temple, would I be required to serve for life?"

"No, the only people who serve their role for life are

temple priests and priestesses," she said. "But that is only because they choose that life for themselves."

I wondered what she meant by that last bit. There was the obvious answer that part of their selection process for ordaining new priests included the candidates volunteering for the position, but it felt like there was more to her words. Had any of them joined the temple by their own volition, or was it a matter of last resort for them as well?

"How long would I have to serve Cuvar?"

"It's not a matter of time but rather a matter of money," Damiana said.

One of my eyebrows arched. However, she continued with her explanation right before I could ask her for clarification.

"We have a ceremony—one you'll partake in tonight, assuming you join us—in which Cuvar will reveal how much money you'll need to secure for him to fulfill your duty as his acolyte. Once that amount has been met, an acolyte is free to leave if they so choose."

I fiddled with my fingers as I processed the new information. Depending on how their "god" valued my work, I would be looking at a few years of service or a few decades. The former would be doable. The latter... I shuddered at the thought.

"Given your role, I wouldn't be too worried about the ceremony," Damiana added. "Even if Cuvar foresees you delivering a higher sum, every theft your inventions are used in would count toward your offering. Honestly, you'll probably be able to complete your service faster than most."

The carriage rocked to a stop.

"Looks like we're here," she said as she peeked out of the slot once more. "So, this is your last chance to walk away.

Would you like to follow me inside, or should I have Romero drive you home?"

It was kind of her to ask, but there was only one option. I no longer had a home. Even if I had them bring me back to San Fernando, then I'd be essentially throwing my mother onto the streets with me. For better or worse, I would have to make this work.

I gestured to the door. "Lead the way, Sister Damiana. I can't ready myself for the ceremony in here."

5

TALLIS

The view of Arremendia from the rooftop terrace of Pozuelo's villa was breathtaking. The luxurious fortress the ianista called home when he resided in the city limits was one of twenty such villas that lined the base of King's Mountain. There were only three ways to acquire such a prime piece of property: through the luck of inheritance, as a gift bestowed by the king, or by spending enough money to make the gods jealous. In our mark's case, it was the first of the three.

"She's a lovely city, isn't she?" asked Pozuelo as he reappeared with a bottle of Azeria Vermouth. "There's a reason we call her the Pearl of the Mountains."

I smiled at his remark instead of telling him the real reason for the name through one of Mother Sienna's history lessons. According to her, our city's name meant "birth between the mountains." However, the mental image of childbirth along the banks of the Beltza was too graphic an image for King Markel IV's weak stomach, and thus, he claimed the city had been named after a simple, pretty thing.

"Aye," I said. "She certainly lives up to the name."

The clattering of practice swords rose up from the courtyard below us. Like the two mountainside villas I had visited in other games, Pozuelo's had a similar layout. Three large stone walls formed a squared-off "u" with the mountain behind it acting as the fourth wall. The only real difference was that he had transformed the standard, picturesque courtyard into a training ground.

Pozuelo gestured to the table his servants had prepared for us, causing sunlight to glimmer off the golden fox on the vermouth bottle's label. "Come, business is far more enjoyable to discuss with a full belly and drunken lips."

"You are far too kind," I said as I made my way toward the table. "Though I must admit it is a philosophy I could see myself getting used to."

The smell of grilled river squid and the white wine used to cook the black ink risotto wafted up to greet me as I took the seat across from my host. My mouth salivated. Although we no longer had enough time to take the whole 100,000 crowns as we had originally planned, at least this meal would account for a minor compensation.

"Will Basilius be joining us today?" I asked as one of his servants, a dark-haired girl masquerading as a woman in a shimmering silk dress, draped herself over me to deliver my plate. Her hand rested gently on my shoulder as she awaited her next command.

One day she would become the stunning woman she was playing at today, but she couldn't have been older than fifteen. Pozuelo was using her as a prop to learn something about me, and the act sickened me for two reasons. The first being that the girl seemed too at ease with the situation for it to have been the first time she performed this task. The second being that this probably would have been Ora's fate if Mother Sienna hadn't taken her and Omar off the streets.

"Oh no, with the games set to begin tomorrow, he'll be busy sharpening our panthers' teeth," said the ianista. "Should I have Raquel bring you anything else?"

Afraid of insulting my host with the words I wanted to say to him, I opted to feign embarrassment. After all, it wasn't every day Master Pierre LeBlanc found himself in this predicament.

"I, ugh, no," I stammered, looking everywhere except at Pozuelo or Raquel. "She has already brought me more than enough."

Pozuelo let out a laugh. "Very well. Raquel, pour Master LeBlanc two fingers of Azeria, and then you may go."

The cloying scent of the lilac perfume they must have bathed her in assaulted my nostrils as she leaned over to fill my cup.

"Let's get to it, shall we?" asked the ianista.

It's about time, I thought as I flashed him a respectful grin.

"I know it is bad business to start with an apology, but I must," I said. "A man as influential and as well connected as you knows the happenings of the world better than most, but I need to ask this question, nonetheless, as it is important to understand the necessity of this deal. So I pray it causes no offense."

Pozuelo leaned forward in his seat, momentarily setting his cup down to encourage me to continue.

"What do you know about the current situation in Gregus?"

It was an important question not only because it laid the groundwork for the remainder of our shortened game, but it would also give me an indication of the only factor we couldn't plan for: his knowledge of the uprising in Gregus. More particularly, if he knew the status of Molino, the small nation's capital city.

The only thing that stood in our way of a nice payday was contradicting his own sources. In order for this to work, I would have to build off the knowledge he had already obtained.

The ianista took a sip of his drink, presumably to buy himself a little time to recall the information. "It's been about two weeks since I've heard from my scout in Molino. Besides telling me about a few fighters of note, he did mention a rebellion brewing in the countryside. Though he seemed quite assured that it wouldn't reach the capital."

"Although I wish it weren't the case," I said with a grimace as I set down my cup, "Molino has been taken by the same religious zealots who roused the countryside. Only the palace has yet to fall, and my master fears for the worst."

"I fear it is my turn to ask an ignorant question, but why would the mob's anger be directed at him? Your master is a beloved marvel across the continent—dare I say the world."

I didn't know if he intended the "ignorant" comment to be a barb, but I stored the information for later reflection.

"You have nothing to fear," I assured him. "As my master says, it is better to ask an ignorant question and be a fool for minutes than to keep it to yourself and remain a fool forever."

"Hear, hear," my mark said, lifting his glass in toast. "It appears your master is as wise as they claim."

"He is indeed, and that is why he sent me here. It is no secret to you that my country has been struggling these past few years and that these hardships have not been felt by our capital."

He nodded his understanding but refrained from cutting me off.

"My countrymen, they..." I paused for dramatic effect. "They wrongly believe that these ills of chance are the result of the Duchy turning his back on our gods to worship the money of foreigners."

The ianista swirled the vermouth in his glass as he soaked in my words.

"It is an obvious falsehood," I continued. "You know as well as I that it is possible to be a man of faith and a man of business at the same time. However, try telling that to a mob."

"I can only imagine," Pozuelo said, letting out a nervous laugh.

"Now try imagining being in my master's stead. A man sent here from another world by gods unknown to us. A man seeming capable of a magic unseen in our world." I dropped my head and lowered my voice. "My master is the epitome of what this mob sees as being wrong with our city."

Pozuelo dropped his spoon, and the silver clanged loudly against his fine porcelain bowl. "Do not tell me that they mean to kill him."

"Not for now, Taide be praised," I said with a sigh. "For the time being, they seem satisfied with the destruction of his art, the burning of his studio, and placing him and his family under house arrest."

"I am so sorry, Master LeBlanc. We need to make the bastards pay for what they have done, but I don't know what I can do about it. It's not as though my gladiators are enough to retake the city and free your master."

There were many ways in which our target differed from the rest of my countrymen, but in this regard, he was one and the same. So many here had a knack for feeling pity. However, very few possessed the will to make the situation better unless it benefited them.

"My master is not requesting you to do that, nor is it needed."

The ianista squinted as he puzzled over my words. "What do you mean? You said it yourself. Master Mosley and his family have been captured. You are here on his behalf, are you not?"

"Yes," I said after clearing my throat. "I am here on the very mission he designed upon receiving word of the uprising in the countryside. Unfortunately, the rebellion moved faster than any of us could have predicted."

Pozuelo rubbed his scruff-covered chin. "And what exactly is this plan?"

"You see," I said, leaning forward and resting my arms on the table, "when word of the uprising reached the capital, many businesses, my master's included, debated whether they should leave the city. Naturally, the Duchy of Molino's response was to forbid them from leaving. He thought he would need their resources for the impending war, but my master saw it differently. To him, it was a sign that the end of his reign was coming, and he decided to plan accordingly."

I took a sip of the vermouth. The floral- and honey-scented elixir warmed my body as it traveled through me.

"Although he couldn't leave the city or send his goods away for safekeeping, he was still allowed to sell his art."

A wicked grin crossed Pozuelo's face. Had he figured out where I was going with this?

"As such," I continued, "he took advantage of this loophole by selling some of his pieces to a series of fake patrons in our neighboring kingdom of Hoppe. It was a delicate process. Sell too much too fast, and the Duchy would be on to him. However, he also realized that each piece he didn't move would be doomed to destruction."

"Such a shame," Pozuelo said with a shake of his head. "At least he was able to save some of them. Does anyone besides you know he did this?"

It was my turn to smile. If he hadn't pieced together our "plan" yet, then he was on the right path now.

"Not a soul."

One only had to glance at the ianista's face to know I had him eating out of the palm of my hand. He stared at me with such intensity that if the ground beneath our feet collapsed, I would still hold his complete attention.

"If we can come to an agreement, then my master would like you to do the following," I said. "The first thing he would need you to do is to fund a voyage to Hoppe. A deal has been struck with the McKinnie brothers to smuggle my master and his family out of Molino. All that is left to do is pay them. Obviously, since his funds have been frozen, this is an expenditure he would like you to cover as well."

The ianista hummed at this, and I liked to imagine he was adding up the figures in his mind.

"Once they have been safely retrieved from the capital," I continued, "my master will direct the crew—which will include as many of your own men as you wish to have accompany us—to the location of the previously mentioned art he successfully snuck out of the city. From there, the crew will load the hidden art onto the ship and return us to Arremendia. Lastly, my master would like you to allow him and his family to live in one of your villas and turn it into a studio where he can then eventually make new living glass creations."

"Is that all?" Pozuelo asked. "With all of those wishes, I am afraid your master has mistaken me for a genie."

I let out a hearty, genuine laugh, which brought a chuckle from my mark as well.

"Seriously, though," said the ianista, easing the conversation back to the business at hand. "Even by the most conservative of estimations, your master is asking me for an enormous amount of money." He covered his heart with his ring-ladened hand. "I feel for your master and understand why he wants these things, but what is in it for me?"

With this question came my time to shine. My art might not have been as renowned or appreciated as my supposed employer's, but I was as talented when it came to my own craft.

"Given my master's unusual entrance into our world and his unique talent, he has found himself in the limelight for every waking moment he spent here. In order to give himself and his family the much-needed respite they deserve, the McKinnie brothers will be faking his death as part of their smuggling mission."

I felt my falsely thickened eyebrow arch. Why hadn't he reacted more strongly to that news? Apparently, I would have to spell it out more plainly for him.

"Tell me, Ianista Pozuelo, what happens to the worth of an artist's work after they die?"

The smile I had expected after my previous line finally crossed his face. "It increases exponentially."

It does indeed.

"Not only that," I added, "you need to also consider how much more his price will increase when you factor in that everyone will believe his remaining work has been destroyed."

Pozuelo had done the sums. I could practically see the

piles of gold crowns he envisioned reflecting in his eyes. If the proposition I offered him had been real, then it would have been a perfectly normal reaction. In this hypothetical scenario, selling one of Mosley's larger pieces would bring him enough profit to afford my proposed voyage twenty times over.

"Given all the expenses you'd have to bear upfront," I continued, "Master Mosley thinks it is only natural that you should receive fifty percent of the proceeds from each sale during his four-year hiatus."

I paused to take a bite of risotto. The creaminess of the ink merged seamlessly with the sweetness of the onions, the earthy complexity of the mushrooms, and whatever his chef seasoned it with to create the perfect amount of zest.

His face pinched as he tilted his head. "It is an interesting offer, but why only four years? Is my saving the lives of him and his family only worth four years of reward?"

In all honesty, that had only been the beginning of my fake offer. Playing a target was a finicky game. Although it was important to have them believe they were getting everything they wanted and more, if you made it appear too good to be true, especially too soon, then the game could end in a blink of an eye. The real art of false facing was having the mark believe they were in control, and I had Pozuelo right where I wanted him.

I swallowed my food then flashed him an innocent smile. "Fear not, Ianista Pozuelo, it was only our planned initial offer. Although I knew you would never accept it, as a servant working for my master's interest, I have to do my part to get him the best deal. If you were willing to do this for a cut-rate, then who would I be to say no?"

"Understood," he said with an appreciative nod. "Then tell me, what's your master's next offer?"

"In addition to the equal splits of profits during his four-year hiatus, my master would also like to grant you ten percent of every sale he makes on his art for the rest of his life. After his resurfacing, of course."

Pozuelo turned his eyes from me, opting to focus his gaze out on the city beneath us as he pondered the offer.

When his pause lasted longer than ten seconds, I knew he wouldn't accept the terms of my fake deal. He was a notoriously shrewd businessman, but he also led with his gut. If he had been satisfied with my offer, then he would have accepted by now. His silence screamed of a man who was still trying to eke out every drop of advantage he could get.

"The deal your master has devised is a fair one," he said, returning his gaze back to me after another minute of silence. "However, as we can both attest, life is everything but fair, and I hold all the chips."

Like the countless marks before him, I had succeeded in tricking him into believing he was the spider instead of the fly. With every word he uttered, he unknowingly entangled himself further and further into my web.

"Given your master's predicament," he continued, "you do not have time to find him another partner in this endeavor. Even if you did have the time, it wouldn't be of use as I would know he was still alive and could easily thwart his plan."

Go ahead, I thought. *Make sure your noose fits tight*.

"Just like you have to work in your master's best interest, it is only natural that I need to work in mine. Though I've earned my reputation for being a calculated man, I am not a cruel one. As such, I only ask for three alterations to the deal you have put forth."

"And those are?" I asked.

He took another sip of his drink. "The first adjustment

we need to make is to the timeline. Although I appreciate the offer of ten percent of the sales for the rest of your master's life, what happens if your master does not live as long as he plans? By those terms, if he were to die a year after his hiatus ended, then I would be left holding the short end of the stick."

"It is a valid point," I admitted. "What do you suggest?"

"If we add an addendum that states that I will continue to receive my ten percent for fifty years in the case of your master's premature death, then I think that would suffice."

Although these terms didn't mean anything in the grand scheme of things, in Pierre LeBlanc's reality, they were everything. He would push back and be careful with each of his words. In order to be him, I had to do the same.

"For clarification," I said, "do you mean fifty years after death, or would this countdown be initiated the moment he returns from hiatus?"

"The fifty years would begin at the start of his resurrection," he said with a laugh.

I agreed to his first amendment and encouraged him to continue.

"My other two alterations have to do with the percentages," said Pozuelo. "To be blunt, I want more."

My fingers danced nervously along the rim of my glass. "How much more?"

"I want sixty during his hiatus and twenty upon his return," Pozuelo said.

I took a few more bites of food as I pretended to consider his offer. "We can do either sixty or twenty, but we can't do both." I gestured with my empty spoon for added effect. "Which would you prefer?"

This time, the ianista didn't miss a beat.

"Twenty percent it is," he said as he raised his glass. "Here's to our newfound partnership."

"Hear, hear, indeed," I said as we clinked glasses and downed their remaining contents.

Pozuelo called for Raquel to pour us another round before he turned to address me again. "I'll have my scribe begin working on the paperwork on the morrow. What would you like to do in the meantime?"

The idea of having to wait another day ate at my insides. Between trying to cope with Mother Sienna's death and all the other bullshit that was happening back at the temple, I needed to be taking things off my plates, not adding on to it.

"I know it would be an abrupt turnaround," I said, "but I want to be sailing toward Hoppe before the end of the week. To do that, I need to start approaching captains with coin in hand as soon as possible."

"Your rush, though ambitious, makes perfect sense," Pozuelo said before pausing to admire Raquel's figure as she filled our glasses with more of the golden fox's special.

As he asked the girl to fetch him a quill and a promissory note, I was once more reminded why we selected him to be our mark. Men like him, who preyed on the powerless, deserved everything we were about to do to them.

"How much do you need?" Pozuelo asked.

"Thirty thousand crowns," I said, launching my original plan of 25,000 crowns off the balcony for the simple reason of *fuck this guy*.

His body shook ever so slightly. "30,000?"

"Finding a crew and readying a ship on short notice is no cheap feat," I said with a shrug. "Once we have that issue resolved, then we have to take care of the necessary supplies for this type of voyage. Plus, we have to account for the McKinnie brothers' payment, any bribes we may need to go about undetected, and taking care of any other problems that may arise along the way."

"I see," the ianista said as he began writing the note. "It just seems like a lot of money."

"That's because it is a lot of money," I admitted. *And consider yourself lucky we don't have time to take you for more.* "But your investment will feel well worth it once my master reaches these shores safely."

Pozuelo finished his looping signature and handed the note over to me. "Well, hurry up and go get him, then."

6

NEREA

With another blink, I'd found myself in yet another new location. However, for the first time since fleeing Binsoro, I found a place that possessed a sense of permanence. That notion in itself should have been a comfort.

The temple gave me a cozy fourth-floor dorm with a view looking up at the rest of Arremendia stretching up to the King's Mountain. In reality, it wasn't much, but I had never needed a vast living space. The barren room covered all the essentials: bed (check), an empty desk and bookshelf (check), an aged wooden wardrobe (check), and a modicum of lounge space (check).

A smile eased onto my face as I painlessly rolled over on my bed to stare at the ceiling. I still had plenty of questions about the temple, most of which dealt with my discomfort over how they *raised* their funds, but this bed alone almost made it worth it. It was like sleeping on a cloud compared to the lumpy pile of garbage I had slept on the last two years.

"Nerea," Damiana called as she knocked on my door. "Are you ready?"

Ready for what? I thought as I pushed myself into a seated position.

However, a glance out the window answered that question for me. The sun had started to set over the King's Mountain, bathing the city in the last glimmers of orange light. Mother Sienna's second night of funeral rites would begin soon, and my initiation would take place shortly thereafter.

I lifted my door's lock and started to push it open. "I think s..."

The words died on my lips as I realized Damiana wasn't alone. As she walked through the door, one of the most attractive men I'd ever laid eyes on strolled in behind her. Was everyone in this place going to be insanely gorgeous?

He was the type of handsome that made you question your own beauty. Not only did he possess high cheekbones, a slightly dimpled chin, and brown eyes like the richest chocolate, but his face was *perfectly* symmetrical. He looked more like a drawing come to life than an actual man.

"Wonderful. This is Omar, by the way," Damiana said, gesturing to the black-haired beauty. "He's the dipshit I told you about on the way over here."

Her exact words didn't come to mind, but I recalled it having to do something with his passion for barmaids.

Omar took my hand in his and planted a light kiss with his bow-shaped lips. "It's a pleasure to finally meet you."

A wave of heat filled my cheeks.

"I assure you that most of what she's said is utter nonsense," he added.

Damiana let out a low laugh. "Would you like to tell her what you said in the hallway or should I?"

"It was only a joke that wasn't worth dwelling on," he

said, taking a step toward the door. "We should head to the temple before we make a scene like Tallis did last night."

The blush that prevailed through his olive complexion indicated his embarrassment, and that was his attempt to change the topic. However, what would be the fun in letting him get off that easy?

"But I love jokes," I said as I walked out the door. I would make him sweat, but not at the cost of making us late. "Why would you deprive me of your wit?"

Omar ran a hand through his neatly styled hair. "Well, you see, ugh—"

"He wanted to see if you'd have sex with him before your initiation," said Damiana. Her words echoed through the dormitory's hall.

A hint of bile reached the back of my throat. "What in the world made you think that I would ever go for such a thing?"

The three of us made our way toward the stairwell at the hall's center.

"For the record, I never asked the question," he said, his words coming faster than before. "The basis of my joke was that we could still technically have sex as you hadn't become an acolyte yet. I know Dami likes to make me out as a halfwit, but I'm not *that* daft."

For a moment, my legs became trees, rooting me to the top of the stairs. "Wait, are you telling me acolytes can't have sex?"

"They can," Damiana said, "but just not with anyone from the temple until they're no longer an acolyte. It helps to keep the acolytes focused on their task at hand, and it also protects them from being taken advantage of by people of power within the temple's hierarchy."

My legs began to work again as relief coursed through

my veins. It wasn't that I was the most promiscuous person in Arremendia, but the thought of giving up control over what I could or couldn't do with my body terrified me.

"Besides," she added, "if Cuvar outlawed sex in its entirety for acolytes, then this one would have blown up years ago."

Omar's brow furrowed for a moment, and I thought he was going to refute the claim until he shrugged. "Yeah, it doesn't happen often, but she's right on that one."

Damiana was in the midst of giving a detailed description of where he could place his remark when we exited the dormitory and entered the hanging gardens. Out of the few places she had shown me on the temple's grounds so far, this had been my favorite. It was a maze of flowered walls and sculptures. Marble fountains and nooks to relax in filled both my eyes and nostrils with delight.

I had to be careful not to gawk at the burst of colors all around me. If I lost track of Damiana and Omar, then I could spend the rest of my life trying to find my way out. Though I guessed there were few places more scenic than this for me to perish.

"So," I said as we rounded yet another corner. "What exactly happens in this initiation ceremony? They're not going to cut me or make me take some weird hallucinogenic, are they?"

"You'll be fine," Omar said before taking in a sharp breath. "That is, of course, unless you're afraid of spiders."

A chill ran down my spine. It wasn't that I was afraid of spiders, but I certainly wasn't fond of them.

"You see," Omar continued, "what happens is Father Roberto will summon the gi—"

Damiana smacked him on the back of his head. "Stop being an asshat."

He winced from the blow and muttered something under his breath.

"It's not bad at all," she continued. "All that happens is you sit on Cuvar's hand, and he weighs your worth to him."

Oh, is that all? I thought with a smirk.

"You'll find out soon enough," Omar said as we turned one last time to find the temple's back side.

My breath caught in my throat as we entered the temple's back door. Although I wasn't religious, it was hard not to be impressed by the grandeur of Cuvar's sanctuary. The entire place appeared as though it had been designed to draw your eye to the giant statue of the deity.

Even with the god being depicted as bending down on one knee, the top of the red stone sculpture still towered at least three stories above us. Cuvar, who apparently had the head of a three-eyed fox and the body of a muscular humanoid figure, stared down past his snout into his awaiting outstretched hand. It rested palm up on the back of the large circular altar.

Damiana led us around the altar's stone railing to a pew in the front row. As I followed her, I sensed the eyes of the entire congregation on the back of my neck. Why were they staring? It wasn't as though we were the last to arrive. Streams of black-clad acolytes were still filing into the room.

"Shit," I muttered to myself when I realized why I drew their gaze.

Everyone here had donned black robes to mourn Mother Sienna's passing. Everyone except me. My simple beige tunic and sage-green long skirt wouldn't have earned me a passing glance on the street, but not here. In this room, they shouted, *I am an outsider. I am not one of you.*

Part of me wanted to curl in on myself, giving them less to see. However, my mother's voice drove it out.

Sit tall and proud, my miracle child, she commanded. *You've survived too much to cower to anyone. Show them why you were chosen to be here.*

I sat up straighter in my seat, pushing my shoulders back into a proper posture. It didn't alleviate the feeling, but I could bear it. I would bear it.

After another minute or two, the stream of acolytes entering the temple came to a stop. I wanted to look around to get a better sense of their numbers, but I kept my attention trained on the altar.

Unlike most altars I had seen, there wasn't a pulpit on it. Instead, everything appeared to be centered around Cuvar's cupped palm. To the left of it stood five wooden chairs that would have made worthy thrones. Each was cushioned and had Cuvar's symbol, part of a human forearm and open hand sitting inside the god's crimson palm, draped over the back of it.

To the right of the hand was an ornately decorated black casket, presumably Mother Sienna's, sitting on a pedestal. Fourteen large white candles, each standing in their own holder, formed a semicircle around the casket. However, only one of them was lit.

I was about to ask Damiana about the candle's significance when everyone in our pew rose to their feet. The reason for this became clear when I rose to mine a second later. The five head priests, and three young acolytes carrying woven baskets filled with small candles, had entered the temple.

No, the five weren't all priests, I realized as they took their seats on the altar. Four of them wore the shinier black robes, double-pointed caps, and crimson stoles of priesthood. The last member seated on the altar wore the plain black mourning robes and the flat white beret of an acolyte.

"What's Tallis doing up there?" I whispered to Damiana as I took a candle from the basket, the feeling of wax already coating my fingers. "He's not a priest now, is he?"

She took a candle from the acolyte and thanked him before tilting her head toward mine. "No, he's representing our finger until we name our successor. Though he might end up becoming a father if Ora doesn't recover in time."

"What do you mean by your 'finger'?" I asked. "That's the second time you've used the term."

Damiana pointed to the symbol of Cuvar that had been etched into her robe. "Every temple of Cuvar is made up of five groups, one for each of our Lord's fingers. Each of these is led by either a priest or a priestess, who also make up the temple's council."

"And which finger are we?"

Damiana didn't miss a beat. "We are the pinky."

"It's a fitting name for many reasons," Omar said, cutting in.

Despite my intuition, I asked him why. The poor bastard wore the stupid grin of someone dying to complete a joke, and I couldn't help myself.

"Besides being overlooked because we're the smallest finger," he said, "we also know how to have a shocking amount of fun when used correctly."

A low laugh escaped my lips as I shook my head. It was even worse than I had feared. Before I could retort, one of the priests rose from his seat and motioned for silence. The father seemed oddly thumb-shaped, which was appropriate given what I had just learned, and had graying tufts of hair that popped out in all directions from underneath his cap.

"That's Father Roberto," Damiana whispered.

"Just be happy you don't have to take his math class," said Omar.

"And why's that?"

Damiana smiled at me as though I were a child asking if the moons shrank because they were really cookies the gods ate every night. "Let's just say he has a knack for cruelty."

"That's putting it mildly." Omar scoffed. "For a while, I thought Ora would give him a long-distance haircut with her bow, but apparently, she reserved those types of warnings for me."

The priest cleared his throat, and Omar's attention snapped back to him.

"We're gathered here today to honor our late Mother Sienna as her soul begins her second day of trials," said Father Roberto. "To help guide her spirit in this endeavor, we'll gather and pass our collected light on to her. I remember when..."

The manner in which I was so easily able to tune out his tale made Omar's comment about his class more poignant. My mind was too preoccupied with other questions to consume his ramblings. Such as what did this ceremony say about their religious beliefs, what were the trials her spirit had to endure, and how would they judge me when I took my place on the sculpture's hand?

All the members of the temple began to sing, and it pulled me back into the moment. Although I couldn't make out their words at first, their melody rolled through me sweet and low like the tide returning to the ocean. I awkwardly hummed along as I tried to piece together the entire looping melody.

After the fourth repeat, I was confident of two lines:

Blessed be the thief

Who stole for you, who gave for you, who prayed for you.

I was on the verge of joining in as the chorus restarted when Omar gave me the slightest nudge.

"What—" I started to ask, but I cut my question off when I saw the lit candle in his hands.

Still singing in his silky baritone, he tilted his flame toward my candle. It lit almost instantaneously, and he gestured with his head for me to pass my flame to Damiana.

Although my candle didn't burn brightly, its subtle heat warmed my fingers as I lit Damiana's wick.

The giant acolyte was the last person in our pew. As such, the task of bringing the flame to the priests fell to her. Tallis met her at the altar's opening to accept the flame. With his candle lit, he turned to the other priest and shared it with them.

Unsurprisingly, the last person to have their candle lit was Father Roberto. Upon receiving the flame, the priest walked to Mother Sienna's caskets and lit the second of the fourteen candles. The moment he pulled his flame all the way from the candle, everyone stopped singing.

Out of all the things that had happened so far, I didn't know why this was the one that caught me off guard. Why had they cut off in the middle of the song? Wouldn't it have made more sense for them to stop either at the chorus or right after it? I filed the questions away to ask my newfound fingermates later.

"May her soul withstand her trial," said Father Roberto as he walked toward the altar's opening.

Trial? What kind of trial did they believe she would face in the afterlife? Surely someone as devout as Mother Sienna would have been in Cuvar's good graces. Unless, of course, she wasn't as pious as she appeared to be.

"May Cuvar show her the way," said the congregation in near unison. Their words echoed off the temple's high slanted ceiling.

"May Cuvar show you the way," I said under my breath a second after them.

Although I was foreign to their ways, nor did I believe them, Mother Sienna had most likely been a believer. If she had helped my mother in the way I thought she did, then the least I could do was offer her this blessing. Who knew, maybe it would tip the scales of her trial in her favor?

Father Roberto stopped walking once he reached the center of the altar's opening and spread his arms out wide. "My beloved children of Cuvar and my dearest brothers of his council, today is more than a day of mourning."

Shit, I thought, *and so it begins*.

"Today is also a celebration of life," he continued. "On this most sacred of nights, we are blessed to welcome Mother Sienna's final acolyte. One more candle, so to speak, whose shining light will be another reminder of her legacy."

If I hadn't felt all their eyes on my way into the temple, then I definitely held the entirety of their weight at that moment.

"Arise, Nerea Zabala," the priest commanded, making the floor shake without raising his voice. "It is time for Cuvar to know your worth."

My heart pounded against my chest as I rose from my seat. I couldn't help but wonder if there was still time to change my mind as I glanced back toward the temple doors. Was I truly destined to live amongst a church of thieves?

I closed my eyes, lowered my head, and took a deep breath. My mother's image filled my mind. It did not resemble her current state but rather the way she used to look before we fled. Back when she was a cat of prey in human form.

My mother had suffered and sacrificed so much to give me a life we could've never had if we stayed. This could be the only chance I would ever get to repay her, and I would not falter.

When I raised my head again, I discovered that Father Roberto had stepped aside. Tallis and his organized mob of black curls now waited for me in his place.

The handsome acolyte offered me his hand as I reached the altar. "I'm glad to see you will be joining our little finger."

His words came out hushed so as not to interrupt the priest, who was still rambling on about the importance of tradition.

A small shock jolted me as I accepted his hand and joined him on the altar.

"To be fair," I whispered into his ear, "you're just lucky no one offered me the middle finger."

He cracked a smile, unleashing his single dimple upon me. "It sounds like we both lucked out. In that scenario, you'd be reporting directly to him." His eyes shifted toward Father Roberto for a moment as we moved toward Cuvar's open hand.

"So why does your god need me to sit in his hand like some baby bird in order to determine my worth?" I asked. "Shouldn't he already know that, being a deity and all?"

He paused in front of Cuvar's thumb, which was as thick as my thigh and rose to just below my waist. "You sure do ask a lot of questions for a nonbeliever."

"You didn't answer my question," I teased.

"Nor will I," he said. "Unless I'm playing a mark, I see no benefits in pretending to know an answer that evades my knowledge or understanding."

"It is time, Brother Tallis," Father Roberto's voice boomed. "Assist your finger's candidate into our Lord's hand and step aside."

"Well, you heard the prick," Tallis said. "It's time to be a baby bird, if only for a moment."

I offered him a smile before climbing onto the sculpture. Cuvar's hand was both smoother and more detailed than I had anticipated. The artists who had created it had taken the time to carefully form the palm lines and even the finer fingerprints.

After crawling across the cold red stone, I sat at the very center of the deity's palm and peered out at the rest of the temple. A wave of black-clad figures stared back at me.

"Almighty Cuvar," Father Roberto continued. "The blesser of thieves and protector of the misfortunate. We bring before you a new soul who wishes to serve in your honor. Tell us, oh Lord, how great is the task you set before her?"

The words had barely left his mouth when the ground beneath me began to tremble. Its force knocked me onto my back and stirred the congregation into an uproar.

This can't be how I die, I thought as I struggled to reach the edge of the stone hand. *An earthquake won't be the end of me.*

I was on the verge of rolling out of Cuvar's grasp when a sight caught my eye. Stone balls of different sizes and colors were rolling along the top of the indented railing toward the front of the altar. I traced their path to discover that the balls were falling out of Cuvar's wrist.

Realization shook me harder than the tremors. The shaking was not that of an earthquake but had come from the statue itself. The congregation's roar had been one of delight, not panic. Most importantly, I realized that these balls were what determined my fate, and it didn't take a genius to recognize they would expect me to contribute a fortune to this deity's endeavors.

The rest of the temple must have realized this as well, as they had fallen silent while my spheres of gold, silver, red, and blue continued to pour forth from the statue.

"This can't be right," Tallis said to Father Roberto.

My spirits lifted at his words. It was a relief to know that I wasn't the only one who had come to that conclusion. Would this mean that they would have Cuvar judge me again?

A scowl crossed the priest's face. "And who are you to question our Lord? Do not tell me you have forgotten what occurred at your own induction?"

Tallis's shoulders sank, and I mirrored the expression. If he, an acolyte on the verge of priesthood, couldn't sway the middle finger's mind, then what hope did I have of accomplishing the same feat?

The rumbling finally subsided, and I looked down in time to watch a string of copper marbles roll to their final resting point.

"Cuvar has weighed our new sister's talents," Father Roberto announced to the crowd instead of turning to address me. "Let us tally his will."

While the other priests set about their task, Tallis made his way toward me.

"What's going on?" I asked, cringing at the simplicity of my question.

"They're counting your worth to the temple," he said matter-of-factly. "Don't worry. Although this was the second-highest number of stones to drop at a ceremony that I've ever witnessed, you'll pay it off quickly given the nature of your role here."

I swallowed the lump that formed in my throat. "I don't know whether I should be flattered or terrified."

"Honestly," he said, smiling as he leaned in closer, "a

combination of the two would be a perfectly natural response."

His words did nothing to alleviate the dread that consumed me.

"Tallis," Roberto called.

The acolyte rolled his eyes. "Duty calls. Wait here. This will all be over soon enough."

If only that were the case. In reality, it felt like seven moon cycles had passed while they counted and recounted the stone spheres. Since my perch was too far away to accurately follow the count, and I couldn't decipher the murmurings of the crowd, I attempted to ease my racing thoughts by figuring out how the ceremony worked. Not the symbology, as that was obvious, but rather the mechanics.

How had they released the stones? They had poured forth immediately after the priest's command. Was there a lever they pulled or valve they released behind the scenes? Also, where had the stones come from? Every angle of the statue I had seen showed no sign of it being connected to any other part of the temple. That would mean the stones were either stored inside the colossus or shot up from the floor.

"My fellow servants of Cuvar," Father Roberto said. The seriousness of his voice pulled me out of my endless series of questions.

I rolled onto my belly and crawled until I could rest my forearms and head on the tip of Cuvar's middle finger.

"The tally has been counted and verified," the priest continued. "Please help me in welcoming Sister Nerea. Our Lord has foreseen that she'll bring this temple 1,213,358 crowns and 17 coppers during her time as an acolyte."

The number robbed my lungs of air. How was I supposed to bring them over a million crowns when I had only held a single crown in my entire life? Even that had been pure chance as one of the actors had found it on the street. The only reason she let me touch it was because she wanted me to check to see if it was real.

Almost the entire temple erupted with cheers at his words. The only people who didn't seem excited were Tallis, Damiana, and Omar. The latter two wore their confusion like a well-fitted cap, while Tallis paled considerably as he approached me.

"Welcome to the pinky," he said as he offered me his hand and forced a smile onto his face. "It looks as though Mother Sienna knew we were destined to work together."

One thought ate at my mind as he helped me down from the statue. *What are you not telling me?*

7

TALLIS

"What's going on?" Nerea asked, her words hushed but intense. "It doesn't take a genius to realize there's something you're not telling me. For fuck's sake, you're paler than most the corpses I've seen."

I couldn't prevent my eyebrow from arching. Just how many corpses had she seen?

However, one look into her monolid brown eyes was enough to prevent me from questioning her. The beauty of her smooth dark skin, her broad, rounded nose, and her sharp cheekbones may have distracted the less observant of the truth, but not me. There was no denying that those eyes had witnessed the horrors of this world.

"Are you coming, Brother Tallis?" Father Roberto asked. His impatience seemed to evaporate by the day.

"It's nothing bad," I said, trying to assure her. "It's a long story. If Damiana and Omar don't explain it tonight, then I promise to tell you on the morrow."

Her mouth twitched. Whatever she planned to say, it wasn't quite ready yet.

"Who knows," I added, "if this meeting doesn't take all night, then I might be able to join your celebration and explain it then."

Without giving her a chance to respond, I turned and made my way toward the other priests.

"Apologies, Father," I said with what little respect I could muster. "I didn't mean to keep you waiting. It would be understandable if our latest acolyte was a little overwhelmed by the honor our Lord has placed upon her, and I wanted to make sure she was all right."

Father Ignacio looked up at me from his wheelchair. His fingers skimmed along the line of his jaw. "How noble of you. I think you may be better suited for fatherhood than you realize."

"It is our actions that matter, not our intentions," Father Roberto said, bristling at the remark. "Now, let us make haste. Cuvar's will waits for no man."

There were so many holes in his logic that I had to take heed not to fall into them. The old bastard was still upset that I hadn't given him his way, and now his grasp on power was teetering on the edge of an abyss. As tempting as it was to knock him over, I couldn't allow myself to fall for his games. One did not become the leader of the middle finger by being a fool.

I gestured to the door to the right of Cuvar's statue. "Then lead the way."

With his need for authority satisfied, the priest spun his back to me with the hint of a smile on his face and began making his way toward the door.

Father David fell into line behind his beloved master, taking Father Ignacio with him by pushing his wheelchair. This left only Father Sebastian, who fell in line beside me as we walked.

"You handled him much better this time around," said the instructor of thievery. "Although I wish Sister Ora a speedy recovery, I agree with Father Ignacio. You would make an excellent priest."

I held my hands behind my back to not appear too appreciative of his praise. Even though Mother Sienna had always been my favorite instructor, Father Sebastian was the only priest who could ever hold a candle to her in my eyes. Though, my reverence for him probably had more to do with him teaching my favorite class than anything else.

"You are too kind," I said, "but my purpose will be better served elsewhere. Besides, Ora will make a better ally and priest than I ever could."

"I pray that you are right."

The expression on his face said he wished to say more, but I was grateful that he chose to let the matter rest.

As we joined the others in the hall, Father Roberto finished pushing open the door to the secret staircase. "You're about to be the first acolyte to walk down these stairs. I hope you'll remember to treat this hallowed space with the respect it is due."

For neither the first nor the last time, his words were utter nonsense. To be fair, he wasn't aware of it on this occasion. I had discovered the secret stairs back when I was twelve, and I frequently visited the lower levels to marvel at the portraits of our previous living saints and read about their deeds in their hidden library.

"Of course, Father," I said, continuing to play my role of the innocent acolyte. "I'll take this matter with the seriousness it deserves."

We followed Fathers David and Ignacio down the wide spiral stairs slowly as they took their time to ensure his wheelchair remained in its guide ramp. The stairs ended at the Hall of Saints, where we took a left.

I had roamed this hall a hundred times over, but the feeling never changed. Every time I looked upon the portraits of the previous living saints in their ceremonial attire, the pull of destiny tugged at my chest. One day, my portrait would hang beside them.

Maybe they would place me next to St. Gaspar II, who once famously stole the heart of Nosorey. Or maybe they would place me beside St. Leon IV, who once seduced Queen Alexandria the Conqueror, the Beauty of Seadiff, only to rob her chambers blind while she slept in orgasmic bliss.

Perhaps they would hang me alongside Cuvar's current living saint, St. Keira, the first of her name. Her legend was chock-full of firsts and onlys. She was the first saint from the Isle of Opara, the first female saint in our history, and the only person who was able to defeat Mother Sienna in the saint trials.

Regardless of where they hung my painting, my portrait would grace these halls. The only thing that stood in my way was time. All I had to do was wait for St. Keira to either pass or retire. Then I would compete in the saint trials and secure my destiny. After all, only the best of Cuvar's thieves could claim the title.

Eventually, we arrived at the council's meeting room. It was an over-simplistic name for a room so luxurious, the focal point of which was the table at its center. It was shaped like Cuvar's hand above in the heart of the temple, with the exception that the fingers were splayed out instead of being cupped. Before the tip of each finger sat a chair better suited for royalty than a humble, pious man.

As I eased myself into my cushioned throne, my mind drifted to Mother Sienna. What thoughts had crossed her mind during the countless nights she sat here? What would she want me to do now in her stead? For the first time, I found myself wishing she had filled me in on the political workings of our temple.

Father Roberto hit his gavel against the table twice, stirring me from my thoughts. "I call this council meeting to order. Father Sebastian, what is on the agenda this evening?"

"Let's see," our thieving master said as he opened the scroll. He sat at the seat in front of the pointer finger. "Cuvar be praised, it's a short one tonight. All we have is our weekly account of sums acquired, news from the rest of Yenra, and a myriad of issues involving Mother Sienna's death that we can now address with her temporary replacement here."

Finally, I thought. Although it had only been days since her passing, the fact that they had provided me with next to no information regarding her murder was beyond frustrating. It appeared as though I would receive some answers at last.

Father David chuckled from his seat at the ring finger. "Our guardian of the misfortunate has lived up to his name yet again."

Both Father Roberto and Father David laughed at his remark, but only Roberto's was genuine. Father Ignacio, our thumb, offered up a smirk.

Did these fools really believe that they were the misfortunates? Did they not see the position of power and privilege to which they had been appointed? Worse yet, had Mother Sienna joked like this as well, or were these comments only now seeping out in her absence?

"I'll get us started, then," Ignacio said. "My finger was on donation duty this week, so we have no stolen funds to report. However, the fine folks of Arremendia did toss 72 crowns, 213 silvers, and 843 coppers into the collection cauldron."

Father Sebastian reached for the gold goblet in front of him. "What fine folks indeed. Let us raise a glass for their charity."

"A splendid suggestion," Father Roberto said. The corners of his lips pulled up to form a faint grin. "I've brought just the thing for the occasion."

A bottle of wine appeared from out of the sleeve of his mourning robes, and he set it in front of him on the table.

"Have you had a bottle of Don Immobile stashed on you all night?" Father David asked with a laugh.

It wasn't an impressive trick, but it was the first time I could remember him flashing a modicum of personality other than being a hard-ass. That in itself was a surprise.

"Some things are better left as mysteries."

Although Roberto's reply was to his want-to-be disciple, I couldn't shake the notion that his words were aimed at me.

"However," Father Roberto continued as he uncorked the bottle of port, "this seems like a natural segue to my finger's summary."

Father Sebastian cracked a smile as he passed his goblet forward. "Please don't tell me you have something to *wine* about."

I cringed internally. With a pun that bad, it was easy to understand how father jokes got their name.

"The only whining we shall hear is that of you lamenting how a Master of Sums and Tongues could out-rob the Master of Thieving," said Roberto.

I swallowed the laughter that wished to pour forth from me. His finger might have out-stolen Father Sebastian's on this occasion, but the priest boasted as though the theft was his own doing. The only thing he was capable of stealing was a pie from the kitchen, and even in that effort he still wouldn't go unnoticed.

"Just spit it out already," said Father Ignacio.

Father Roberto's eyes narrowed for a moment on the leader of the Thumb before he returned to gloating. "A merchant from Sirrom traveled across the continent to secure sixty caskets of Don Immobile's port batch of 638. We diligently separated them from his care on his way home through the mountain pass."

Although playing highway robber wasn't our style in the pinky, the scent that wafted up from the half cup he poured me made me appreciate his finger's work—if only for a moment.

"Their going rate on the market today is a hundred crowns per case. Though that value shall only go up over time."

"Well done," Father Sebastian said, raising his glass yet again. "Here's to another of Cuvar's blessings."

I joined in the toast. Notes of ripe berries and bitter chocolate consumed my palate as I took a swig. If this was how all their meetings went, then it was no wonder they were notoriously long.

Both Fathers David and Sebastian went on to explain they hadn't brought in any funds this week. The former claimed that would soon change as his finger's next game would begin in a matter of days. Sebastian, on the other hand, opted to play it coy.

"We have something in the works," he said. "You'll see soon enough."

Their eyes then fell to me. Although they didn't voice the question, one would have to lack a pulse in order to miss it. *What had we stolen this week?*

"I'm pleased to announce that we brought Mother Sienna's final game to a close today," I said before setting down my goblet and lowering my eyes. "Unfortunately, given the circumstances, we were only able to take Ianista Pozuelo for a fraction of our original plan."

Father Roberto smiled into his cup, the wine flushing his cheeks. "It's all right, young Tallis. I'm sure Mother Sienna would have appreciated it nonetheless. She knew, as we all know, that not every week will feel like a victory. Your time will come again."

I had the condescending prick right where I wanted him. The time had come to wipe that smug look off his face.

"Wise words are easily said but harder to follow," I said solemnly, pulling out my receipt from the coffer. "We had planned to take upwards of 100,000 crowns off him, but we only managed a measly 30,000. Hopefully, Cuvar will still look upon this small offering with pleasure."

While the others toasted the pinky's success, I basked in watching the color leave Roberto's face before taking another sip. After all, wine always tasted sweeter after silencing a rival.

"Let us move on to the news from the continent," Father Roberto said, not-so-subtly changing the topic of conversation. "Father David, what do our birds have to report on the rest of Yenra?"

Our Master of Combat's face pinched as he read from the scroll.

Members of the Council,

Although this is a preliminary report, we believe we have stumbled upon a matter that you must all be alerted to straight-

away. Trusted members of our network have given us reason to believe that the uprising in Gregus is more complicated than we initially thought.

The skin on the back of my neck stood on end as he read those words. Perhaps being forced to abandon the Pozuelo game early had been a good thing.

Although it is true that the uprising was started by an extremist religious movement, Father David continued, *new information has come to light that suggests the rebellion has been backed by the faithless Osigren Empire.*

We will delve into this matter further and be sure to update all of Cuvar's councils in the process. However, if validated, this development will prove our domino theory true. That the Osigrens seek to topple every religion on our planet one empire at a time until the world blindly worships science just as they do.

Gregus may be a small domino in the grand scheme of things, but even the slowest of children know that a small domino can topple the larger ones with enough momentum.

The room fell into an eerie silence as we all absorbed the weight of those words.

As dire as my message is, I encourage you not to act in haste. Time is needed to either confirm or rebuff this serious allegation. With that said, we need to be wary of any actions that threaten the relationships between our temples and our respective empires' governments.

I threw back the rest of my drink, but it did nothing to relieve me of the weight of the last sentence. There was no denying that we had recently experienced one of those such actions.

Blessed be Cuvar, and may he always be,
High Father Gravadain
The Keeper of Birds

I looked to each of our temple's councilmen, waiting for them to break the silence. There was no way that I could have been the only one to see the connection between Mother Sienna's murder and the contents of the bird keeper's letter.

"I've known Gravadain for nearly sixty years," Father Ignacio said, ending the silence that had lasted far too long. "That's going back to when we were newly confirmed acolytes terrorizing the streets of Corusa. In all our years of friendship, I have only known him to be wrong on one occasion. I pray with all my heart that this will be the second."

I sat there stupefied as they all echoed his sentiments. This was not because their concerns were unjustified—for in truth, I held them as well—but rather that none of them addressed the giant in the room.

"Is no one going to say it?" I finally asked.

Father Roberto raised one of his bushy eyebrows. "What is there to be said?"

His question felt like a punch to the gut. How could I be the youngest in this room and the least naïve?

"Be wary of actions that threaten our relationship with our empire's government," I said. "Does that not describe the very act of Mother Sienna's murder?"

Only Father Sebastian held my gaze. "You're right, Tallis, but there isn't much we can do about it at this stage."

My knuckles whitened as I gripped the stem of my goblet. I usually cloaked my emotions well, but I had to bite my tongue to prevent myself from screaming at him. Out of all of our council members, he was the last one I ever expected to turn his back on me.

"Besides," Father Roberto said, "High Father Gravadain commanded us not to act in haste."

It was too much. It was *all* too much.

"There is a difference between not acting in haste and not acting at all," I spat. "Tell me, have you done anything about her murder? It certainly seems that way given your refusal to tell me, or the rest of my finger, anything about the circumstances of her death."

"Listen here, child," Father Roberto said as he rose from his chair and slammed his fist into the table. "Do not forget your place. Sienna may have been your mother for years, but she was our sister for far longer. We are doing all that we can."

I scoffed. "Yeah, and what is that?"

Father Sebastian motioned to our Master of Sums that he would take it from here, and I set my glare upon him.

"We've already reached out to the royal family, Tallis," he said. His eyes pleaded with me to believe him. "They informed us that they were unaware of any such meeting with Mother Sienna. Our birds are looking further into the matter as we speak, and, obviously, this new information will be a part of their search."

Was this really all they had to offer me? The woman who had saved me from the gallows and raised me as her own told me to my face that she had a meeting with royalty. That was not something she would've lied about, and they simply took the royals at their word? Did he truly think that answer would satisfy me?

"Good fathers," a cheery foreign voice said from the doorway. "I hate to interrupt your meeting, but I'd like a word with Mother Sienna's acolyte."

Who in the world could have broken into the temple's secret chambers? The voice surely belonged to an outsider as I didn't recognize it as anyone from our temple. My head snapped to see who stood before us.

"Cuvar's cock," I muttered.

Although I had only ever seen a portrait of her, and she had clearly aged some since its creation, I would've recognized the black-clad woman before me anywhere. We stood in the presence of Cuvar's living saint. The one and only St. Keira.

8

NEREA

During my four years in Arremendia, I had rarely ventured to Cuvar, the neighborhood that surrounded my new Lord's temple, because of its location. In a city comprised of hills, it sat atop the largest. This left you with two ways of reaching its summit: a winding series of roads that wrapped around the outer portion of the city or the Ghent Stairs. Both options were an absolute bitch to climb. Fortunately for us, we were traveling down the ancient architect's thousand-step behemoth.

From the top looking down, even I had to admit that Ghent's creation offered a mesmerizing view. Although the darkness of night shrouded the hilly city's architecture, between the various lampposts and the flickering candlelight that shone out of strangers' windows, it looked as though we were plunging into a rolling wave of fireflies.

Despite the beauty that surrounded us, one question still plagued my mind.

"Sorry to change the subject," I said as we reached the bottom of another one of the many sets of stairs that comprised the monstrosity, "but why did you two and Tallis seem shocked by my number of stones when the rest of the temple celebrated it? I tried to ask Tallis, but he got pulled away before he could explain."

Omar, who had traded in his funeral robe for a pair of well-fitted black riding pants and a fancy white tunic that left little of his chest to the imagination, looked up at the sky as though the answer to my question had been written amongst the stars. "It's complicated."

If the answer was amongst the stars, then he was either shit at finding it or he wasn't searching very hard.

"Not really," said Damiana. Unlike our show pony in the form of a human male, she had opted for a simple lavender dress. Though maybe it wasn't as comfortable as it appeared because she picked at it like she was trying to destroy the thing.

I didn't press her to continue. During our limited time together, she had always preferred to dive into a subject rather than test the waters. If the trend continued, then it was only a matter of moments until she explained herself.

Damiana peered around to ensure no one in the pastel-colored apartments that flanked either side of the stairs was paying us any heed. Apparently content with her search, she brought her attention back to me. "The reason why we were also stunned by your total is because it matches Tallis's remaining debt to the copper."

"To the copper?" I asked.

Their initial surprise made sense. The odds of our debts matching exactly had to have been astronomical. However, it still felt as though I was missing the entirety of its significance. If their reaction had been due to a simple alignment of numbers, then why had Tallis's interaction with me after the ceremony felt so forced? Also, what had he meant when he said we were destined to work together?

"Yeah," said Damiana, "except for the leader of a finger, it's uncommon for anyone to know an acolyte's remaining dues."

The sound of laughter and the scent of fried pintxos and beer reached us from the plaza below. It wouldn't be too much longer until we left the stairs behind for Old Town.

"If it's so uncommon, then why do both of you know the remainder of his debt?"

My fingermates, if that was even a term, exchanged a look.

Omar smiled at me like a flower monkey. "Now that answer is *truly* a bit more complicated."

"And better suited to hear away from prying ears," Damiana added. "Let us get our drinks and some privacy. Then we'll explain."

Their decision proved to be prudent. As we rounded the stairs' final bend, more than just the plaza became visible. So many people filled the square that dozens of them had chosen to sit on the steps to enjoy their fermented beverages.

Despite the lateness of the hour, it was common practice for the residents of Arremendia to socialize at this time. The days, especially in the summer, rivaled the temperatures of the Binsoro savanna. Since the sun kept them away, it was only natural for them to wish to socialize in the cooler night air.

"You've got to enjoy the King's Day festivities," Omar said over the crowd once we reached the plaza.

Was he being sardonic? We were still two days away from the official start of the King's Day Festival, but the swell of visitors it drove into the city had begun. If he was being serious, then I could only assume that had to do with there either being more targets to rob, more women to bed, or a combination of the two.

The walk to Marzana from Ghent's Plaza usually took ten minutes if you were moving at a leisurely pace. However, the added weaving caused by the crowd doubled the time.

"Cuvar's cock," said Damiana once we reached the bar. "Is all of Yenra trying to drink at Marzana's tonight?"

Omar stepped forward, pushing his hair into place. "Fear not, fair ladies. Go claim that section of stairs by the Luna tree while I fetch us the first round."

"Blow me, gentle sir," Damiana teased. "That chivalry crap isn't fooling me. We both know you only want to go in there so you can hit on the barmaids before I can."

He clutched his chest in mock offense before shrugging it off. "Alas, you know me too well."

"Why don't we all go in together?" asked Damiana. "We can consider it your first mission as a part of the pinky."

Her notion, while sweet, was unappealing. The bar looked more crowded than a watering hole during a drought, and it probably smelled as bad.

"Tonight is supposed to be in honor of me, is it not?" I asked.

When neither of them disagreed, I plowed ahead with my reasoning. "I'd rather enjoy the fresh air by the Luna tree than wade into that swamp. Damiana can fetch us some beers while you explain the *truly* more complicated story to me."

"You heard her," Damiana said before bolting to the bar as though she was worried I would change my mind.

I took a seat on the step closest to the tree and leaned my back against its rugged bark. Out of all the plants in this city, these were the only things that could come close to challenging the beauty of the flora of my homeland.

This was due solely to its flowers. They looked like five-pointed stars with deep-purple centers that ombred to white at the tips of its petals. While aesthetically pleasing by day, they earned their name, and my awe, by night when they glowed under the light of the moons. With the twin moons being a sliver of themselves that night, the flowers above my head only let off a faint glimmer.

"I'm sorry to disappoint," Omar said as he sprawled out on the step beside me, "but I fear your plan to seduce me while Damiana's away is doomed to fail. I have to deny you carnal knowledge of me until both of us are no longer acolytes."

Although I knew he was joking, his words left a sour taste in my mouth. He may have been as handsome as the gods, but he appeared to be equally as vain. Did his little ruse work on anyone?

"Based on the size of your debts," he continued, "that may be a long time, so I hope you are not aroused by things you cannot possess."

I tsked him. "Please, I've known monkeys like you my whole life. Even if I was interested—which I am not—you wouldn't be able to handle me. You've spent so much time climbing branches that you wouldn't know what to do if you got your little paws on a trunk."

"Are you calling yourself a tree?" he asked, staring at me blankly. He shifted his body closer, if only by a fraction. "I honestly don't get it."

I cracked a smile. "Nor will you."

A flush crossed his face. Had he finally understood my meaning, or was he simply embarrassed? Regardless of the reasoning, his dwelling on either thought served no purpose to either of us, and I changed the subject to put him out of his misery.

"So are you going to tell me why everyone knows about Tallis's debt, or am I going to have to pry it from your lips?"

Resting his elbows on his inner thighs, Omar leaned forward toward me. "There are three things you need to understand. The first, and Damiana could tell the story better as she was actually there, is that Tallis drew the greatest debt anyone can remember Cuvar granting. We're talking about an amount so immense that scholars across the continent had to check their sources to see if it had ever been bested."

"And this is necessary for me to know because..."

"I did warn you it was complicated. Do you want to know the answer or not?"

I sighed. "Fine, what are the other two?"

"Has Damiana or anyone else explained to you how we pay down our debts?"

"No, but I guess it has something to do with stealing our way to freedom."

His laughter danced on the breeze. "There is a little more nuance to it than that but not by much. You see, any common man can pick the pocket of a fool on the street. However—"

"Let me guess, you're no common man?"

He unleashed an easy, too perfect smile at my barb. "Those were your words, not mine. Now, if you would refrain from interrupting, I'd really like to finish—"

"Are you already sharing the most frequent complaint you receive from your lovers?" Damiana asked as she returned with the beers. "That's odd. I thought I would bring that up before you did."

The sound of our laughter and the clinking of our glasses drowned out his attempts to rebuff the claim.

I took a sip of the foamy drink and savored the bitterness of its hops.

"As I was trying to say," Omar continued. "Because our scores are significantly larger and require multiple people to pull them off, it is only natural that we divvy the earnings out equally amongst those who participated in the game. Once divided, that money is then put towards each person's respective debts."

Damiana cleared her throat. "Unless of course everyone agrees to divide their shares differently. Like we've been doing to help pay down Tallis's debt."

"Wait, why aren't you taking equal shares?" I asked. My eyes flicked back and forth between them. "Don't you want to pay off your debts as soon as possible?"

"I was about to cover that with reason number three," Omar said.

"Aww, look at you listing your lines of reasoning," Damiana said as she reached out to pat him on the head. "Father Roberto would be so proud of you."

He batted her hand away before it could disturb any of his lovely black locks. "Fuck off. Why don't you go play with that ant?"

"Where?" she asked with a smile that rivaled the brightness of the flowers above us as she scanned the ground for her new little friend.

"Can you finish answering my question?" I asked before they could spiral away from the topic any further. "Why aren't you taking equal shares?"

Damiana nodded at Omar. "Go on, tell her your third reason."

"The last thing you need to understand is that very few people get to stay at the temple once they complete their acolyteship," he said. "In fact, unless you become a priest or are a tradesperson, like yourself, you're essentially forced to either retire or spread Cuvar's word abroad."

I replayed his three explanations in my mind. How did Tallis's unworldly debt, the payment method, and their faith's exit policy have to do with them knowing his debt?

No sooner had the question formed when the answer came to mind.

"Let me get this straight," I said. "You all know his debt because you're actively paying it down so he can leave sooner?"

Omar offered me half a grin. "That's not *too* bad for a first guess. I'm glad to see your mind is as sharp as your tongue. That'll bode well for you here."

Damiana smacked him on the back side of his head. The force of which caused him to lose a few drops of precious beer.

"Hey," he said. "What in Potami's murky depths was that for?"

She simply raised her eyebrows and lowered her nose while she stared at him. Whatever their silent language was, the message was received loud and clear.

"My apologies," Omar said. "What I meant by that was we're not trying to get him out earlier. Rather, our goal is for all of us to leave here together."

Damiana shook her pointer finger. "You mean all of us except for Ora. She has wanted to be Mother Sienna's successor since I was around twelve or thirteen."

As Omar rambled on about their childhood plans, I realized two things. The first was that I had been thrown into a family, not a finger. These two, despite their taunts, and Tallis were not related by blood, but they were bonded by an even deeper connection. It was the connection of a chosen family.

As lovely as the first realization was, the second tore at me. "What will you do now that my debt is as great as Tallis's?"

It didn't take a genius to see the two options that lay before them. They could either pitch in to help a stranger pay off their debt sooner and force themselves all to stay here longer in the process or continue to do things as they had always done.

"You're part of the family now," Damiana said, not even taking a moment to think it over. "It might be a fucked-up family, but we look out for our own."

Omar grunted his agreement.

"If you wish, then we'll help you and Tallis equally," she said.

A lump formed in my throat. These two had no reason to treat me the same as they did Tallis. They had known him for far longer than me, and I assumed they had been through more together than I could imagine. The fact that they were even willing to assist me meant the world to me.

"Thanks," I said as I dabbed away the tear that had started to blur my vision. "I have no idea how I could ever repay you for your generosity."

A grin flashed across Omar's face. "I have a few ideas."

Damiana went to smack him again, but he managed to block the blow this time and spare his beer.

"What was that for?" he asked. "I didn't do anything that time."

Damiana cracked her knuckles. Each one seemed to pop louder than its predecessor. "Keep your ideas to yourself. We're a temple, not a brothel."

"You cut me too deep. Just because I like to enjoy myself from time to time doesn't mean all my thoughts are perverse."

Based on her smirk, it was clear Damiana would beg to differ.

"What were these *innocent* ideas of yours, then?" I teased.

The effects of the beer started to make their mark on me. Its warmth spread throughout my body, melting the day's tension away with it. I brought my glass to my lips once more to hasten its spread.

"I just thought that you might be willing to return the favor by inventing something for us while you wait for our next game," he said.

There was nothing funny about his words, but there was something in the way he said them that caused me to laugh.

"Obviously you don't have to," he said, trying to backtrack his previous comment. "I only thought—"

I waved him off. "It's fine, honestly. What would you like me to try to make?"

His slack-jawed expression could have been from surprise at my acceptance or a sign of his brain's struggle to form an idea. Damiana had no problem filling the silence.

She pointed down toward the Beltza. "We need a stealth escape boat for that thing. Too many of our games have ended with us diving into that murky bitch, and I'm not the best swimmer."

"I'll add it to the drawing board," I said with a shrug before turning my head to Omar. "And what about you? According to the barmaids, it sounds like I should invent something that would make you last longer. Then again, I'm only an inventor, not a miracle worker."

Damiana let out a bark of approval.

Omar shook his head. "If I'm stuck with you two teaming up on me for the foreseeable future, then the least you could do is make me something to block out the noise."

"I'll see what I can do," I said.

"Spoken like a true member of the pinky," Damiana said, raising her glass. "Here's to joining our fucked-up little family."

Her words made my skin crawl. How could I be a true member when I wasn't a thief? Did I even want to become part of a family of thieves?

Despite my unease, I echoed her toast, and we spent the rest of the night drinking and laughing along the banks of the holy Beltza.

9

TALLIS

Me? Cuvar's living saint wanted to talk to me? The notion seemed too good to be true. Worse yet, her expectant blue eyes fixated upon me.

My mouth grew dry under that stare, and it felt as though a weight had trapped my tongue. What in Cuvar's name was wrong with me? It was as though all the moisture that had vanished from my mouth had decided to reemerge in my palms.

"St. Keira," Father Roberto said, composing himself before the other priests. "We were not expecting you. To what do we owe this honor?"

The saint started to untie her ceremonial mask as she strode to the heart of the room. "I had just finished emptying one of Osigra's Imperial vaults when I caught word of Mother Sienna's passing. Although the priestess was my most fierce rival during our trials, she also earned my respect through that process."

With the knot undone, Keira removed the cloth, fully revealing her pale face, sharp beak of a nose, and wavy hair that was streaked with more gray than brown. She crumpled the mask and set it on Cuvar's hand. "That respect grew to a correspondence. Which then grew to a friendship over the years. So, Father..."

Whether she intended the pause to come across as a power move, I could not say. However, it certainly had that effect.

"Roberto, Father Roberto," the priest stammered after a pause that lasted far too long.

"As I was saying, Father Roberto," the saint said, "I am here to pay a dear friend my respects and support through her final trial. I know she would've done the same for me."

Out of all the words she said, four stood out above the rest: *through her final trial.* Did that mean she planned to stay until all fourteen days of her funeral rites had been completed?

My pulse quickened. Getting the opportunity to learn from her felt like stumbling upon a small island of hope in the middle of this sea of shit my life had become. Although it wouldn't alleviate my problems, it could provide me with a few much-needed mental respites. That alone would be worth all the gold in our vaults.

"Your gesture is much appreciated," said Father Sebastian, rising from his seat. "I am confident Mother Sienna would have been as touched by your presence."

A sad smile crossed St. Keira's face, and her eyes glazed over as if a memory danced before them. "Thank you, that means more than you know."

"And what does all this have to do with the boy?" Father Roberto asked. "You did say you wish to speak with him, did you not?"

It took all my effort not to snort. He might have been three times my age, but his whole you're-still-a-child-in-my-eyes routine had grown tiresome. I was twenty and three, and if I survived another half dozen years, then I'd be the same age Mother Sienna was when she officially became a priestess.

St. Keira shrugged. "I'm quite interested in finding out the reason for it myself as well."

"What is that supposed to mean?" Father Roberto asked.

"When I entered the temple grounds, Cuvar told me that I would find him down here and that I should talk to him in private," said the living saint.

The Master of Sums shook his head but was unable to rid himself of his stupefied expression. "Our Lord wishes you to speak to *him*?"

Although Father Roberto's blatant disregard for my value would have enraged me under different circumstances, a portion of myself agreed with his sentiment. I could only see three potential reasons for St. Keira's words, the first being that she was simply bullshitting them to get out of this conversation. Hopefully, that was the case as the other two reasons were much more alarming.

The second possible reason was that Cuvar's living saint had lost her mind and believed our Lord was talking to her. If my idol turned out to be a lunatic, then it would be the bile glazing on top of the feces-filled pastry that was this week.

However, the worst possible option was that she spoke the truth. That Cuvar was actually real and that he instructed her to find me. Despite being raised in the temple, the idea that the gods and goddesses of Yenra were real seemed as likely as the world being flat. Everything about the notion seemed illogical. However, if it were true, then I stood on the precipice of a life-altering paradigm shift.

"Do you find Tallis unworthy of our Lord's attention?" St. Keira asked.

"Wha—" Father Roberto started, but our visitor continued over him.

"Is he not the same acolyte who stole two priceless Rollet masterpieces? Is he not the same acolyte who successfully stole from Potami's temple even before his indoctrination?"

I gulped. It was not surprising that word of our completion of the Gunderson game had spread throughout the continent's temples. After all, it was not every day that long-lost artifacts were found, let alone stolen. However, Mother Sienna must have told her much if she knew of the act which sent me to the gallows as a child.

"He is one and the same, but—"

St. Keira cut him off again, this time with a wave of her hand. "If the acolyte is as accomplished in the ways of our Lord as you admit, then is it Cuvar's judgment that you are questioning?"

There was no mistaking it. The question was a dagger thrown to put the priest in his place and end the conversation entirely. I joined the rest of the council in watching Father Roberto, bracing both for the damage and his response.

"Apologies, St. Keira," said the leader of the middle finger, hanging his head. "I did not intend to question His will. These past few days have been testing, and your request caught me unprepared."

Stunned silence consumed the air as St. Keira walked around Cuvar's hand. She stopped in front of the middle finger and lifted the priest's head by his chin with one hand until he met her gaze.

"Fear not, Father Roberto," the saint said. Her smile

reminded me of a calm ocean after a storm. "Our Lord will forgive you. I'm sure of it."

As the priest stammered out a thank you, I wished Ora were here to witness it. We had all faced our share of his power trips, but he seemed to delight in demeaning her. She would have relished getting to watch someone get the upper hand on him for once.

St. Keira spun on her heel and made her way toward the Hall of Saints. "Come along, Tallis. Let us discover what Cuvar has planned for us."

"Well, this was an exciting meeting to say the least," I said, rising from my seat. "I hate to leave early, but"—I gestured in the direction the saint had gone—"it seems as though I'm off to do our Lord's work."

I sped toward the hall, but I didn't get there fast enough.

"Tallis," Father Roberto called, bringing me to a stop. "I expect you to give us a full report on your return."

He'd like that, wouldn't he? "As you wish. Unless our Lord forbids it, of course. He is the higher power after all."

I could hear the steam whistling out of the priest's ears as I turned my back on him once more. Oh well, it was a problem that future me would have to deal with, if at all.

"There you are," St. Keira said once I reached her at the foot of the stairs. "I was beginning to worry Father Whatshisname wasn't going to allow you to come."

A puff of amusement escaped through my nostrils. "If it wasn't for Cuvar's order, then he'd probably strap me to that chair before letting me join you."

She pushed the hidden door open and turned to enter the heart of the temple.

"Speaking of which," I continued, "did Cuvar truly command you to find me? It all seems..."

"Like a massive load of shit?"

"Well, was it?"

St. Keira paused in front of the temple's doors, momentarily letting her gaze fall upon the statue of Cuvar before focusing on me. "Fear not, Tallis, I have yet to lose my mind. However, there are too many prying ears here to speak plainly. I'll explain everything once we reach a more secure location."

I gestured to the door. "Lead the way."

With a flick of her wrist, she unlocked the door, and we bolted into the clinging summer night air.

A myriad of questions flooded my mind as we descended Cuvar's hill and cut through side street after side street in the city's lower level. Where was she taking me? Why weren't we safe to speak freely at the temple? Why did she, or Cuvar, wish to speak with me alone in the first place?

By the time he finally stopped, we had traveled across three neighborhoods to find ourselves at the foot of the library in the University District. Although I had never previously stepped inside the domed marble masterpiece, we had frequently visited the bars in this neighborhood as they were some of Omar's and Damiana's favorites.

"Is there a book you'd like me to read?" I asked as I watched her run her fingers over the building's facade.

"There are so many books worth reading that I wouldn't know where to make you begin," she said as she continued to pace the side of the library. "However, there's a private place Si—Mother Sienna showed me the last time I was here. Ah, there it is!"

Was there a hidden room built into the side of the library? I took a step closer to take a better look.

"How are your climbing skills? Or would I have been better off finding one of the Sandovals for this?"

It took a moment for me to process what she had rediscovered. There were the slightest indents in the marble barely large enough to work as foot- and handholds for an experienced climber. "I'm no temple squirrel, but I can handle—wait, how do you know about the Sandoval siblings?"

"I did say Mother Sienna and I were close, did I not?"

Before I could respond, she began climbing the side of the five-story building.

Despite my lack of faith, I said a little prayer asking the gods to make sure I wasn't too drunk to complete the climb. Fortunately, scaling a large building with your fingertips proved to be a surprisingly sobering activity.

When I reached the top, the living saint helped pull me over the ledge. Sucking in a breath, I rolled onto my backside to discover we were on the flat section of roof that wrapped around the library's dome. The corner we were on was as deep and wide as a king's bed, while the path that skirted along the dome to the other corners was just wide enough for a person to walk across.

"You said Mother Sienna brought you here?"

St. Keira sat down beside me and leaned her back against the dome. "Unlike you, she could outclimb the temple squirrels, and this, *this*, was one of her favorite views of your city."

A soft laugh escaped my lips as I soaked in the view. From this vantage point, we could take in the whole of Potami's Temple, which sat directly across the Beltza from us. The large metallic structure dedicated to the worship of the river goddess had been designed to resemble a series of rolling waves. It wasn't a perfect recreation. However, it still produced an undeniable sense of awe, especially when it reflected the neighborhood's light at night.

"What's so bloody funny?" asked the saint. Her Oparian accent came out stronger than before.

I sighed and shook my head. "I knew her for almost my entire life, but I never once pictured her as an avid climber. It makes me wonder what else I didn't know about her."

"That's just the nature of humanity. It's rare for us to show more than a few sides of ourselves to anyone, and Sienna was no exception. We should count ourselves blessed to be included in the small circle of people who she let in close enough to see more than one of her sides."

Despite the truth of her words, the comfort they provided was not enough to keep me from wondering about all of her unknowns.

"You never answered my earlier question," I said to change the topic. "Did Cuvar tell you to find me, or was that a load of rubbish to get Father Roberto off your back?"

It was her turn to laugh. "As insane as this may sound, the answer is a bit of both."

My eyebrow fought to arch its way off my face.

"Cuvar informed me of Mother Sienna's murder and sent me here to prevent the temple from being destroyed," she continued. "The bit about his command for me to find you was proper bullocks, but it did the trick. Nothing silences our Lord's righteous servants quite like telling them he's given you a direct order."

Her response did nothing to answer my question. It only created a plethora of new ones that tried to shoot out of me at once.

"Wait, you've talked to Cuvar? Does that mean you know who killed Mother Sienna? Hold on, did you say our temple may be destroyed? Does this have something to do with the Osigren Empire? How do I factor into all of this?"

If she hadn't raised her hands, then I probably would never have stopped spouting off questions.

"Let me try to answer these before you ask me more questions than I can count."

A blush crept its way across my face.

"Prior to my sainthood ceremony, I was a nonbeliever like yourself. However, once my spirit was connected to his, he had the ability to communicate with me. The first time he entered my mind, I thought I was going insane."

"Does that mean you can talk to him right now?" I asked.

She sighed. "No, I'm afraid it's a one-way path in that regard, and with his weakened powers in our realm, he can only easily communicate with me when I'm in one of his temples."

"Isn't he a god? How can his powers be weakened?"

"Ever since the gods were locked away by Zolten and his rebels, their abilities to influence our world have been tethered to the strength of our belief in them," St. Keira said. "Although many people appreciate the work of temples, fewer and fewer believe in the deities they were founded for."

Despite my doubts about the alleged demigod coup being real, her final words rang true for me. I had been raised in the temple to become a disciple, and I hadn't even believed in Cuvar. If I had doubts, then surely many others outside our walls did as well.

"As for your question about Mother Sienna's murder," she continued, "I wish I knew the answer so I could kill them with my own hands. However, Cuvar has told me what it was in relation to."

A jolt ripped through my core. I leaned forward so the sound of her words could reach me even faster. "And it was in relation to what, exactly?"

"What I'm about to tell you needs to stay between us," she said, seemingly stilling the air on command. "If this information reaches the wrong person's ears, then the consequences could be unfathomable."

I held my hands to stop myself from fiddling with them. "Your secrets are safe with me."

"The warning sent from the keeper of birds is even more pressing for your temple than you realize. Princess Amaya, the Osigren Empire, and at least one member of your very own temple are plotting together to not only outlaw religion in Arremendia, but they also plan to overthrow the king."

Her words drove the air from my lungs. How could any of that be possible? Why would the princess wish to overthrow her father? Why would any member of our temple wish to have religion outlawed?

If I hadn't heard High Father Gravadain's urgent warning, or if I hadn't held St. Keira in such high regard, then I would have laughed this idea off as being preposterous. Unfortunately, it now seemed all too plausible.

St. Keira ran her fingers through her thick curls. "Apparently, Princess Amaya hungers for power but does not wish to play second fiddle to a stranger in a foreign land. Obviously, the odds of her overthrowing her father and skipping her brother in the line of succession on her own without severe consequences would be slim."

"If what you're saying is true, then it would make sense why she'd look to the Osigrens for assistance. Not many countries would want to see King Kepa removed, and even fewer would keep that knowledge to themselves if they opted not to help her."

The living saint grimaced as she shook her head. "You'd think the opportunity to remove your enemy's leader would be enough for them. However, my crew discovered that they only agreed to help her if she would outlaw religion upon her coronation."

I nodded as I pondered her words. Her explanation answered some of my questions, but it had come nowhere close to answering all of them.

"But why would the princess wish to dethrone her father, and how would they bypass Prince Ander? Also, I still don't understand how this involves our temple."

"I wish I knew the answer to your first question, but I can answer the others," St. Keira said as she pulled out a piece of paper from inside her shirt. She flipped it over in her hands. "How do you think the people of Arremendia would respond if their new queen made them give up their religion without any significant justification?"

"Some people wouldn't give two shits, the zealous would riot and refuse to recognize her, and those who enjoy chaos would help it spread."

"They'd refuse to recognize her," she said, touching the tip of her nose with one hand and pointing at me with the other. "In order for her to gain power herself and fulfill the Osigren demands, she'd need to do it in a way that removed her brother and father and would also lay the blame for their fall on the city's temples."

"So you think someone in our temple is helping her frame us?"

"Not just us, all of Arremendia's major temples," she said as she passed me the paper. "It's why Mother Sienna died. She was getting too close to the truth."

The letter, which initially felt as light as a feather in my hand, suddenly outweighed our temple's statue of Cuvar. My hands shook as I opened it.

"She addresses me by my given name," she explained as I started to read.

My breath got stuck in my throat. I would recognize Mother Sienna's tiny, slanted cursive handwriting anywhere.

Dear Laura,

I fear this may be the last letter I ever send you. Two weeks ago, I stumbled into an Osigren plot to dethrone King Kepa and place his daughter in his stead. To make matters worse, it appears as though the princess herself and members of our own temple are willing participants in this scheme.

When you receive this message, ride here at once. Although I will meet with the king's ear on the morrow to share my findings, we will need your help should things go awry. If they claim my soul before your arrival, then you can find the evidence I've hidden away at our last sunrise.

Forever the better thief,
Sienna

PS, you can trust the members of my finger. The rest of the temple I cannot speak of with such certainty.

The letter verged on being too much for me to comprehend. Who in the temple did she fear was in on this? Did she meet with the king's ear, or did one of our own cut her down before she ever had the chance?

However, it did make two things abundantly clear. We were wading into a pile of shit that was way over our heads, and she wanted us to work together to get to the bottom of it. If that was her last wish, then I'd make sure we followed through for her.

"She mentions there being evidence at your last sunrise," I said. "Have you already looked for it?"

She made a sweeping gesture to the area around us. "This is it. It was the first place I came when I arrived here at dusk."

"And?"

"Nothing, well, nothing up on this roof anyway. She might have meant something we could see from up here, but I'll have to follow that lead tomorrow."

I scanned the area for other landmarks. Besides Potami's Temple, from our vantage point, we could see the outline of our temple up on the hill, the river markets, and a slew of other buildings sprawling out in all directions. If her evidence was out there, then it would be like trying to find a needle in a haystack.

"Whoever these traitors at our temple are behind this, be they singular or plural," St. Keira continued, "they would have to value power over their love of our Lord and his traditions. It may be bloody deranged, but it's the only plausible reason I can think of for anyone to do this."

Her description brought one name to the front of my mind. It didn't ripple through me but rather crashed with the strength of a tidal wave. "Roberto, it has to be Father Roberto."

My fists clenched at the thought. He was the one who had denied me information about her death. He was the one who wished to separate my finger without following our church's tradition. Unlike the other council members, he seemed to be the only one who hungered for power.

"You may be right, but we need the evidence before we can make our move," said the saint. "If we move too soon and turn out to be wrong, then we will find ourselves in a proper pile of shit. Not only would we have to start over, but in that scenario, the real culprits would know that we are onto them."

Despite almost every fiber of my being wanting to march back to the temple and begin interrogating our middle finger, I could not deny her reasoning. "Then what do you suggest we do?"

"My crew are currently scouring Osigren for evidence that we can use to prove this treason to your king. As talented as I may be, it is not the best idea for me to search for evidence here by myself. That is why I need you and your finger to help me find this proof before it is too late."

If Cuvar was as real as she claimed, then maybe her presence here was the answer to my prayers. I had asked Him to put Mother Sienna's killer and Ora's attacker in my path, and it now appeared as though I was one step closer to wringing their necks.

"Not that you need the pot sweetened," St. Keira continued, "but I do have the ability to pardon the debts of you and your finger if you choose to assist me."

The chance for revenge, to save the kingdom, and even earn my freedom stared back at me. To think, only a few hours ago, all hope seemed to be lost, and now my cup appeared to runneth over. Time had a strange ability to steal from you one moment and bless you the next.

"Alas, it is not for me to decide," I admitted.

"Are you not the acting leader of your finger?"

"I am many things, but I am not our leader. As confident as I am that the rest of the pinky will agree to help, I cannot decide for them."

St. Keira's easy smile turned into a firm line. "Although this delay pains me, I respect your decision. Go and collogue with your finger, but make haste. Time is a fleeting creature, and there's no telling how much of it we have left."

10

NEREA

When I was ten years old, my father asked me why I spent so much time trying to solve problems. His question was well intended. Life in the savanna did not allow children to be children for long, and he saw his precious daughter not spending this time participating in the common games of youth.

"You'll have all your life to work, my clever one," he said. "Don't you want to have fun?"

My little brow furrowed at that, wrinkling like a wild hairless boar. Up until that point, I had no idea that others didn't find making inventions and solving problems enjoyable. Even back then, I was stubborn. If my joys marked me as different, then I would paint them on my skin like an honor.

"It is more than fun, Papa. It gives me peace."

It gives me peace. Those words were true then, and they rang truer with each passing year.

Some people lost themselves in the fantastical wanderings of a good book, others in the arms of a lover, and far too many lost themselves trying to reach the bottom of a mug.

Our realm probably held as many variations of escapism as the people who roamed it. My variation just happened to take the shape of problem-solving.

When I was in the midst of inventing a solution to a challenge, it was as though the rest of the world melted away. Beyond the therapeutic release they provided me was the added benefits of helping my loved ones and community. Add in the heaps of praise and it was no wonder why I got hooked.

"And that should do it," I said to myself as I finalized my first plan as an official member of the pinky.

A smile stretched across my face as I imagined showing it to Damiana. During her drunken ramblings about her desired escape boat, I doubted she ever pictured anything as dynamic as the sketch that lay before me.

Something touched the back of my shoulder, and I nearly jumped out of my new acolyte's robes. With a startled yell, I spun around, sending papers and charcoal sticks flying off my workshop's desk in the process.

"Sorry, sorry," Damiana said with her palms up to protest her innocence. "You didn't respond when I called your name, so I didn't know what else to do."

In an attempt to quell my racing heart, I forced myself to take a deep breath. "You're fine. Sometimes I forget that my surroundings exist when I'm focused on a project."

"Just don't let Omar know that," she said with a laugh as she dropped to the ground to pick up my things. "Otherwise he'll be trying to scare you on a regular basis."

My fingers brushed against the cold concrete floor as I scooped up the plans I designed for her.

"So what had you so distracted that you didn't hear my loud mouth calling your name?"

I rolled the scroll flat against the smallest of my workbenches. "Seeing as I don't have any major projects yet, I thought I'd get started on your escape boat."

The faintest gasp escaped her lips.

"Don't get too excited," I said. "There are certain aspects of this, like pedal-driven propellers, that I've never attempted before. Even if the trial-and-error stage goes well, we'd need to find another place to make it. The basement you all have set me up in is amazing, but I doubt Cuvar himself could pull off the miracle of getting a boat this size through that door."

"I'm sure my Lord could find a way, but I have a solution that will make it unnecessary."

"And that is?"

She smirked. "One of my former flames has a dockyard in a little village up the Beltza. I can have your plans sent to her to build it for you. If you don't mind, of course."

I chewed on the inside of my bottom lip. Never in my entire time as an inventor had I had someone complete a project for me. The whole notion felt like trusting a stranger to raise your child.

"Besides," Damiana said, picking up on my hesitation, "I think you're about to have your hands full with another project."

"What makes you think that?" I asked, rearranging the charcoal sticks until each was in its correct place.

"Tallis has summoned the pinky to meet at our rendezvous point as soon as possible. We're to dress in civilian wear, so you'll want to change quickly before we go."

Thank the stars. My basement workshop was the coolest place on the temple grounds, and I still found it sweltering in this heat. Sure, the savanna was far warmer, but at least we had enough common sense to wear breathable clothes instead of these glorified blankets.

The change in clothes proved to be needed as the cafe on the outskirts of the city that served as their meeting point offered less shade than a tree stump. Besides its lack of coverage, it looked like it was a solid gust away from collapsing in on itself. If it weren't for the scent of their pastries, I'd be hard-pressed to name one positive thing about it.

We had barely sat on the rickety chairs when Omar appeared.

"Sorry I took so long," he said, peering around as he joined what remained of our table. "I had to wait until Sebastian's blades could cover Ora for me. Do you have any idea what this is about?"

Damiana shrugged. "I'm not sure, but the only thing that would make sense is he got a lead on what happened to Mother."

"But why discuss that out here?" I asked. "Couldn't we talk about that at—"

A loud whistle cut off my question, and my fingermates rose to their feet at the sound. I was about to ask them what they were doing when I spotted Tallis. He was guiding a gondola through the river toward us.

"Grab me a badgerpaw and hop on!"

Omar snagged a few pastries off the counter, and Damiana sent a few coppers flying like songbirds in the barista's direction.

"So why did I have to design an escape boat from scratch when you have this thing waiting around?" I asked as I stepped into the boat. Its unsteady surface made my heart seize in my chest, if only for a moment.

Tallis's brow creased. "What makes you think we own this vessel, and what escape boat?"

"You should have seen the sketch she made," Damiana

said. "Well, I've already sent it to Violeta. So you'll see the final result soon enough."

Our makeshift gondola driver shook his head as he pushed us back toward the center of the Beltza. "I guess we've spent money on more futile projects than that."

"That's the spirit, Brother," said Omar, lounging against the curved front of the boat. "Life is all the more pleasurable when you embrace the frivolous with the delight it deserves."

If those words came out of any other mouth, then I would have written it off as sarcasm. However, his joke landed like a secretly admitted motto.

Tallis laughed. "Never in a million years. Besides, we have more pressing matters at hand."

"This better be good," Omar said as he fanned his face. "I love traveling the Beltza as much as anyone, but at high noon with no shade is a different story altogether. Especially considering I had to leave Ora to be here."

As much as I enjoyed watching him melt under the heat, I found myself in agreement with him. Was his information truly that dire, or was he the type who possessed the need for dramatics?

"We have a lead on Mother Sienna's murder," Tallis whispered as we passed through the arched gate of Arremendia's outer wall. "I must warn you, it's far worse than any situation I imagined since the attack."

My mind went to work on what little information he provided. What was the worst thing a servant of Cuvar could imagine? Did their faith believe in demons? No, that wouldn't make sense. He had told me he didn't believe in the gods on the night we met. If that were true, then he surely didn't believe in the supposed monsters either.

"That's marvelous news," Damiana said before tossing

me one of the badgerpaws, "but I must agree with Omar. I don't see why you had to bring us out here to enlighten us on the matter."

I hadn't realized earlier that the pastries were covered in a gooey glaze, but the stickiness that coated my fingers no longer concerned me. Damiana's words had unlocked the riddle for me. During our limited interactions, Tallis had struck me as a reasonable man, and there was only one logical reason for why he would be afraid to share this discovery within the temple walls.

"Her murderer resides in our temple."

The moment the words escaped my lips, I sensed the weight of their gaze shift back and forth between Tallis and me as we awaited either his confirmation or denial.

Tallis peered around once more to ensure none of the boats that left the city with us were within earshot. Although his scan proved to be satisfactory, he still opted to lower his voice. "A lot has happened since Nerea's ceremony last night. Trust me when I say I know how crazy this sounds, but I need you to hear me out."

My words might have caught their attention, but his held it. Even though I had found him charming before, I had never noticed the magnetic nature of his demeanor until that moment. With every word he uttered and movement he made, I felt myself wanting to be pulled farther and farther into his world. It was no wonder why the rest of the pinky were enamored by him.

"I understand why you found that alarming," Omar said after Tallis finished explaining the letter from High Father Gravadain, "but I don't see how the Osigrens' ploy confirms that one of our own was behind Ora's attack and Mother Sienna's murder."

Our acting father flashed a grin. "That's only because patience isn't your forte."

"Does he have a forte?" Damiana chided.

Omar appeared to let the comment roll off him like water on a well snake's skin before unleashing a nonchalant bite of his own. "Restraint is certainly one of them. Without it, I would have taken your tongue many years ago."

"That's due to your lack of skill, not your lack of trying."

I shook my head. The remarks were clearly a game neither took too seriously, but did they have to be at it constantly?

"If it wasn't High Father Gravadain's warning, then what was it that revealed your lead?" I asked, hoping to bring the conversation back on task.

"St. Keira showed up at our council meeting unannounced," Tallis said.

Who? The way Damiana's and Omar's heads snapped to attention, she had to have been someone of repute.

"She told the council that Cuvar sent her to speak to me alone," he continued, "but in reality, it was because she couldn't trust the rest of them given the contents of Mother Sienna's letter."

Everyone on our boat grew silent as we waited for his explanation.

"In it, she wrote of stumbling upon a conspiracy. One in which Princess Amaya, the Osigren Empire, and at least one member of our clergy are plotting together to overthrow the king."

My jaw dropped with such ferocity that I expected to find a punctured hole in our gondola. Nothing about his statement made any sense. I may not have been well versed in the politics in my city of refuge, but the idea of a princess allying with a foreign enemy to overthrow her own father seemed like a stretch. And that wasn't factoring in the odds of the role our temple may have been playing in this alleged debacle.

However, what surprised me more was how eagerly both Damiana and Omar ate up his words. The way they nodded along without questioning it had my stomach in knots.

"Maybe this is just my naivety showing, but who in the world is this St. Keira person, and why do you believe her?" I asked. "If this boat had as many holes as her story, then we would have drowned minutes ago."

Damiana was the first to shake off her shock. "St. Keira is Cuvar's living saint. The title is an honor bestowed upon the greatest thief in all of our Lord's temples."

I was about to ask them why they would trust arguably the greatest thief in the world when I recognized the stupidity of the question. Of course they would trust her. They were all thieves, after all.

"As to the matter of trust," Tallis said, "I don't trust her. I trust Mother Sienna."

I saw my eyebrow arch in the reflection in his mossy-green eyes.

"When she first told me of their plot, I saw its flaws and questioned her on them. Although her answers made sense, it was reading our mother's letter that convinced me."

"And how do you know it's not a fake?"

By the looks on their faces, one would have thought I had questioned a child's belief in San Giovanni. While they might believe in a mythical gift bringer, I was not about to attach my wagon to this horse without proof.

"Skepticism is the best friend of a thief who wishes to live another day," he said, simultaneously affirming my stance while quelling their discomfort. "With that being said, I would recognize her handwriting anywhere."

Damiana let out a soft laugh. “I remember being baffled by her penmanship when I first arrived at the temple. Her letters were so small and precise that I thought they were written by ants.”

“I’m sure St. Keira will have the letter on her. If you all choose to join me for this meeting, then you may read her letter for yourself and draw your own conclusions.”

“If we join you?” asked Omar.

A splash sounded beside me as a fish jumped alongside our boat.

Tallis drove his pole into the water once more, correcting our course. “St. Keira needs to gather more evidence before she can take this to the king. Her own crew is scouring Osigra for evidence on that end as we speak. Mother Sienna told her that we were the only ones in the temple that she could trust, and that is why she is asking for our help to do the same thing here.”

The only solace his words provided me was the confirmation that the saint was no fool. Not only did this letter represent a threat to their way of life and the security of the kingdom, but it also provided them with a reason for a loved one's tragic death. Despite these emotional pulls, Keira possessed the clarity of mind to recognize that one letter from a priestess would not be enough to convince the crown to act against their own blood.

“I understand that, brother,” said Omar, “but you still haven't answered my question. Why did you say ‘if we join’ you? It is as though you doubt our willingness to help.”

Tallis sighed as he brushed a curl away from his face. “I know I am temporarily holding Mother's position as we wait for Ora to recover, but I am no father. As such, I cannot speak for any of you.”

That was good to hear. Even as a child, I did not like others making decisions for me.

"You all have the choice to make," Tallis continued. "Either you may join the living saint and me in gathering evidence to save our kingdom and temple and avenge our mother, or you may opt out of this challenge. If you choose the latter, then I will drop you off onshore, and I promise you will face no judgment."

Damiana didn't need a moment to think it over. "You can count me in."

"I'm in as well," said Omar.

All their eyes shifted to me. I was sure Tallis knew that the others would join him in a heartbeat. As I was new to this, I must have been the only question mark in his mind.

Sweat greased my palms. "I guess that makes three of us."

As far as first missions went, this would be as good as it could get. Compared to their thefts, which were morally gray on the most generous of scales, trying to prevent a coup might be the most positive contribution I would make for years to come.

"Perfect," said Damiana, cracking her knuckles. "Now that we're in the middle of nowhere, where exactly are we supposed to meet her?"

Tallis kept his eyes trained on the water. "There is a fishing village after this next bend in the river. We are to dock there and wait for her."

"And just how long are we supposed to wait?" I asked.

"As long as it takes," he said with a grunt as he guided us toward the right bank. "Given the urgency of the matter, I can't imagine that she'll make us wait long."

Our gondola hugged the outer bank of the Beltza as we

rounded the bend. Sure enough, the little fishing village that Tallis had promised would be there came into view.

"From this point forward," Tallis said, "we need to keep a tight lip on our purpose here. We'll know that it is safe to talk openly when St. Keira does. Until then, follow my lead."

Although he played it off as a reminder for everyone, I couldn't help but feel as though the real message had been directed to me. After all, I was the one who was new to this lifestyle, not the others.

Tallis pulled us into the first open dock, and Omar went to work tying the boat to it with only a slight look of distaste on his face.

While he turned up his nose at the scent of fish that filled the air and the sight of all the structures made from warped wood, I marveled at it. These were my type of people. There was no luxury here; there was nothing that had been gifted to them. Compared to most, these people had little to nothing and still survived anyway. They scrapped and fought each day for their existence, and I would show them nothing but respect and admiration in return.

After a few minutes of waiting, a cloaked old man with a long gray beard slowly approached us as he struggled to walk even with the aid of his cane. "Her net is ready for you." His shaking voice mirrored the tremble of his hands. "If you follow me, I'll take you to it."

Our eyes turned to Tallis.

He nodded. "Lead the way."

The old man moved at a pace that made slugs seem lightning fast. Even though the walk to his shack couldn't have taken more than ten minutes, it felt as though hours had passed.

"She'll join you in a moment," the old man said as the door creaked open, revealing the small empty room inside.

Tallis slipped the man a copper. "Thank you for your service. It is much appreciated."

Without another word, Tallis stepped inside, and we followed.

The state of the shack made my years at the refugee camp look like they had been spent in a palace. Besides the cot one could not pay me enough to sleep on and a large chest tucked in a corner, the room was barren.

"Careful where you step," Omar said. "I don't feel like dying underneath a pile of trash."

Damiana grinned. "You need to look on the bright side. There's a good chance I could find some termites here to add to my collection."

My brow furrowed. Did that mean she already had a collection of termites that she wanted to add to, or would these termites be a new addition to her collection of other bugs?

"I don't know about that," Tallis said with a laugh. "I am a little disappointed, though, that there isn't a net in here."

"What were you expecting to get for one bloody copper?" a female voice with an unfamiliar accent asked from behind us.

I spun around to see the old man had entered the room. However, he no longer hunched over his cane. He stood as tall and as proud as the mountains that flanked my new home.

"I didn't realize Mother Sienna raised a crew of penny-pinchers," she continued.

"She raised us to be generous, not excessive," Tallis said. "What's with the disguise?"

If I had any doubt that it was St. Keira who stood before

us, then one look at Damiana and Omar would have removed all doubt. The latter looked as though he was on the verge of fainting while the former struggled to appear nonchalant. It was the fidgeting of her hands that gave it away.

St. Keira peeled off her beard. "I doubt you were followed here, but caution is what has kept me alive all these years."

Her words caught me off guard. I had expected someone who was supposedly her Lord's greatest thief to be eager to praise herself. Was she as cautious as she implied, or was this simply a dose of feigned humility?

"I take it the rest of you have been brought up to speed?" asked the saint.

"For the most part," I said while the other two confirmed in near unison.

St. Keira tossed her beard onto the crate. "Brilliant, then let's not waste any more time."

"What can we do to help?" asked Tallis.

"Keep an eye on the princess for me. She'll be attending tomorrow's games along with the rest of the royal family." She pulled three slips of paper from under her cloak. "Getting you in the same box with her would be too risky, but these should get you close enough to observe her while remaining inconspicuous."

I cleared my throat. "And what will you be doing during our trip to the games?"

"Excuse me?" asked the saint, taking a half step back.

"There's only three tickets here." I pointed to the papers in Tallis's hand. "Since you need our help tracking down evidence, it only makes sense for all of us not to be in the same place at once."

St. Keira bowed her head. "Of course. Apologies for the

misunderstanding. While three of you track the princess, I will break into and scour her chambers. If there is no evidence to be found there, then I will see what I can find in the rest of the Hanging Palace."

How she planned to break in was beyond me, but I swallowed the question. Time was of the essence, and I didn't want to be the one to pull us from the game trail.

The saint stared down at me past the beak of her nose. "Mother Sienna never mentioned you in her letters. You must be the new member. The inventor, correct?"

"You may call me Nerea," I said, emphasizing my name, "and yes, you are correct."

Her fingers brushed the underside of her chin. The moment I had been waiting for finally arrived. What would she need me to invent for their task? A way to listen in on people from a distance? A contraption to climb up walls faster? Maybe she'd need me to come up with a way to determine what the princess touched in a given room?

"This here is a potent dose of spavati." St. Keira pulled out two glass spheres with gray smoke in them and held them between her fingers. "It's a fast-acting sleeping gas."

Gas? Why would we need sleeping gas? For the first time in years, my tongue felt like a boulder inside my mouth.

"There is no need to be alarmed, Nerea," she said.

Apparently, my ability to cloak my emotions was not up to her level.

"I generally only use these for escape purposes, but—"

"But this time is the exception?" I cut her off.

She smiled at that, sending a wave of thin wrinkles across her pale face. "Yes, but for good reason. Hopefully it doesn't come to this, but what say we needed to take a suspect in for questioning whose forces outnumber our own? Sure, we might be able to take them in a fair fight, but at what cost?"

That was an oddly specific scenario. My mind raced to decipher its meaning.

"In that situation," she continued, "we wouldn't be able to chuck these and run like I would usually do, and I don't like the idea of waiting around for the smoke to clear."

I felt my eyes light up as if I had been shocked by an eel. "So you want me to create you a device that will keep you safe from the smoke as you kidnap the princess?"

The tension consumed the room like a wildfire and dissipated just as quickly.

"I'm glad to see one can't easily pull the bag over your eyes," St. Keira said with a laugh. "Kidnap, though? That feels like a bloody loaded term. I prefer to call it our last-ditch-only-if-all-other-plans-fail option."

"I don't know. That sounds a little too wordy," Tallis said.

I glared at him. This was serious. Why did they always have to make a joke out of everything? Was I the only one among them who was uncomfortable with the idea of potentially having to kidnap the princess?

St. Keira's blue eyes softened as my gaze fell upon her once more. "Your concern is valid, Nerea. I assure you we would not do that unless the most dire circumstance were to arise."

Her wide-eyed plea registered with my gut as being genuine, but could I trust it? The reasoning she laid out for his plan was understandable enough. However, I didn't know if we could fully believe someone renowned for being the world's greatest thief.

"Can you make a device like the one you described?" the saint asked.

The simple answer would have been "probably, yes." I

had designed a charcoal water filter for many members of our village. Assuming some of those principles were transferable, then there was a chance I could pull this off.

"I won't make any promises," I said, "but I will see what I can do."

Despite the reeling in my gut, another part of me eagerly awaited the chance to test my skills. My fingers twitched as design possibilities floated through my mind.

"Brilliant," St. Keira said while the others made various noises of approval. "Let's get on with the rest of the plan."

11

TALLIS

The black sands of the Stadia Zaharra shook with the roar of the crowd.

That only looked a little painful, Damiana signed from the box opposite me. She had disguised herself as a man and, like me, sported the purple and black of Pozuelo's Panthers.

I guessed that was one way to describe it. However, it didn't quite grasp the grotesque nature of witnessing a man bleed out from a strike that didn't completely sever its victim's head.

Focus on what we came here for, I signed back.

She didn't risk making direct eye contact with me, but she did unleash a smirk. *It's called multitasking. Ever heard of it?*

There were many times when multitasking was not only feasible but necessary. This was not one of those times. Between the energy and pageantry of the crowd and the spectacle of an "entertaining" death, it wouldn't take much to make one lose sight of our true purpose.

We were here to track Princess Amaya, not lose

ourselves to the glorified bloodlust before us. The plot she devised brought a premature end to my mother's life. I would do everything in my power to see those scales balanced.

Remember the priority.

Based on the scowl that crossed her face, my message had been received.

Apologies, Father, please forgive me. She hasn't done shit this whole time, and I got bored.

Despite my best efforts, I cracked a smile. Fortunately, I managed to play it off as being satisfied by the butchery on display.

Her signed words were an oversimplification, but there had been some truth to them. During the two hours of battles, the princess had barely moved from her seat. To this point, the whole task had been a rather dull affair. The only thing of note had been Prince Ander's late arrival, but that had probably been caused by his desire to personally support every brothel in the city.

Damiana scratched the space in front of her right tear duct. *Who is that?*

It took all my self-control to not snap my head toward the princess. She had been in my periphery this entire time, and I would need to keep it that way to avoid getting caught gazing at her. Instead, I turned my head a mere fraction to bring her into plain view.

Not only had a member of the royal guard joined the box, but the lines that crossed his brow suggested that he either always had a dagger up his ass or this matter was of importance.

Be ready to move on my signal.

Damiana straightened at my warning.

Princess Amaya turned and leaned so that her round face was practically inside her father's ear.

The moment the king nodded, I flashed the symbol and made my way toward the exit. Royal guards were trained to spot threats. We needed to be already moving in the hall before them to appear as though we weren't following them.

By the time I reached the exit, the princess had risen to her feet. My pulse quickened. The chase was most certainly on.

I walked as fast as I could without raising suspicion. This hall of the sporting cathedral was reserved for the Arremendian elite, which was both a blessing and a curse. Although the barren hall meant it would be easier for us to follow her, it also gave us few options for hiding our intent.

The four guards blocking the hall to the royal box watched me as I crossed their path. Despite the flutter in my chest, I stood tall and pretended as though I hadn't noticed their existence. A man who grew up frequenting this hall would have grown accustomed to their presence, and that was who I needed to be.

"Dario," I said as Damiana stepped into the hall. "I thought that was you. You aren't heading out to gamble your inheritance away before it reaches your coppers, are you?"

Footsteps echoed through the hall behind me as I finally reached her. The only question now was which direction would they turn?

Damiana laughed as she pulled me into an embrace. "Please, I *left* that life behind me long ago."

They had taken a left out of the hall and were moving toward us. That meant she would be exiting the stadium's east side. The other direction would have put them closer and on a more direct path to the Hanging Palace. Where were they heading if not back home?

"Where are—"

"Make way for Her Highness," a guard bellowed.

Damiana and I stepped aside in time to avoid being given assistance in finding the wall.

I spun around, bowing my head in respect of her presence. As a result, I only caught sight of the train of her green dress following her like a tail and, more importantly, four sets of armored boots surrounding her.

Four guards by her side didn't seem like enough protection given the heightened numbers in the city. What were they up to?

"I think I've witnessed enough bloodshed for the day," I said as they stomped away. "Why don't we catch up over a bottle or five?"

Damiana wrapped her arm over my shoulder. "Lead the way, good sir."

We walked behind them at a rate that made tortoises look like hares until we were far enough away for them not to worry about us.

Although we continued to talk to keep the charade going, we sent our real questions through signs.

Where are they going? I asked as we trotted down the stairs.

Fuck if I know.

That made two of us. At least we were clueless together.

The roar of the crowd echoed through the hall at the announcement of the next sets of gladiators to fight. Somehow, after hours of bouts, their hunger for death had still not been satiated.

"Shit," I muttered, as we reached the exit after a few more minutes of walking.

The princess and her guards may have only been twenty yards ahead of us, but we were on the verge of losing them entirely. A pristine white carriage stood waiting for them with two horses ready to sweep her away. If they took off at a faster rate than a leisurely stroll, then keeping up with them without blowing our cover would become an immensely more challenging task.

Damiana's ever-widening eyes suggested that she had arrived at the same conclusion. "What do we do now?"

I was about to answer when the carriage door swung open and robbed me of my breath. Two priests sat inside the carriage, awaiting her arrival. Their crimson robes belonged to our order, but the men who wore them did not. These bastards had to have been part of her plot.

"Prepare to move," I hissed. "We must follow them at any cost."

Fortunately for us, wherever they were going, they did not appear to be in a hurry to get there. The carriage moved at such a pace that you'd wonder why they bothered using it in the first place.

I shook my head. Although I didn't believe St. Keira's tale of Cuvar, maybe, *just maybe*, this was a sign that our Lord was aiding our effort. If that was the case, then I couldn't waste the gift he had bestowed upon us.

Out of Her Highness's four guards, only one of them had joined her inside the carriage. The others clung to its outside as they scanned the crowds for danger. Surely they had seen us in the hall, and the last thing we needed was for them to wonder why we were still in their sight. A change of wardrobes would be required.

They turned onto a road that bordered a river market trying to take advantage of the swelling crowds that turned up for the festivities. The usually empty street was now partially swallowed by row upon row of tents, stalls, and motivated merchants.

Go change, I signed. *I'll keep following them.*

She didn't bother with a response. One step she was beside me, and with the next, she had vanished. However, she would not keep me waiting.

"What do you think?" she asked as she reappeared by my side before we reached the end of the block.

Damiana had kept her original pants but ditched her Panthers top for a large white shawl with a bizarre brown pattern on it. Her hair, which had previously been up, now fell freely around her face.

"Did you steal a tarp right off a table?" I asked.

"Fuck off. If you wanted to go on a shopping spree, then you should've brought Omar. Our pretty boy probably spends as much time comparing fabrics as the princess."

"Be nice now. I'm sure the princess doesn't spend half the time Omar does."

"Speaking of which, you should go."

I nodded in the direction of the carriage. The moment she confirmed she had eyes on it, I disappeared into the crowd.

The first matter of business was removing my false, line-thin mustache. With a flick of the wrist, I ripped it clean off. Ignoring my smarting skin, I slicked back my hair with wolf flower resin as I plunged into the heart of the market.

As I weaved around the stalls, I ditched my shirt. It was a general rule of thumb that the more people there were in the crowd, the less people seemed to care about changing in public. Between that and the heat, no one batted an eye at the sight of me roaming around in my undershirt.

After a few more seconds of wandering, the opportunity I had been searching for presented itself. A red-faced vendor had lost his mind over an offer that he viewed as being insultingly low and was too engaged in his tirade to notice my approach. I swiped the gray silk tunic at the edge of his stall and didn't bother putting it on until I reached Damiana.

"What did I miss?" I asked as I slipped into my new shirt. It was a little big on me, but that was better than the opposite problem.

She shrugged. "One of the horses took a shit. Speaking of which, you need to stop using that flower gunk. You look weird with gray hair."

"I look different than before. That's the whole point."

"Different doesn't mean hideous. Between your hair and your shirt, someone might mistake you for pocket lint come to life."

I glanced down to fasten the shirt's wooden toggles on its collar and sleeves. "I guess I'll have to focus on your deeper meaning. It's so nice of you to describe me as a walking miracle."

Damiana laughed. "Whatever you have to tell yourself."

We continued to trade barbs as we followed the carriage down the cobblestone street. If it hadn't come to a stop before reaching Old Town, then we would have kept up the banter all the way to the end of the continent. As it was, we halted with them, and I pretended to admire the Beltza while Damiana looked over me at them.

"Has anyone gotten out?" I asked. "It doesn't sound like they've started up again."

She dropped her voice to a whisper as though she feared the wind would carry it to them. "I don't have a clean look, but I think so. Two of the guards have gone to its far side, and I can only think of one reason for that."

My mind leapt to a single conclusion as well: to open the door. The only question that remained was would Princess

Amaya exit with the priests, or would she be whisked away after their departure?

"Looks like they're leaving," said Damiana.

Instead of asking who, I turned to face the street to see for myself.

The two guards had returned to their positions atop the carriage, and the hooves clicked on the street as they continued to their next destination. However, we wouldn't maintain the slowest chase of all time.

As the carriage had rolled forward, I had caught a glimpse of those frauds in our crimson robes entering the building in front of where they had stopped.

"I've seen that look before," Damiana said as she started to follow the carriage. "What are you thinking?"

I motioned for her to wait. "Leave it. We have a better chance of finding the information in there than we do following that thing."

"But St. Keira told us to keep an eye on her."

"That is our task, but it is not our mission."

Her brow furrowed.

Even as a child, she had been that way. Always hesitant to go against the rules at first. However, if you gave her a remotely good enough reason, she changed her tune in a heartbeat.

"Our mission is to save our temple and the kingdom and avenge our mother. We need answers to do that, and our odds of finding those answers are far greater in there."

She nodded. "You're right. Let's get the others first. We have no idea what we're walking into."

"There's no time. They could be gone by the time we get back."

We need to be safe, she signed. "What good is finding an answer if we can't return to spread the word?"

As much as I didn't want to accept it, her words rang as true as our temple bells. At the same time, we couldn't allow this opportunity to slip through our fingers.

A boy, five or six years my junior, was walking toward us from the direction of the old town. He bore the armband of a messenger on his left sleeve. The moment I saw him, I knew what I needed to do.

With the aid of one of my hands, I whistled to get his attention, and with the other, I waved the three-finger salute to ensure he understood my meaning.

"Sorry," the messenger said, shaking his head. "I'm off for the rest of the day."

I let a silver coin fall into my hand and made a show of rolling it along my knuckles. "How much is your time worth to you?"

Apparently, it wasn't worth too much as he closed the distance between us in a blink of an eye. "Are you really offering me a silver for delivering a message, or is this some sort of sick joke?"

"I love to joke as much as anybody, but this is too serious a matter. See for yourself."

He snatched the coin I flicked toward him out of the air with one hand and immediately tried to bend it with his teeth.

"Well, would you look at that," the messenger said, his smile stretching past his ears. "It looks like I have time for one more message today."

Damiana forced a smile. She must have seen where I was going with this, and my solution didn't please her. "All praise the Trinity."

"All praise them indeed," echoed my newly hired hand. "Now, what is your message, and who do I have the honor of delivering it to?"

"The message is for my brother, Omar. He's an acolyte at Cuvar's temple. Be sure to deliver it to him personally as I don't trust his associates to send him my word in a timely fashion."

The messenger raised a thin eyebrow. "What, you don't trust the priests of the misfortunate?"

At the moment, I trusted them about as much as a mouse would trust a serpent. "Not when it comes to urgent matters that could make or break my career."

"Understood. What would you like me to tell your brother?"

I cleared my throat. "Tell him that I've been given an opportunity to make our mother proud. I'll be cooking for a party of elites at 2 Parroco Ugaz. Dario and I will get started right away, but I need you to bring my knife roll as soon as possible. I don't know how many guests we may be serving."

The messenger looked back and forth between Damiana and me. "So you want me to interrupt a priest so he can go fetch you your cooking supplies?"

Damiana's fingers danced dangerously close to the hilt of her hidden dagger. "Do you not feel the weight of that coin in your hand?"

"I, ugh, yes," he stammered, wilting under her glare.

"Then do what you've been paid to do, or I'll see to it that you're incapable of delivering a message ever again."

"Yes, sir," he said with a gulp.

After making him repeat the message back to us, we sent him on his way. The poor bugger sprinted toward the temple when we released him.

"How long do you reckon I'll haunt his dreams for?" Damiana asked with a laugh.

I shrugged. "I don't know about his dreams, but I doubt this was an encounter he'll ever forget."

My eyes fell back on the building our phony priest had entered. Except for the boldly painted white number two above the black double doors and the knocker fashioned after the royal coat of arms, nothing made it stand out from any of its neighbors. It might have consumed half the city block, but there wasn't anything that would make me want to look at it twice. It made it an ideal hideout.

"So what's the plan?" Damiana asked. "Should we head around back and see if we can find a way in?"

The door stared back at me, throwing out the challenge.

"No, we're entering the same way they did."

Before she could protest, I had casually slipped my lock-picks from my waistband and began making my way toward the door. The wrought iron door handle and lock had blended in with the rest of it from our previous position. I gave it a jingle, which confirmed it was locked.

Damiana stepped behind me, blocking most of the view that any suspicious onlookers may have possessed. "Go on. Be quick and get it over with."

"Not to sound like Omar," I said as I slid my tension wrench and short hook into the lock, "but that's the only way I know how."

As if on cue, the door unlocked with a satisfying click.

I pulled the door open and motioned for her to step through.

Play it safe, she signed as she stepped past me into the building.

Always, I replied, closing the door behind us.

What the hell is this place? asked Damiana.

I couldn't have phrased the question better myself. Not only was the room darker and colder than I had anticipated, but large, bizarrely shaped structures covered by tarps dotted the entire floor. The stale air that danced on my tongue didn't provide any further clues.

No idea, I signed back. *I don't hear anyone. There must be stairs around here somewhere.*

Damiana pulled out a pair of daggers and motioned for me to do the same. She would have preferred to have had her custom curved swords, but the sight of any blade in her hands always had a calming effect on me.

Follow me, I signed after freeing my own dagger from its sheath around my calf, *and stay close.*

We skirted around the structures, only pausing periodically to listen for any hint as to where our wannabe compatriots were located.

After weaving past another three structures, we stumbled across one that wasn't covered. Realization struck as I stared at the remains of the largest block of marble I had ever seen. All the other structures must have been completed sculptures, but why would these frauds hide in such a place?

I took a step closer to admire the sculptor's handiwork. With over half of the sculpture yet to be finished, it was difficult to imagine. However, the finished portions were breathtaking. One in particular caught my eye. It was some type of canine trapped inside a net.

Losing myself in the moment, I allowed my fingers to brush against the cold white stone. How had the sculptor been able to craft such a fine distinction between the net and the beast? The way they had textured the fur poking out of the gaps in the meshing was mind-boggling.

All sense of wonder died the moment I saw the creature's face. It was no canine. It was a three-eyed fox, and its meaning sent a shiver down my spine.

Look, I started to sign, but I stopped myself short when I realized Damiana wasn't there.

Where was she?

My pulse quickened as I scanned the rest of the room. Nothing. Had she wandered to the other side of the sculpture?

I circled the entire marble block to no avail.

My fingers tightened around the handle of my dagger. I took a deep breath in an attempt to slow my racing heart. It didn't work.

Where the fuck was she? It wasn't like her to disappear, especially in this type of scenario. The only thought that provided me with an ounce of confidence was the knowledge that she wouldn't have gone down without a fight, or quietly for that matter. Then where had she gone?

The last place I had seen her was when we had paused two structures ago. I crept back with the hope that something had simply caught her eye.

She wasn't there either. The knot in my stomach turned over, squeezing any hope left in my gut.

"Dami—"

A weight crashed into me from somewhere up above. It drove me head-first into the hardwood floor. The force caused me to drop my blade.

Before I had any hope of gathering my wits, someone with a hideous tattoo of purple dragon wings pressed a damp cloth against my face. Other arms seemed to appear out of nowhere as I choked on the chemical fumes.

One of my attackers called out something in Osigren. It was one of my weaker languages, but I recognized two of the words before I passed out: Amaya and happy.

12

NEREA

Thuuuth... thuuuth...

It was hard to tell which was more disturbing, the way my breathing sounded with the gas mask on or the way it looked in the mirror. While I was tempted to go with the former, any unsuspecting witnesses would have chosen the latter, especially if they stumbled across me in the dark.

The brown leather cap was creepy enough by itself the way it made my face appear like the drawing of a skull. However, it was the combination of the glass eye sockets and the attached filter that truly gave it its eerie, otherworldly feel.

Although I had yet to test it against Keira's sleeping gas, the signs had been promising so far. For starters, the cap might not have fit my head perfectly, but it did fit. I was able to breathe with it on, which was kind of important. It had also steered clear of my biggest concern, which was that the added weight of the filter would make it too awkward and uncomfortable to wear. While it wasn't a walk in the park, the slight strain it added to my neck wasn't torturous either.

As much as I wanted to be the one to test it, I wouldn't be one of the people who would have to rely on it.

I untied the strings that held the contraption together on the back of my neck. The skin on my face danced for joy as the cool basement air greeted it as I pulled the mask off.

"Now what?" I asked the empty room.

It didn't make sense to make more of the masks until I could properly test the two prototypes. The only other project I had, the escape boat, didn't require my attention. This left me with the age-old problem of too much time on my hands and not enough activities to do.

The concept of having nothing to do was unheard of in my former life. My world had been consumed by my work and taking care of my mother. On the few occasions it occurred, I had one tried-and-true rule I could fall back on: when in doubt, sketch it out.

After returning all my tools to their proper locations and double-checking the shop to make sure I hadn't forgotten anything, I snagged two charcoal pencils and a sketch pad and set them inside my canvas bag on top of the gas masks. The thought of daydreaming of inventions from the comfort of my own bed was the change of scenery I needed.

With all my necessary possessions gathered, I made the short journey from the school's basement to the dormitory almost unnoticed.

As I began my ascent up the stairs toward my room, footsteps and unknown voices echoed down to greet me. My right hand flew to the top of my bag to partially close it. Could these people be working with the traitor?

That question had plagued my mind with each acolyte and priest I had crossed paths with since our meeting with the saint yesterday. Each unknown voice or face I had come across sent both my thoughts and heart racing. It was yet another reason I had chosen to speed back to the safety of my room like a cat to its den.

“Cuvar’s cock, that was uncomfortable,” said a man. “If I can still hear Omar crying through the walls when we get back, then I’m going to be sleeping in your room.”

What? I paused for a moment, unsure if I had heard him correctly. Why was he crying? Could they be talking about a different Omar? Wasn’t he supposed to be with Damiana and Tallis at the games?

A deeper male voice responded. “For starters, that might have been the worst proposition to enter my temple that I’ve ever heard.”

“Fuck off. You know what I meant.”

The voices grew louder. They must have been getting closer. I lowered my eyes to avoid startling them into silence.

“Give him some slack,” said the man with the voice as deep as a well. “How would you react to our father being brutally murdered and having your sibling on the precipice of death?”

The two finally came into sight. Based on their white robes, the pair of them were acolytes. However, I was unable to deduce more information as I kept my eyes glued to the step in front of me.

The first acolyte sighed. “Couldn’t he at least spend the day sobbing in his own damn room? I swear those walls are so thin that it’s like he’s crying into my ear.”

I made a mental note not to be too loud in my own room, especially about important matters.

“You used to love those thin walls,” his friend teased.

He laughed as they walked past me. “Can you blame me? Ora’s noises were so much more enjoyable.”

My blood boiled as I fought off the urge to vomit. “What the fuck is wrong with you?”

The pair halted a few steps below me and looked up. Both acolytes had easily seen thirty suns, and this realization only intensified my disgust.

"Excuse me?" asked the creep, his face growing paler with each passing second.

My eyes threatened to burst from their sockets. "You heard me just fine, pervert. If I ever, *ever*, hear of you doing creepy shit like that again, then I swear to Cuvar that I'll sever that sad needle you call a penis from your body and bask in having the whole temple listen to your cries."

The little prick just stared at me with his mouth open while his friend's face turned bright red.

"Do you understand me, or do you need me to write all that down for you?"

When he still couldn't find his voice, his friend spoke up. "I'm sure this is a moment he'll never forget."

"Good," I spat as I allowed my fingers to wrap around one of the charcoal sticks in my bag. "Get him out of my sight before my blade gets any itchier."

The acolytes didn't need any further encouragement to leave. Like a herd of spooked cattle, they stampeded down the rest of the stairs.

Just as the idiots had disappeared from my sight, any thought of returning to my room had similarly vanished. How could I focus on inventions that might never be needed when a member of my finger was suffering? The least I could do was check on him first.

According to Damiana, my room had been Ora's old one as she had been given a new chamber on the third floor last summer. Besides that tidbit, I had no other information that would aid me in finding him sooner. All I could do was pick a direction and meander around the square hallway until I came across him.

As I turned to the right to begin my search, I moved quieter than a hunter approaching a cougar's den. My best bet was to hope Omar was still crying and I could hear him from the hall. However, this tactic proved to be a gigantic waste of time. When I rounded the second corner in silence, the door belonging to Ora's room became abundantly obvious.

Her door stood about halfway down the corridor. Bouquets of flowers and a surprisingly high number of little brown bags surrounded it. Out of curiosity, I picked up one of the bags. Its contents jingled as I lifted it from the floor.

I shook my head as I set the coin purse back in its rightful place. Of course the protector of thieves would accept coins to watch over his chosen ones. Did this mean that all of these bags had been stolen?

In an attempt to not dwell on the thought, I opted to listen for Omar. Based on the silence that greeted me, he had either left the room, run out of tears, or the jackass from the stairwell had been filled to the brim with shit.

"Omar, are you in there?" I asked after rapping my knuckles on the dark-brown door.

Although I didn't receive a verbal response, I heard someone shuffle around the room. Somebody was definitely in there. If it wasn't Omar, then who could it have been?

I pounded on the door once more. "Omar, it's me, Nerea. I just want to make sure you're okay."

His footsteps grew slightly louder before stopping altogether, but the door remained shut. The only logical explanation for this was he must have been looking through the peephole to confirm it was me. However, what would cause him to be *that* paranoid?

Whatever he saw must have been satisfactory as the door finally opened.

"Never been better," Omar said as he stood in the doorway. His puffy red eyes and his red nose stood out like bloodstains against the pure white of his tunic. "Why, ugh, why do you ask?"

My hand reached out to his shoulder to comfort him. Which was a strange gesture in itself as it was the first time I ever wanted to lay my hands on him in a way that wouldn't inflict pain.

"I overheard some acolytes in the hall who said you were crying in your sister's room. If the idea of you expressing other human emotions outside of horniness wasn't alarming enough, I recalled that you were supposed to be at the fights with Tallis and Damiana."

He sniffled and tried to cover it with a laugh.

"I figured if something was keeping you away from making bad jokes at their expense, then it had to be serious," I continued. "Given we're fingermates and all, I thought I should check on you."

Omar smiled at me weakly. His unnaturally white teeth appeared even brighter against the backdrop of stubble that covered his face. "Thanks, that means a lot."

New voices echoed through the hall, and Omar peered out. In doing so, a new figure caught my eye. Someone was lying on Ora's bed.

"Is that..."

I couldn't get myself to finish the question. The sight of their motionless body reminded me too much of my own father's passing.

"Yes," he said, stepping aside and motioning for me to enter the room. "The doctors at Potami's deemed her stable enough to return. All there's left to do now is feed her mush, give her water, and hope she wakes up."

Given Ora's current state, hope was the key word in that sentence.

Although I had come to comfort him, I couldn't keep myself from focusing on her. My stomach ached as I examined her bruised and swollen face. A multitude of little scars that peppered the right side of her face. What had caused them?

"She landed face-first into shards of glass," Omar said. "Or at least that is what the doctors told me."

"What?"

"You were wondering about her scars, were you not?"

Heat rushed to my cheeks. Why had I been so blatant with my gaze? This was his sister, not some totem to be scrutinized. "Sorry, I—"

"It's all right. I did the same thing when I first saw her with the bandages taken off, and I'm sure she'll do the same when she wakes up."

His attempt to comfort me after my slipup would have gone over better if a painfully long and awkward silence hadn't followed it.

"I should go," I said when I couldn't take it any longer. "I shouldn't have interrupted your time together."

"Wait," he said as I took a step toward the door. "Could you please stay a little longer? This whole situation has brought back... well, it's stirred up some dark memories I thought I had banished. I, I, um, I just don't want to be alone with my thoughts right now."

My legs became rooted to the floor. Was there more to him than promiscuity, childishly bad jokes, and thievery?

"You can even take the chair and ask me anything you like," he said, gesturing to the cushioned wicker reading chair in the corner of the room.

I sank into the chair's cushion, which was far more comfortable than it appeared. "Anything?"

Omar cracked a smile. "Anything within reason. I don't want you to think that you can tempt me out of my vows during this moment of weakness."

"Don't worry," I said with a soft laugh. "I wouldn't allow that to happen even in my worst nightmare."

He let out a sigh of relief as he pretended to mop sweat from his brow.

"If you don't mind me asking," I said, leaning forward in the chair, "you said you were being plagued by some bad memories. Would you like to talk about them?"

His mouth formed every geometrical shape as he searched for the right words.

"It's okay," I said. "We don't have to talk about it. I didn't mean to pry."

Omar smiled faintly as he took a seat at the foot of Ora's four-poster bed. "You did, and it's fine. Burdens are easier to bear when you're not the only one carrying them. I just don't know where to begin."

I nodded and gave him a moment to gather his thoughts.

"Do you know how most of us end up as acolytes for our Lord?" he asked once I repositioned myself.

"The temple rescues homeless children with thieving potential off the streets, does it not?"

"It's a little more complicated than that, but you're more or less right."

I couldn't help the smirk that crossed my face. Every explanation he ever gave seemed to start with that precursor.

"Mother Sienna rescued Tallis from the gallows after hearing of how he nearly got away with robbing from Potami," he continued. "She took in Damiana after witnessing her beat up three older boys in a failed attempt to steal the pigeon she killed for dinner. Ora and I, however, joined through the most common route. We were orphans who were found by Cuvar before the slave traders could get a hold of us."

My eyebrows knitted together. "Isn't slavery illegal here?"

"Many things are illegal, but that doesn't stop them from occurring."

Wasn't that the truth. Wickedness knew no borders. My family had learned that lesson the hard way.

"Did you arrive in Arremendia before or after the gorria plague?" he asked.

My left eyebrow arched as I tried to recall if we had talked about my arrival to the city before. "I'm guessing this happened before my mother and I arrived in the area as I've never heard of this plague. We've only been here for four years."

"That makes sense," he said through a sniffle before giving me a slight grin, "as it occurred nine years before your arrival. Are you familiar with gorria at all?"

I shook my head.

"Pray you never have to as it's a gruesome way to die. It starts like most common colds, you know? Chills, congestion, and scratching at the back of your throat. However, that's just the bastard gestating inside of you. By the time the bleeding starts, you're fucked. All you can do at that point is sit back and watch them slowly bleed out of all their orifices until they're all dried out."

He stared down at his hands as if he could still see blood on them.

"Is that how your parents died?"

I cringed the moment the words left my mouth.

Although the question had been begging to be asked, I threw it out there with all the grace of a drunk falling into the Beltza. How had I been so careless? Surely there was a more thoughtful way I could have asked it.

His face turned toward mine, but his glazed-over expression suggested he was mentally elsewhere.

"Sorry," I said after another awkward moment of silence. "I shouldn't have asked."

Omar shook himself out of his trance. "No, no, it's fine. I just lost myself in a memory."

Slipping out of Ora's chair, I eased myself onto the bed beside him. My toes curled as our thighs momentarily touched. Ew, what was wrong with me?

"My father came down with it first," he continued as he fiddled with his fingers. "Like other plagues, by the time he realized he brought it into our home, it was much, much too late. My mother, she... she started to bleed out the day after he did."

He buried his head in his hands and tried to palm away the tears that threatened to flow down his face.

Before I realized what I was doing, my hand found his knee. The thin fabric of his breeches left little to the imagination of the muscles that hid beneath them as I massaged them with my thumb. "It's okay."

"No, it's not. My parents would have halted the moons for us if they could. Everything they did was to give us a better life, and do you know what I did as they bled out before my eyes?"

My voice refused to leave my throat under his gaze. The pain etched into his brown eyes was undeniable.

"Nothing," he said. The word eked out of him as though the word itself had stabbed him in the back. "They had given me the world, and I did nothing for them in the end but watch on in horror."

"But you were, what? Ten years old? Potami's doctors can barely do anything for plague victims. What were you supposed to do?"

He stared at my hand. "Anything would have been better than what I did. Ora was only eight, and at least she knew enough to clean up their blood and give them water."

My gaze wandered over to her body. If she were awake for this moment, then what would she tell him?

"The day my parents died, I promised that I would never do nothing again. That I would do everything in my power to protect my family. I guess it shouldn't be a surprise that I failed to keep that vow."

His words tore at my stomach with the ferocity of a leopard's claw. He blamed himself for not being there to protect his sister from her attacker. Worse yet, just like the death of his parents, there was nothing he could have done to prevent Ora from being in this situation. Somewhere deep down he probably knew that, but it was clear he wasn't ready to accept that reality.

A knock on the door launched both of us to our feet.

"Are you..." My words drifted away like the breeze. One look at the steel in his hands signaled that he hadn't been expecting anyone.

Thud. Thud. Thud.

"Omar, are you in there?" asked an unfamiliar female voice. "There's a messenger here for you."

He held out a hand for me to stay where I was while he inched toward the door. "I'm a bit preoccupied, Jemma. Have him deliver the message to you, and I'll get it from you later."

"I'm sorry to disturb you, but that simply won't do," said a higher-pitched male voice.

Judging by Omar's creased brow, I assumed he hadn't recognized the man either.

"Your brother was clear that I had to deliver the message to only you, and his brute of a friend, Dario, promised to render me incapable of working if I failed in this task. These types of threats are sadly not uncommon, but he struck me as one of the few willing to follow through on his word."

A smile crossed Omar's face. "That does sound like them. I'll be out in a moment."

He dashed over to Ora's nightstand, pulled a dagger out of the drawer, and gave it to me.

"What do you want me to do with this?" I asked.

"Hopefully nothing," he whispered. "This messenger sounds legit, but I want you to bar the door shut behind me."

I was about to ask why when the answer came to mind. He'd do everything in his power to protect his sister. If they weren't who they claimed to be, then I was the only one standing in the way between Ora and her premature death.

"You'll know it's safe to unlock the door if I mention needing beauty sleep," he continued. "If anyone else tries to open it, or I try without mentioning that, then throw every piece of furniture in front of it and call for help from the balcony, understand?"

It sounded like an idiotic code, but now wasn't the time to question it. "I've got it."

As I promised, the moment he closed the door behind him I slipped the lock into place. My heart pounded in my ears as I listened to him send Jemma to the stairs.

"So what message did my brother find so urgent that he'd interrupt my life's work over it?" I heard Omar ask.

My grip tightened around the hilt of the dagger as I searched for what I could put in front of the door first in case this all went to shit. The bookshelf would cover the most space, but could I manage to drag it across the room in time? Her dresser was on the wall adjacent to it. I could probably push it into place rather quickly.

"Your brother said that he has been given an opportunity to make your mother proud. He'll be cooking for a party of elites at 2 Parroco Ugaz. He and Dario will get started right away, but he needs you to bring his knife roll as soon as possible. Lastly, he stated that he doesn't know how many guests they may be serving."

The message was obviously coded, but what did it mean? Was there any significance in their cooking references or was that just the first thing that had come to Tallis's mind? The one part I felt confident about was the first line. They had found evidence that pertained to Mother Sienna's death.

"Is that all?" asked Omar.

"Of your brother's message, yes. However, he did also state that you'd double my pay."

Omar's laugh seeped under the door. "Of course the cheap prick would throw his bill at my feet. What do I owe you?"

"As this is an urgent matter, and I was off duty when he summoned me, he said you'd pay me a silver for my trouble."

I stifled a gasp. It was no secret that the temple had money to spend, but a silver for a single message seemed more than excessive. Omar sounded reluctant as well, but he paid the man nonetheless.

"Looks like I won't be needing beauty sleep after all," Omar said once the messenger's footsteps had faded away.

I unbarred the door and pushed it open. "What the heck was that about?"

His eyes flicked back and forth between me and his sister's motionless figure. Was he unsure where to begin? Why had my question made him appear conflicted?

"It's Tallis and Damiana," he said. "They found something regarding Mother Sienna, but they may be in danger."

13

TALLIS

Where in Potami's murky depths was I?

It should have been a simple enough question, but the haze of sleep still clouded my senses. The orange of evening lights poured through a window off to my left, blurring my vision. Although I couldn't recall much, I knew one thing for certain. Whoever had selected the chair I sat in really needed to acquire new furniture. Its fraying wicker design scratched at my bare back.

"The fu—"

The cuss stuck in my throat. I needed to scratch my back, but I couldn't move my arms. Why couldn't I move my arms?

The question launched my mind into full alert, making everything clear and confusing at the same time.

I knew this place. That bow and quiver of arrows, those stacks of books that formed looming towers around the desk, and the random eclectic furnishings could only belong to one person.

"There you are," Ora said. Her voice rolled through me. It felt like years since I last heard her speak, and I didn't realize how much I missed it until that moment. "I was wondering when you were going to wake up."

Ora stepped in from the balcony. A simple white dress hugged her figure, but she made it look immaculate.

"This doesn't make any sense. I was with Damiana. What the fuck is happening?"

"You realize you're dreaming, right?" She shook her head and flashed an all-too-familiar smile. "I know Mother says there's no such thing as a stupid question, but I guess you do have an affinity for testing limits."

"Wait, if this is a dream, then why am I naked and tied up to your chair?"

She shrugged. "I don't know why you're asking me. It's your fantasy, after all. Though, if I had to guess, then I'd say it's because you either have a secret bondage kink, or those fake priests tied you up that way."

Heat burned my cheeks.

"However, you won't know which one it is until you wake up, and that's assuming you remember any of this at all."

"It must be the fake priests, as I've told you before that I—"

"Only view me as a sister," she said, cutting me off. "I remind you too much of Omar, et cetera, et cetera. Please spare me your blatant lies."

"They're not lies!"

She leaned her face dangerously close to mine and smirked. "You do realize I'm your subconscious, not her. I know everything you know. So if I say you've been forcefully preventing yourself from pining after me since you were fourteen, it's because it's the truth."

It dawned on me that this was the closest our faces had ever been. Her bow-shaped lips were mere inches away from my own, and it took all my willpower not to reach out and savor them.

I swallowed the lump in my throat.

"Now do you really want to continue to waste your time arguing about feelings we both know you have, or should we

discuss how you might be able to get out of the predicament you decided to waltz straight into?"

"Waltz? I don't recall either Damiana or I dancing our way into trouble."

Ora sighed. "With jokes like that, maybe priesthood would suit you. However, that's beside the point. Let me be clearer so you don't mistake the mountains for bushes. You are a great thief and improviser, but you're a rather atrocious planner."

"Oh, how you wound me." I wanted to gesture for dramatic effect, but the coarse rope digging into my wrists spoiled the moment. "Is that what you've visited my dreams for? To point out my shortcomings?"

"Don't be ridiculous," she said as she moved away to sit on the edge of her bed. "I have the rest of our lives to taunt you. I'm here because you need a plan."

"And what would that be, exactly?"

Ora leaned forward, sending her wavy, raven-black hair tumbling over her shoulders. "The way I see it, you have two choices. You can either try to delay the Osigrens with the hope that Omar finds you before they can do too much damage, or you can find a way to escape."

"Too much damage?"

"What do you think they sedated you and Damiana for? To whisk you away to a surprise party? They're clearly going to try to extract information from the two of you, and I can't imagine they'd do that in an enjoyable fashion."

I nodded. Sadly, the reality she painted was undeniable. "Since we're being brutally honest, escape seems unlikely—unless they're completely inept, of course."

Ora moved to her desk and grabbed something that had been hiding amongst her stacks of books.

"Which leaves us with only the option of delaying them and hoping Cuvar intervenes so he can continue to profit off my tan

ass," I continued. "However, if they moved us to a new location, then how am I supposed to stall them for long enough?"

When she turned to move toward me again, I saw the item she had grabbed was an apple with a peel as red as our priests' robes. "You've spent the majority of your life spewing nonsense that people fall for. If there was ever a moment for that skill, now would be the time. Speaking of which—" She held the apple a fraction in front of my mouth. "Take a bite. It's time for you to return."

"Return? But I thought we were here to plan."

"There's nothing else for us to determine as I am unaware of your location or your surroundings. You know your options. It's up to you to determine which one best suits your needs."

Ora moved the apple even closer to my lips. "Take a bite and you will wake up."

"But I'm not ready to leave you," I said, imploring with my eyes to let this moment last a little longer. "I've only just got you back."

She planted the softest of kisses on my forehead. The faint scent of her lavender perfume cloaked me like a blanket on a rainy winter night.

"I'm a figment of your imagination, not her," she said. "Take a bite and find a way to survive. It's the only way for you to see the real her ever again."

I needed no further encouragement. Before I could give myself the chance to conjure another question, I bit into the crisp apple and immediately regretted it.

The flavor of rotten fish filled my mouth in an instant. I gagged. Vomit rushed up to join the putrid mixture. If Ora hadn't covered my mouth with her hand and tilted my head back, then I would've spit it out.

I stared at her through my watering eyes. If this was my imagination, then why did the apple have to taste so revolting?

"Take a deep breath through your nose," she commanded. "You need to be calm when you wake if you don't want to alert your captors."

I tried to follow her instructions, but it did little to improve my circumstances. It was difficult to ignore the mouthful of vomit and the worst-tasting apple in human history.

"I know the taste is repulsive," she whispered into my ear, "but it'll all be over as soon as you swallow it."

Despite every urge to do the opposite, I gulped down the horrid concoction.

Ora was wrong. She disappeared when I woke, but the flavor remained. If I hadn't been acclimated to it, then I surely would have gagged on the soiled rag they'd shoved down my throat.

Along with Ora, her room vanished as well. In its place stood a large, dark room whose walls were covered floor to ceiling in a patchwork of random tapestries. If it hadn't been for the assortment of lit torches scattered about, then nothing would have been visible.

What the hell was this place?

"*Fotwi nach!*" said a voice as rough as stone.

I didn't know much Osigren. However, I was fond of being able to cuss in other tongues, and "fuck off" was always the first one I tried to learn.

Laughter followed behind me along with the sound of clinking coins and the shuffling of cards. So my captors were busy gambling, and at least one of them was from Osigra.

Slow and steady, I thought as I eased my head to the right. The last thing I needed was to draw their attention. Who knew what they would do if they knew I was awake.

My chest seized. Before I could turn my head far enough to see the game, I found another figure to my right staring at me. I instantly pretended to fall back asleep.

Shit, shit, shit. What do I do? What do I do?

I repeated the phrase over and over again in my mind until it became its own melody. It wasn't until the fifth refrain that I realized that the person hadn't raised an alert upon noticing me. Why was that?

After a deep breath, I risked another glance.

It was Damiana. My makeshift gag prevented me from letting out a sigh of relief. She was all right. Well, as all right as anyone could be in these circumstances. They had tied the Giant of Gecho in the same fashion as myself with the exception being that her chair faced the card game.

As our eyes locked, there was a multitude of things I wished I could have expressed to her at that moment. Apologizing for getting us into this mess would've been at the top of that list, but there was no way of knowing how much time we had left. We needed to make every second count if we wanted to leave this place alive.

Okay? I signed.

It was far from my most eloquent question, but with our hands tied behind our backs, we had limited options.

No, she responded.

How many?

Her eyes darted back toward the Osigrens. *Four.*

Four wasn't too bad. We'd still be outnumbered if Omar showed up by himself, but we'd have close to even odds if he brought St. Keira with him.

However, that was wishful thinking. This room seemed nothing like the workshop where we had been caught. Besides, if these Osigrens were the same ones who attacked our temple, then it was safe to assume they were professional enough to move us to a secure location.

Understand them? I asked.

While I had been sent to Molino to learn the ins and

outs of royal courts, Damiana had been shipped off to a village in Osigra for specialized combat training. If her grasp of the language was still sharp enough, it could provide us with the edge we needed.

Yes, she signed.

Explain.

No.

My brow furrowed. No? It took me a moment to realize she probably meant that she couldn't explain it through signing given our limited range of motion.

What to do? What to do? What can I do?

I scoured my line of sight for anything that could help us and came up blank. What on Cuvar's cock was I supposed to do with an obscene number of tapestries and a few torches? Unless one of them turned out to be a magic carpet, then the only thing they would be useful for would be burning this shithole to the ground.

Despite the gag, I managed to crack a smile. We could burn this place down.

The more I dwelled on the idea, the better it sounded. Given our condition and their superiority in numbers, fighting them head-on would send us to the afterlife. However, dodging them as we spread the fire was a far more manageable feat. Then there was the bonus that a large fire would send people throughout the city to our aid. If we could get out of these ropes, then that would be our best bet for survival.

What were the odds they'd removed the blade hidden in the sole of my shoe? I couldn't feel any of my other hidden weapons that had been holstered to each of my calves. As I tried to lift my leg to judge my shoe's weight, the chair's leg shifted and let out a loud eek.

The only thing more noticeable than that dreaded

squeak was the silence that followed. Gone was the sound of laughter and shuffling cards that had filled the room seconds before.

My mind proved the diversity of the word fuck as I slumped over to feign sleep once more. How had I managed to mess this up prior to getting a chance to try to escape?

A few agonizingly long seconds later, their game continued. I cracked my eyelids open to peek at Damiana. Her fingers pinched together to form the greatest sign of all. *Safe.*

Was her chair as rickety as mine? If I smashed mine, then would she be able to break hers as well?

Destroying my chair would only be a viable option if she could do the same. Otherwise, they'd threaten her life to subdue me.

Sit strong? I asked.

Her raised eyebrow asked the question for her.

To be fair, it wasn't a great question, but it was the best I could come up with given I couldn't form the sign for chair.

I rocked my chair ever so slightly. *Sit, sit.*

Mother Sienna had forced us to not talk from sunrise to sunset for an entire year to perfect our understanding of our nonverbal codes. Now our lives rested on interpreting a bastardized version of them.

Okay, sit, she signed.

Did that mean she got it?

A bead of sweat trickled down my face. *Sit strong?*

Was her chair sturdy or not? My pulse raced as I awaited her response.

Right before I repeated the message, she rocked her chair. Although it didn't squeak, the corner of her lips turned upward.

Sit strong? I asked again.

No.

My heart tried to leap from my chest, but I reined in the rush of excitement that pulsated through me. *A hothead will find you dead.*

I smiled at the irony of Mother Sienna's sage wisdom given what we would have to do next. Or was it technically a paradox? The distinction between the two was one I never fully understood. If our know-it-all, Ora, was here, then she'd happily set me straight.

Focus. If I could've slapped myself, I would've done it in a heartbeat. We were nowhere close to safety. I needed to keep my head in the game.

Fire, I signed through the wiggling of my fingers.

Fire?

I nodded my head in the direction of the nearest torch. *Yes, fire.*

She shrugged her shoulders.

Not for the first time, I cursed our restraints.

Fire, I signed once more before trying to pull my hands apart from each other. Hopefully she'd get the message of using the flames to free ourselves.

How? she asked.

Follow.

If I was lucky, she would copy my actions and not literally follow me, but that was out of my control. If Cuvar was real, then this would be the perfect opportunity for him to prove it.

The Osigrens burst into another round of laughter. Nothing they did would perfectly mask the sound of my crashing chair, but it was worth a shot.

I rocked onto the balls of my feet. The back of the chair forced me to hunch over as I quickly waddled toward the closest torch. I launched myself, chair legs first, into the wall.

"*Scheitong!*"

The words that followed the Osigren curse never reached my ears as the satisfying snapping of wood drowned them out.

Unable to brace myself, I fell face-first into the floor with a thump. Heat blazed at my back. Rolling over, I discovered I had knocked the torch free during my collision. Better yet, it had lit the bottom of the tapestry on fire.

Another loud splintering of wood rang out across the room. Damiana must have flung herself against the wall opposite of me.

There was no time to lose. The rope that once bound my legs now tethered me to nothing, but my hands still needed to be freed. I rolled toward the flame and shove my restraints into it.

"Fuuuuuck!" I groaned as the flames licked my hands and forearms.

"*Fotwiar!*"

The Osigren roar came from right above me. I rolled out of the way in time to hear steel slice the air and slam into the spot on the floor I had just abandoned.

Pushing myself onto my feet, I bolted toward the next closest torch.

"You cannot outrun us, *hungae Arremendi*," said the attacker. His Osigren accent made each word sound unnaturally coarse.

Fortunately for me, that wouldn't be required.

As I reached the next torch, the ember had burnt through enough of the rope for me to rip my wrists free. I snatched the torch off the wall and spun on him.

"Shit," I murmured into my gag.

I was dealing with two of them, not one. The bastard who had been talking was a mountain of a man with a large enough gap between his front teeth to drive a carriage through comfortably. His wiry, dark-haired friend, who I recognized as one of the fake priests, drifted to my left to flank me. While the giant oaf armed himself with a pair of hatchets, his compatriot held a dagger in each hand.

Damiana said there were four of them. Did that mean the other two were after her?

My eyes danced past them as I yanked off my gag. One of them was wrestling Damiana next to the ruins of her chair, while the other was busy stamping out the fire I started. I needed to get to her fast if we were to survive.

"I know Arremendians are stupid," said the mountain, "but you do not believe your stick of flame can defeat our steel, do you?"

His comrade laughed. "You trapped with us. Stop now, and we gift you a quick death."

I loosed a maniacal laugh the likes of which only a cornered animal could muster. The more unstable they thought I was, the greater our odds would improve. Most people didn't know how to handle the irrational.

"What is it? Do you find your death funny?" asked the mountain.

"I'm not trapped with you," I said, twisting my face into what I hoped was a deranged smile. "You're trapped with me, and we'll all burn together."

Before they could react, I charged the mountain, as he was probably the slower of the two.

He swiped at me with his hatchet. Instead of parrying the blow, I slid underneath it feet first and thrust the torch into the tapestries I passed in the process. They ignited like kindling.

A weight drove into my gut as I popped back onto my feet. No, not a weight, I realized a beat too late. It was the shoulder of the Osigren prick who had been stomping out my previous fire.

I gasped as my back slammed into the floor. His tackle robbed my lungs of air.

"Fu—"

A boot collided with my ribs before I could begin my verbal assault or elbow the prick in the back of the head.

"You can beat him senseless later," said the tackler as he rolled me onto my stomach and yanked my hands behind my back. "I've got him. Put out the fire."

"Dario!" I yelled.

The man on top of me laughed as he dug his knee into my spine. "Dario? Do you really think your friend can still save you?"

I went to give him a piece of my mind, but he punched me in the same spot the other one had kicked me.

"It was a rhetorical question," he said, repositioning himself above me. "He's tied again like the dog he is."

I turned my head in time to see two of the Osigren scum finish hog-tying her. A small gash on her forehead poured rivulets of blood down her face.

"You, though, you proved too clever to be a dog," he continued. "The fire was a nice touch. Tell me, rat, what is your name?"

My teeth clenched with my fists. "Your flattery knows no bounds. I'd rather be a rat than the pile of feces you are anyway."

He sighed and gave a command in Osigren. "I fear I have overestimated your cleverness. I asked you a simple question, and you've answered with a pathetic insult one would expect to be conjured by a prepubescent boy."

The heavy footsteps of the mountain and his companion

started to move toward us. They must have already finished putting out the fire.

"This will be the easiest question I'll ask you," continued the man on top of me. "Answer them truthfully and you'll experience less pain before your death. Now, what is your name?"

I strained my neck to lift my head off the floor. "I am nothing but a rat."

"If that is so, then you are a rat who is about to be maimed. Kladin, Jomed, bring a sturdier chair and some rope. If he squirms too much, then he might bleed out faster than I'd like."

A lump formed in my throat. What the hell could I do? I was not in favor of waiting for divine intervention, but it appeared more and more like my only hope.

As the mountain and his minion secured me to my new chair, I got my first real look at the man who had tackled me. He was a sturdy man around his early thirties who had a crop of thin black hair, a goatee, and a nose as sharp as one of Damiana's blades.

"I'll only ask you one more time," he said, standing over me. "I'll even show you how easy it is to answer. Kladin, ask me for my name."

The mountain banged one of his meaty paws against his own chest as he cleared his throat. "What is your name?"

"I am Hadul," he said while unsheathing his gold-hilted dagger. "Now it is your turn to answer. If not, then I will play one of my favorite games. It is called 'remove your limbs one at a time.' Have you heard of it?"

"Fuck off," I spat. "I am a rat, and that won't change regardless of how many times you cut me."

Hadul's eyebrow arched as his face twisted into a smile.

My stomach squeezed itself into a knot. What idea had I just given him?

"Cut *you*?" Hadul snickered. "Since that is too easy, I guess I'll have to start by cutting your friend instead."

My blood boiled. It was one thing to threaten me but another to threaten my fingermate. "If you so much as touch a hair on her head, I'll fuc—"

Hadul backhanded me across the face, causing me to bite my tongue.

"You are not in control here!" he said, spraying me with spit. "I'll do whatever the fuck I want until you start answering my questions. Just watch."

"Don't!" I said as he strode toward Damiana.

My eyes locked onto hers. The intensity that burned in them pleaded with me to hold my tongue.

He grabbed one of her hands and began tapping her fingers with the point of his blade. His colleagues laughed as he uttered some stupid Osigren rhyme.

"*Wahuda siesin*," said Hadul. His smile stretched farther as his blade stopped on Damiana's ring finger.

My heart tried to burst through my throat when I finally recognized the words "I choose you." The sick bastard was not only going to torture her, but he was also making a game of it.

"My name is Tallis Mendoza. I'll answer your other questions. Just-just don't hurt her."

Hadul walked back to me and fixed his muddy-green eyes upon mine. "See, that wasn't so hard. Was it, Tallis?"

"No, it wasn't."

"Next time I expect you to answer right away. Let this be a lesson for you."

Before I could ask, he grabbed my left hand. Pain and

heat blazed up my forearm as he severed my middle finger at the second knuckle.

"Fuuuuuuuck!" I screamed.

"Silence!" Hadul said as he backhanded me across the face once more. "No one has asked you to talk. You will only speak when I ask you to. Understood?"

Damiana's eyes flooded with rage. One of us would make him pay for what he had done. I could promise Cuvar that much.

"Do you understand, or do I need to remove another one of your fingers?"

"Yes," I said, grimacing through the pain.

Hadul booped the tip of my nose with my bloody nub. "Good, now the real fun can begin."

14

NEREA

Omar pounded his fist into St. Keira's door. "Are you in there? It's just Nerea and me. For the love of Cuvar, please be in there."

After he had explained Tallis's message to me, the first course of action had become abundantly clear. We needed help, and we needed to find it quickly if Tallis and Damiana stood any chance. However, our options for assistance were sorely lacking.

With the rest of the Order cast in doubt, there was only one person we could trust. She had been given Mother Sienna's former chambers for the duration of her stay, but if she wasn't in there presently, then what would we do? How long could we let Tallis and Damiana take on the unknown without us?

"For fuck's sake, please be in there," said Omar.

"What should we do now?" I asked. "We could trick the blackcoats into—"

The door swung open.

St. Keira stood in the doorway, wrapped in a towel. Fresh

bathwater glistened on her pale skin, and she dabbed it away halfheartedly. "What the bloody hell is going on?"

"It's Tallis and Damiana," I said, drawing my eyes up from the array of black lines that covered her revealed skin. Were they tattoos, or was there something wrong with her veins? "They might be in trouble."

The saint arched an eyebrow as she peered up and down the hall. "Come in. This sounds like a private matter."

Although the luxurious nature of Mother Sienna's former chambers was undeniable, it wasn't the room's contents that filled me with awe. It was impossible for me to keep my mind off the woman who had occupied it less than a week ago. What could her belongings tell me about the woman who altered the course of my life?

"What's this trouble you speak of?" Keira asked as she stopped in front of a portrait of the priestess with her adolescent fingerlings.

A single rose lay on the mantel, and a pair of lit candles sat on either side of the painting. Had the saint placed those there, or was that common practice for the deceased in the temple?

Omar stepped forward. "Tallis sent us a coded message. He and Damiana discovered something at the gladiatorial games, and it led them to a building on Parroco Ugaz. They don't know how many enemies are inside, but it sounds like they're not waiting for backup."

"Then we have no time to lose," Keira said, finally slipping into her clothes. "Do you know the exact address?"

Omar repeated the address from Tallis's message while the saint hopped into her shoes as she made her way toward the four-poster bed across the room.

"Perfect," said the saint, pressing her hand against the headboard. A hidden door appeared in the wall beside the bed. "This tunnel will put us down the right side of the hill. Hurry up and grab a weapon. Be careful with their edges. Mother Sienna had an affinity for coating them with hilketa."

A weapon? The room had been neatly littered with many things, but I hadn't noticed any weapons. It wasn't until Keira stepped aside that the array of potentially poisoned swords, daggers, axes, and spears lining the left side of the tunnel became apparent.

Omar stood frozen in place. At least I wasn't the only one caught off guard. How had she known of a hidden door in a room she'd hardly spent any time in when one of the priestess's own students had no idea of its existence?

"What? Don't just stand there. Are they in trouble or not?"

Although Omar snapped into action, I couldn't contain the question. "How did you know of this door and where it leads?"

"Well, you see..." St. Keira said as she stared at her feet. "Bugger it, I guess there's no point in lying."

Omar arched an eyebrow. "Lying about what, exactly?"

"Sienna and I were far more than close friends. She is, was, the closest I have ever come to loving anyone."

The dots started to connect. Not only did this explain how she knew of this tunnel, but it also explained why she wrote to her in the first place and why she had arrived in Arremendia so quickly.

"The first time I knew I loved her was during the second round at our trials," she continued. "She had such a way of transforming obstacles into advantages in a moment's notice that it was hard not to fall for her. I find myself often reliving the first night we—"

"Yeah, I need you to not finish that sentence," said

Omar. "She was like a second mother to me, and the last thing I need to hear is what I think you were about to explain."

St. Keira's brow furrowed for a second before her eyes shot wide. "No, no, no, I wasn't going to say—"

"And let us leave it that way. I know you're the voice of Cuvar and everything, but boundaries are a healthy concept."

Something told me that might have been the closest thing to wisdom that ever exited his mouth.

Omar picked up a sheathed sword and strapped it around his waist. "Nerea, have you ever handled a weapon before?"

"Technically speaking, I have held multiple weapons. Have I been trained to use any? That's another question entirely."

He nodded toward a row of daggers. "Take one of those and strap it to your calf. We can't afford to draw any suspicion."

I was about to point out that his sword was out for the world to see when his meaning hit home. Of course a man could be armed in this city and no one would bat an eye. A woman, however, was preposterous. Regardless of the fact that we needed steel to fend men off, no man could fathom us being capable of defending ourselves.

"I have just one more question for you before we go," I said to the saint as I picked up a blade with an ornate silver handle. "Why did you lie to us about your past with Mother Sienna?"

St. Keira pinched the bridge of her nose. "It is a matter far too complicated to get into at this moment."

"Try again," I said, taking a step forward.

Omar's jaw practically fell to the floor. I guessed questioning their beloved saint was not a practice he had considered possible.

"How can you expect me to trust you if you can't bother to tell me the truth?"

My question clamped down on her like a pair of restraints. I would not let her get out of this one.

Keira nodded once she realized I was serious. "There are so many layers to this, but I'll try to make it brief."

We'll see about that, I thought as I took a knee to strap the holster to my calf.

"For starters," Keira said, "our relationship would have caused many political problems throughout the church."

My brow furrowed. "Yeah, that's a little too vague for my taste. You need to give me more than that."

"How much do you know about the saint trials?"

"She knows next to nothing about them," Omar said.

I smacked him on the shoulder, causing him to yelp.

"What the fuck was that for?"

"You don't speak for me."

"Well, am I wrong?"

"No," I said with a sigh. "Not in this case, anyway."

The saint cleared her throat. "For the sake of saving us time, I won't detail every facet of the competition for you. The key thing for you to know is this contest determines who the next living saint will be."

I knew this already but resisted the urge to derail her.

"Although there aren't many rules in the trials," he continued, "the one that is enforced with the most strictness is that you can't receive help from another competitor or their crew."

My head cocked to the side. "Did you get assistance from Mother Sienna during the trials?"

"No," Keira said, "we were very careful not to let any

information about our plans for the trial slip between us. However, because our intimacy began during that time and no other woman had been the victor of the trials before, there would no doubt be accusations that we aided each other in the competition. For some members of our faith, that would be enough controversy by itself to strip me of my rightfully earned position."

"So you couldn't tell us about your relationship with Mother Sienna because you were worried we'd rat you out and you'd lose your standing?"

The saint visibly bit her tongue. "No, what I am saying is that is one of the political complications that would have arisen should our relationship have become public. And even if people did side with us in the end, the amount of bullshit we would have had to deal with would have been endless."

With the harness holster fastened, I rolled my pants leg back down and returned to my feet. "As troublesome as that could have been, it still doesn't justify your actions. If you were willing to trust us with a conspiracy of this magnitude, then you should have been fully capable of entrusting us with this tidbit of information as well."

Omar raised an eyebrow. "I would like to know the truth as much as you, but is now really the time for this?"

The fact that he even had to ask that question proved it to be false.

"Yes," I said, "all she needs to do is give me a satisfying answer to one question, and we can fly down that tunnel. If she can't trust us with the truth, then what else could she be lying about?"

The saint rested her hand on Omar's shoulder. "It's fine. Her questions are justified."

No shit.

"Although my spirit has been tethered to our Lord's, I am still merely a woman. I am riddled with flaws, and trust me, you'll see more of them before all is said and done."

Omar nodded along as the saint spoke.

"I wish I could give you an answer that you'd find satisfactory, but the truth is that it doesn't exist." Her blue eyes dipped to the floor before finding my own. "I wasn't sure how to approach all of you about the totality of Sienna's and my past, so I took the coward's way out."

"What do you mean?" Omar asked.

It was about time he didn't force me to do all the digging.

"Si—your mother, back when she was among the living, she didn't want you to know about me. She thought it would distract you too much from your training."

Just how highly did they regard her for her presence to be considered that problematic?

"I know it's a poor excuse," Keira said with a wave of her hands, "but I convinced myself that not telling you about us was honoring her wishes. However, that couldn't be further from the truth. I kept that information private because it was too much for me to bear, and I was afraid of your reaction."

Omar's brow furrowed.

"What was I supposed to say?" Keira asked. "Hi, I've been secretly watching you from a distance for the majority of your life? Do you remember that Walking Lotus you found in your room, Damiana? Well, I left that there for you as a present to add to your collection."

I exchanged a look with Omar as she continued to rattle through other tokens she had snuck to them throughout the years.

The saint threw her hands in the air at the end of her rant. "I'm sorry for withholding the entirety of the truth, but this has all been overwhelming for me, and I can't afford to be overwhelmed given what is at stake."

My lips curled into a smile. She was right. Her flaws were out there for all to see, and that was something I could work with.

"Then let's focus on the task at hand," I said, gesturing to the tunnel. "Go on and lead the way. We might have some acolytes to save."

During my four years in Arremendia, I had walked up and down Parroco Ugaz dozens, if not hundreds, of times. Never in all that time could I recall noticing the building that stood before us. In a city filled with color and carefully crafted designs, the blandness of this place was in complete contrast to its surroundings. The gray stone structure appeared as though it had been built to be forgotten.

"How do you think we should enter?" Omar asked. "I prefer windows as they're generally easier than doors, but we'd have to climb to reach those."

That would be problematic. While this street wasn't overly busy under the heat of the summer sun, she was on her way down for her nightly rest. With her departure, the Arremendians came out in droves. The people that streamed past us, to and from the festivities, would certainly have noticed us if we tried to scale our way to those windows.

Keira shook her head. "There's no need for that. We will enter through the loading gate round back."

"What makes you think this place has a loading gate?" I asked.

"It might have been a long time ago, but this place used

to be a storefront. You can tell from the bolts above the door. Do you see them?"

I had to squint, but eventually, I spotted the two rusting bolts.

"Those were used to hold up a sign," Keira continued. "If my assumption is correct, then the odds are good that we'll find a more private entrance in the alley."

Our trip to the alley soon proved her right. About a quarter of the way down it, we stumbled across a large wooden black gate with a smaller door built into its center.

"Wait," I said as the saint pulled out a set of lockpicks.

Omar arched an eyebrow. "Um, you do realize this is something we want to do quickly, right?"

Spoken like a true man, Damiana's chiding voice rang in my ears.

"Obviously, but what is the plan?" I asked. "In case you forgot, I've never gone snooping into a building to rescue anyone before."

Keira glanced up and down the alley. "Keep your blade ready and follow us closely. We're going to sweep the first floor, and if they're not there, then we'll head to the top floor."

"Why straight to the top floor? There are at least three stories in between. Shouldn't we check them all?"

My questions brought a smile to her lips. "It's what we'll do because of the windows."

"The windows?" asked Omar.

"All the windows on the top floor have something covering them from the inside," Keira explained. "The windows on the other floors are not covered. So if there's something we are not meant to see, then it must be up there."

Our position in the alley didn't enable me to step back

and confirm her observation, but her attention to detail impressed me nonetheless.

"Once we find Damiana and Tallis," the saint continued, "Omar and I will create a distraction."

"And what will I be doing during this distraction?"

"Staying out of sight until they are solely focused on us," she answered without hesitation. "If they're not aware of your presence, then our chances of freeing them will go up significantly."

The logic behind her plan seemed pretty straightforward, so there was no sense in questioning it any further. All I had to do was follow them, hide during the start of their attack, and then run in and cut Tallis and Damiana free. It all sounded simple enough.

I removed my dagger from its sheath. The creamy shades of sunset orange reflected off the blade. "Let's do it, then."

Omar echoed my sentiments as Keira turned to face the door. The speed at which the saint picked the lock, one would have sworn she had used the key to the building.

"Remember," Keira whispered as she eased the door open and motioned us inside, "stay close."

The first floor of the building was nothing like I had anticipated. Towering structures covered in tarps filled my field of vision. It wasn't until I noticed the chisels and hammers carelessly strewn about the room that I realized the storefront had been repurposed into an artist's studio, which begged another question. Why were the conspirators hiding out in an art studio?

Keira pulled the door shut behind us and slipped the lock back in place. The three of us stood in silence for a moment before Omar and the saint began exchanging a series of gestures, which must have been their coded language.

My knuckles tightened around my dagger as they continued to trade signals. Why in the world were we still standing here doing nothing? Surely it would have been more effective for us to have actually started looking for them.

Omar nodded. It appeared as though they had made a decision. At least they had been considerate enough to include me in their decision-making process.

"We don't hear anyone down here." Omar leaned over to whisper into my ear. His pleasantly faint musk wafted up to greet my nostrils. "We're going to check the walls for stairs. Stay close to me."

Omar nodded once more, and Saint Keira took off.

Prior to watching them creep across the room, I didn't know it was possible for humans to move simultaneously so quickly and so quietly. They could have sprinted toward their prey on the savanna without so much as disturbing the grass beneath their feet. Why they had found success as thieves was becoming more and more apparent with each silent step.

If I had learned to move as noiselessly as them, then I might have been able to sneak back and see my dad's body one last time.

I had to physically shake off the random thought. Now was neither the time nor place to relive that memory. This moment required all of my attention.

In reality, my footsteps were not that loud. However, in the silence of the room, and in comparison to the professionals leading the way, each time my foot kissed the floorboard, it sounded like a wounded leopard crying out in pain. Each step also found my heart in my throat as I prayed I wouldn't be the one who gave us away.

When we found the stairs on the other side of the room, Keira raised her hand to stop us.

My heart pounded in my ears as she checked to make sure the coast was clear.

I took advantage of the momentary pause by wiping my sweaty palms against my pants legs. What I wouldn't have given to go back to my shop at that moment. As nice as everyone in the pinky had been to me, I barely knew these people. What was I doing risking my life for them?

Fortunately, I didn't get time to dwell on the question. The saint motioned for us to join her on the stairs. Right before I placed my foot on the first step, a scream rang out from above that sent my heart racing even faster than before.

It took a split second for me to register the roar as coming from a male. Could that have been Tallis? The thought tore at my chest.

Omar's eyes widened. "Tallis," he whispered before bolting up the stairs.

A lump caught in my throat as we chased after him. If that was Tallis, then had my questions caused his suffering? We could have gotten here sooner if I had just kept my mouth shut.

Keira managed to stop Omar by grabbing a handful of his shirt just prior to him ripping open the door.

Omar whirled on him, nostrils flared.

"Take a deep breath," Keira whispered. "They'll need you to keep a cool head."

Omar opened his mouth, but no words came out.

"Remember your blade is poisoned," the saint continued. "One slice, even if it's shallow, will be all you need. And you." She turned her face to mine. "Stay here when we enter. I'll call out where they are in the room."

I nodded.

Keira tested the doorknob. It turned freely. Apparently, their captors were confident that they wouldn't be disturbed.

A loud smack sounded from inside the room. "Answer me, Tallis. I'm not—"

The saint pulled open the door only to find a silver tapestry covering it on the other side. If its presence surprised either of them, then they didn't show it. Omar brushed it aside and ran into the room with a primordial roar. Keira chased after, following him closer than his shadow.

There goes our element of surprise, I thought as the tapestry swished back into place.

Our enemies echoed his roar, and the clattering of steel soon followed.

"Tallis, strapped to chair, straight ahead!" the saint yelled over the commotion. "Dario, floor, right side!"

Her words jolted me into the moment. I was about to throw myself into this chaos. The gravity of what I had to do sent my heart racing.

Instead of running blindly into the room, I peeked out from behind the tapestry. Sure enough, Tallis and Damiana had been where Keira said they would be. While Tallis's bindings were unremarkable, Damiana's had caught me off guard. They had her lying on her stomach with her feet and hands tied together behind her back like some captured boar. Blood poured down her face and twisted my stomach into knots.

From what I could tell, there were only four enemies in the room. Despite my companions' skill, I needed to act hastily. It didn't take a genius to realize that two-on-one combat favored the side with greater numbers, and there was no telling how much longer they would last. The faster I could free them, the greater our chance of survival would become.

My heart threatened to fall out my ass as I made a beeline for Damiana.

"I've got you," I said as I dropped to my knees beside her.

My hands shook like a pup at the sound of thunder. It made sawing through the rope all the more difficult. I berated myself for not cutting fast enough, but I needed to be careful. The last thing I wanted was to nick her with the blade and allow the poison to take her.

After what felt like an eternity, her legs were free. The boom of steel colliding with steel continued to ring out from behind me as I unwound the rope from her hands.

"I could fucking kiss you," Damiana said after she wrenched the gag out of her mouth.

"There's no time for that. Grab a weapon and help the others. I need to free Tallis."

Damiana leapt to her feet. "It's your loss."

Before I could utter a remark, she grabbed a long spear that had been leaning against a nearby wall and charged into the fray.

I stole a glance toward the chaos as I sprinted to Tallis. Our adversaries had encircled Omar and Keira in the back of the room. The pair danced around each other as they continued to defend against blow after blow. Hopefully, Damiana could provide them with the assistance they needed.

"He's free," one of them bellowed as I went to cut the rope by Tallis's ankles.

"No, no, no," Tallis said.

I glanced up. Did he really not want me to cut him free?

"Start with my hands. Hurry, we don't have much time."

Although I didn't see what difference it would make, it didn't seem like the right time to question it. I scurried behind him and began to saw the rope.

"Shit, shit, shit," Tallis said. I felt his bloody wrists strain against the rope as I continued to slice through it. "Are you almost done back there?"

"How's this for an answer?" I said as my blade finally tore through the remainder of the rope. "Sit still and let me free your legs."

"There's no time. You need to run."

"I need to what?"

However, my question became pointless. The moment I raised my eyes, a man capable of towering over mountains was charging right at me with his sword drawn.

"Run!" Tallis yelled.

Before the mountain could swing his blade, Tallis launched his body and chair at the man's knees. I barely managed to stumble out of his way, dropping my blade in the process.

A string of curses escaped my lips. Where was the exit? I knew the door was behind a silver tapestry, but I couldn't remember which one. Tapestries covered almost every inch of wall in the room, and dozens of them were silver.

I sprinted to the closest silver one and ripped it aside. My heart sank. There was nothing but a solid wall behind it.

"Guess again, little birdie," said a man with a low, accented voice.

I turned to find the mountain only a few feet away from me, smirking. He took a sideswipe at me, and I fell to the floor to dodge the blow.

Tears warmed my cheeks as I crawled on my back. My

hand desperately searched for a weapon as I pushed myself away from him. I couldn't go out like this. I couldn't die without putting up a fight.

My hand made contact with something other than the floor. For one fleeting moment, I thought I stood a chance. I heard the mountain laugh as I looked down to discover I had found the wall, not a weapon. Worse yet, I had crawled myself right into the corner.

"Don't worry, little birdie, I will grant you a quick death." He chuckled to himself as he raised his sword above his head. "Tell your—"

A blade burst through his open mouth, cutting his threat short and splattering the wall behind me with blood.

Damiana ripped her spearhead out of the mountain's head and spat on his body. "You will do no such thing."

There were a million things I wanted to say at that moment, but none of them found a way out. It had been six years since I had last faced the prospect of a violent death. At least this time I had done something about it.

Damiana gave me her hand and pulled me to my feet. "Come on, we need to get the fuck out of here before the rest of them show up."

15

TALLIS

The absence of adrenaline rushing through my veins brought back my agony. I grimaced as each beat of my heart sent a new wave of pain from my middle finger down my left forearm. However, what stung worse than the pain were the questions that plagued my mind.

I was born to be a thief. Not just any thief but the greatest to have ever walked the mortal plane. How would this injury affect my performance? Had my dreams been severed in a single blow?

Keira closed the tunnel door behind us. The lock clicked into place.

"Are we going to keep walking in silence, or would one of you like to tell me what in your God's dick just happened?" asked Nerea.

Omar chuckled. "Close, but it's Cuvar's cock. It's the alliteration that makes it fun."

If looks could strike, then Nerea's would have knocked Omar off his feet. Fortunately, she didn't have to resort to violence as Damiana smacked him in the shoulder for her.

"Now is not the time to be a smart-ass."

"Damiana's right," St. Keira said as she rejoined us with two lit torches in hand. She gave one to Omar and kept the other for herself. "Did you two learn anything prior to, or during, your capture? I'd hate to find out that you're a pair of bloody idiots who'd put yourselves in harm's way for nothing."

Although she said it with a jovial tone, the message was loud and clear. She thought we were foolish for not waiting for assistance.

Her words cut deeper than Hadul's blade. I had grown used to being chastised by my teachers, but none of that came close to realizing I had disappointed my idol.

"It wasn't for nothing," I stammered.

Cuvar's living saint motioned for me to explain.

"We were able to confirm your theory. When Princess Amaya left the stadium, we followed her. She got in the carriage with two men disguised as Cuvar's priests."

A rat scurried past us and quickly disappeared in the dark.

"How do you know they were in disguise?" asked Nerea. "We know someone in the temple hierarchy is working with Osigrens, but we don't know which temple. Couldn't that have been them? Couldn't they be from another city?"

I shook my head. "One of the men you freed us from, the bastard that took my finger, was one of the two disguised as priests. Him and the rest of the shits up there were from Osigra. So that rules out that possibility."

She seemed to accept this explanation, so I didn't bring up our religion's customs. It was common practice for traveling priests to stay in our temple's walls. If there were other priests of Cuvar in town, then we would have known about them.

"And you confirmed that how, exactly?" St. Keira asked.

"I became fluent in Osigren during my special weapons apprenticeship there," Damiana said. "Clearly our captors were not aware of this as they spoke openly about their plans in their native tongue."

A smile rippled across my face. I knew she understood what they were saying, and now we had reached the moment I had been waiting for.

"The statues downstairs were made by a sculptor who was hired by Prince Ander to make a series of statues in honor of the king's birthday. What the prince doesn't realize is that the sculptor is loyal to Osigra. One of the statues has a chemical compound that will be used to kill the king."

The plan was genius in its simplicity. King Kepa would never suspect a gift from his son, and when the public learned the cause of their king's demise, they would surely seek to put the princess in power.

"The poison is set to be released during His Majesty's masquerade," Damiana continued. "If that fails, then their backup plan is to disguise themselves as the prince's guard and force-feed the king poison in his own chamber."

The joy that coursed through me was overwhelming enough to momentarily block out the pain. We had done it. We had actually done it. All that remained now was to catch them in the act and figure out which one of the bastards was personally responsible for Mother Sienna's death. I was positive the king would grant us some alone time with her murderer as a reward for saving his life and kingdom.

Nerea laughed. "Well, I'm glad to hear I didn't almost die for nothing. How are we going to get this information to the king?"

"We can't, not directly anyways," said St. Keira. "Even if

we could, I'm not sure if we have enough evidence to sway him."

My jaw nearly bounced off the floor. "How can you say that? We found the Osigrens' base and their means of attack. Given all of that and Mother Sienna's letter, how can you claim we don't have enough evidence?"

The saint ran her fingers through her hair. "What we have is hearsay."

I picked at my ear to make sure I had heard her correctly. "Hearsay?"

"Yes. We have a story, and a convincing one at that. However, all our witnesses are dead, and I highly doubt that their bodies or the statues will remain there once the others find them."

Damiana sighed. "I hate to admit it, but I think she's right. Even if we were somehow able to reach the king's ear, our credibility would be shot if they followed our lead and found nothing. That would put us back at square one, and the king's life would still be in danger."

"It's better than doing nothing," I said.

Damiana threw her hands in the air. "I'm not suggesting we do nothing."

"Then what are you suggesting?" asked Nerea.

"We have three days until the king's ball. That gives us two more days to search for evidence. If we can't find anything, then we'll have to go to the masquerade and save him ourselves."

I winced as a new round of pain shot through my hand. "If the Osigrens move their base, then what makes you think we will find it again? The moment they see those dead bodies, they're going to become a shit ton more careful. This is probably our best chance to stop them before the masquerade."

Omar, who had been silent since Nerea's glare, cleared his throat. "Why can't we do both?"

"Both?" asked St. Keira.

"Why can't we send a warning and try to gather more evidence?"

"I hear you, I truly do," said the saint, "but I don't think that's our best use of time or resources. Because we can't give our message directly to the king, we can't trust that it will make it to him at all. Look at what happened to Mother Sienna."

Omar loosed a devilish grin. "Who said anything about the king? He's not the only one with something to lose."

"The prince." I gasped at the realization.

St. Keira mulled over his suggestion. "That could work, but we would need to get to him tonight. What makes you think that would be possible?"

"The night is still young," said Omar. "Given the festivities, there's a good chance our prince is visiting a brothel as we speak. I have crossed him quite a few times at the Scarlet Villa."

That was putting it mildly. The prince had seen Omar there so frequently that he mistook him for one of the prostitutes. Listening to him explain to His Highness that he was one of the customers was one of the most awkward and hilarious moments of my life.

"That settles it," I said. "I'll search the brothels tonight to warn Prince Ander. Omar, you'll keep an eye on the princess in case she meets with anyone suspicious during tonight's festivities. St Keira, as you're our best tracker, I think you should watch their hideout. That way, if they change locations, we'll know where to send the king's men."

The saint's nod of approval sent a wave of pride through

me. Here was one of the greatest thieves to have ever served our Lord, and she had agreed to my plan.

"Why can't I check the brothels?" asked Omar. "I know them like the back of my hand."

I had to stifle a laugh. "That's the problem. I understand how your mind works, and we can't risk you getting distracted in there."

Omar turned bright red under Nerea's questioning gaze.

"And what about me?" asked Damiana.

"I could use your help," Nerea said before I had the chance to respond. "I finished the prototype of the gas masks this morning, and I need someone to test it. If this works, then I could get the others made for the masquerade."

Damiana agreed to assist her as I shook off the pain in my hand. It looked as though we were in for another long night. Hopefully, I wouldn't lose any more of myself in the process.

16

NEREA

As I sat in the hall outside Damiana's room, I wrestled with how much of my past I should share with her. What I needed to say was perfectly normal in my culture, but was it in hers?

The word "normal" reminded me of my mother, causing me to crack a smile. When I would complain as an early teenager about not being normal, she would tell me that normal is an illusion. "It is different for everyone. What is normal for the viper is chaos for the mouse." I didn't fully understand it then, but her words had rung truer and truer with each passing year.

A door creaked open, and I turned to find Damiana's masked head peering into the hall.

"The gas is gone, and I'm still awake," she said. "I guess we can call this a success."

The mask muted her words, forcing me to strain to understand her. It would have been a major design flaw in almost any other situation, but given the time crunch and their use of hand signals, it would have to do for now.

Damiana tried to slip one of her meaty fingers underneath the mask. "How do I take this thing off again?"

"It's tied shut at the back. I can help you with it if you want."

"I've got it, but thank you," she said before disappearing back into her room.

I pushed myself back onto my feet and followed her inside.

Stepping into her room was like stepping into another world. If it weren't for her bed, then I would have no idea that it was a bedroom at all. While her arsenal of weapons consumed the wall closest to her balcony, almost every other inch of wall space had been dedicated to her bug collection.

Terrariums and jars in all different shapes and sizes filled shelf after shelf, and each one contained a different collection of insects. Never in my entire life had I seen so many types of bugs in one place, and that was really saying something as I had grown up exploring every inch of my savanna.

I couldn't help myself. Like a bug to the flame, I had to move in for a closer look.

"I see you found my infamous collection," she said with a laugh. "What do you think?"

Although most of her critters were still knocked out from the gas, my breath caught in my chest as I watched what I thought was a purple lotus walk across a branch to reposition itself. "It's stunning. What is that?"

Damiana peered around me. "Oh, that's technically called a walking lotus, but I like to call her the floral queen."

"Why?"

"The cunning bugger makes all the insects she comes across serve her. Do you see that flower on her back?"

I nodded. The shades of purple that swirled together on its pristine petals were practically spellbinding.

"What it does is draw in pollinators," she continued. "However, instead of releasing nectar, it puts out a chemical that makes the pollinators loyal to her above all else. They're incredibly hard to find, let alone collect, as the infected bugs are willing to die to protect her."

My eyebrow rose. "So how did you manage to collect one then?"

"It's a mystery," she said with a shrug. "I guess you could say it was a birthday present of sorts. I found it in this jar sitting on my bed when I returned from lessons on my thirteenth name day."

A smile stretched across my face. Although I knew it had been a gift from St. Keira, I wouldn't spoil the mystery for her.

"I sometimes wonder if I am her infected one as I am the one who keeps her safe and fed."

We both laughed faintly, but the noise was soon drowned out by our awkward silence.

"Sorry," I said after a deep breath. "I'm not very good at beating around the bush, so I'll just say what I came here to say."

Damiana visibly stiffened. "What is it?"

"In my culture, we take saving someone else's life very seriously."

She grinned at me. "I'm pretty sure that's a universal thing."

"Stop, this is important. The only reason that I joined Cuvar's temple was because I owed my mother a life debt. She saved my life from being kidnapped by Rondu's forces when I was fifteen years old. My father died trying to protect me, and my mother barely escaped with her life.

She wanted me to join the temple, and I honored her wish."

Damiana's smile vanished in an instant, and she placed her hand on my shoulder. "I'm so sorry. I had no idea."

"It's okay," I said, dabbing away a tear. "You had no way of knowing."

She gave my shoulder a squeeze.

"The reason why I'm bringing this up is because in my culture, if someone saves your life, you owe them yours in return."

Her eyes widened. "Nerea, I am not a walking lotus. You don't owe me anything. You're my family, and that's what family does."

I shook my head. "Regardless, I wouldn't be standing here if it wasn't for you, and I'm truly grateful for you because of it. I owe you a debt that can never be repaid. So if you ever need anything, whether big or small, or anywhere in between, all you have to do is ask."

Damiana took a seat at the edge of her bed and began to fidget with her fingers. Had I said something wrong?

"Instead of owing me your life," she said, "could I entrust you with a secret?"

"Of course you can."

"And you won't share it with anyone? Not with the pinky, your mother, or even with the gods in your prayers?"

She certainly didn't need to worry about the last one as I had never gotten into the habit of praying and had no intention of starting anytime soon. However, the sincerity of her concern had grabbed my full attention. What did a thief, one who I had witnessed kill a man, fear others might find out?

I sat on the floor across from her and gazed into her big blue eyes. "I will tell no soul, mortal or divine, what you want to share with me. This I swear on the spirits of my ancestors and any descendants I may bear."

"Shit," she said with a nervous laugh. "That sounds serious."

"So does your secret."

"Touché."

A long silence followed as Damiana rubbed the back of her neck and glanced around the room.

"It's okay if you don't want to tell me or don't feel ready. I will completely understand."

"No, no, it's not that," she said over her wakening insects' soft music. "It's just difficult for me to explain."

I gave her a comforting smile. She was normally a blunt person, which meant whatever was bugging her had to have been eating at her for a while to make her this flustered. If that meant she needed me to be her rock, then that was what I would become.

"I'm not really a woman," she said before covering her face with her hands. "No, that's not what I mean. I was born with all the parts of a woman, but I've never *felt* like one. I've always felt like a man trapped in a woman's body. Does that make any sense? You must think I am insane."

I took her–or rather, them–by the hand. "You're not crazy at all, nor do you sound like it. You're a *faniska*, and there's nothing wrong with that."

Damiana's head cocked to the side. "A fanny-what?"

I fought the urge to smack my forehead. Of course, my friend was unfamiliar with the word. They had spent almost their entire life in Arremendia and its surrounding countryside. When would they have ever come across my native tongue? It was not like the refugees in San Fernando had anything Cuvar would consider to be worth stealing.

"It's the Binsori word for firefly," I said.

My newly revealed brother glanced over their sturdy frame. "I hate to break it to you, but I'm pretty sure I'm human."

"No," I said through a laugh. "That's not what I meant. *Faniskas* play an invaluable role in our society because they have the courage to be who they know they are instead of what the world told them they were. The term might literally mean firefly in our language, but it's used as a title of honor that comes from one of our fairy tales."

Their mouth formed a variety of shapes while searching for his question. "Will you tell it to me?"

"Uh, sure," I said as a bit of heat flashed across my cheeks. "Sorry, I'm not the best storyteller, so you'll have to bear with me."

Damiana made a joke as I tried to remember the story my grandmother told me as a child.

"Once upon a time—"

"Of course it starts with that. Can it even be considered a fairy tale if it doesn't start with 'once upon a time'?"

I cracked a smile. "Do you want to hear the story or not?"

They apologized and encouraged me to continue.

"Once upon a time, there was a faniska, a firefly, that knew it was a star."

"A star?" they asked. I couldn't tell if it was a hint of amusement or disbelief that clung to their words.

"That's what the other fireflies said," I said, transitioning back to my story. "When it told the other fireflies what it was, they all laughed and sneered at it. 'You can't be a star,' they said. 'You are a firefly like us. Do you not see your antennas? Have you not seen your wings or your abdomen? Stars do not have these things.'"

I released a sigh as I sank further into the story. "And sadly, for a split second, it believed them."

"And then what happened?" Damiana asked.

"The *faniska* did what most people do when they're confronted by conflict. It struggled.

"For days and days, the faniska battled with itself. Deep down it knew it was a star. After all, its light shone brighter than all the others, and it felt at home in the night sky. However, when it looked at its body, it saw what the other fireflies saw. It had wings, it had antennas, and it had an abdomen. None of the stars in the sky had those things.

"But then a new thought entered the faniska's brain. What if stars had all those things, but they were just too far away for them to see?"

Damiana leaned so far forward off the edge of their bed that I would've sworn they were about to fall out of it. "And then what did it do?"

Their question reminded me of the time I spent with my grandmother as a small child. I would curl up with her every night and listen to her stories. The entire time, I would pester her with questions as I was eager to know more but too impatient to lie still and listen.

"The faniska devised a plan," I said. "It figured that if it wanted to be a star, then it would have to fly up and join them.

"When dusk began to settle the next day, the faniska told the other members of its tribe that it was leaving them to join the other stars. At first, they laughed because they thought it was joking, but when they realized the faniska was serious, they told it that it couldn't be done.

"'Don't do it,' they said. 'You are a firefly, not a star.'

"'It's dangerous,' another firefly said. 'You'll get eaten by a bat or bird if you try to join the stars.'

"A host of other reasons for why it was a bad idea were rained down upon the little faniska, but it didn't listen. It knew it wasn't a firefly, and the time had come to prove it once and for all."

Damiana nodded along as I spoke. The way they fixed their gaze on me, one might have thought they could have seen the words coming out of my mouth.

"Before the other fireflies could weigh it down with more words of warning," I continued, "the faniska soared into the sky.

"Right before the sun bid the delta good night, the faniska reached the edge of the sky. The stars then appeared and welcomed their newest member with open arms.

"To this day, you can still see the faniska in the night sky," I said. "It is the brightest of all the stars because it remained true to itself, even when the world told it no, and that is also the reason why my people trust it to guide us during our travels. When you are ready to let your light shine, it will have the same effect."

Their face might have remained stern, but I noticed the tears welling in the corners of their eyes. "You're right. You are shit at telling stories."

"Can I ask you a question?" I said through my laugh.

They wiped away their tears before they could fall. "You just did, but you can ask another if you like."

"I'm sorry if this is an ignorant question, but why are you keeping your true self a secret? I'm confident that Tallis and Omar would accept you for who you are."

Damiana sighed. "They might accept me, but I can't say the same about the rest of the temple. You probably realized this already, but Arremendia is not Binsoro."

That was quite the understatement.

"I was only nine years old when I told my mother I

thought I was a boy," they continued. "When she told my ass of a father, and they realized I meant what I said, they tried to sell me into slavery."

My heart broke at the thought. I figured they had to have gone through something terrible to end up as an acolyte of Cuvar at such a young age, but this was more than my heart could handle. It ached for them.

"Fortunately, I managed to run away before they could sell me. I ended up living on the streets of Gecho for over a year before Mother Sienna found me, and the only companions I had at that time were the bugs I found around the neighborhood. It was with her and in the temple that I found my new family. One that embraced my masculine side and even allowed me to live as a boy, if only for a few hours at a time. I guess I'm afraid that if anyone in the temple finds out, then I'll lose my family all over again. I love my new family, even that little shit Omar... I couldn't go through that again."

I reached out, took one of their hands, and gave it a gentle squeeze. "No matter what happens, I'll always be your family, Dami... wait, do you still want me to call you Damiana? What pronouns would you like me to use?"

"My pronouns are he and him, but please still refer to me as Damiana around others. When it's just the two of us, you can call me Dario."

We sat there in silence for a moment, still hand in hand.

Dario sniffled. "Shit, it feels so good to not have to keep this to myself anymore."

Unsure of what to say, I smiled and continued to rub his hand.

"Remember, this needs to stay between us," Dario said.

"Of course, but can you also promise me something?"

Dario shrugged as a wide smile stretched across his face. “I don’t recall you saving my life, but I guess.”

“When you're ready to let your light shine, promise me you won't hold it back,” I said. “Life in this world is far too short, and you deserve to experience it as your true self before it's all said and done.”

“All right, Mother Nerea,” he teased. “I promise.”

17

TALLIS

As far as Arremendian brothels went, the Scarlet Villa was on the nicer end of the scale. Well, at least it seemed that way compared to the other establishments I'd fished Omar out of over the years. I would have been willing to deem it the best of the bad bunch if they hadn't embraced the scarlet portion of their name with such vigor.

The moment I pushed through the door, a nauseating wave of scarlet decor hit me. Even the half-naked men and women eagerly waiting to please were covered in tiny bits of scarlet fabric.

"To what do we owe your noble presence, Tallis?" said a woman with a sultry voice as she took me by the arm. "You are aware that Omar isn't here tonight, right?"

I looked down to find a gorgeous redheaded woman wearing a silk scarlet slip that left absolutely nothing of her slim figure to the imagination. So many freckles dotted her fair skin that she looked like a pointillism painting come to life.

I offered up a teasing grin as I led us toward the closest

empty table. "Come now, Freya. What makes you think I'm here for him? Couldn't I be here simply because I miss our charming banter?"

Instead of sitting in the chair next to or across from me, she sat on my lap and slowly wiggled her way into a comfortable position.

"You're so full of shit that it's a miracle Cuvar hasn't turned your eyes brown," she whispered into my ear while placing her hand on my chest. "You've left me wanting *far* too many times. If you ever want me to believe you, then you'll have to do more than talk to me while you wait for Omar to finish."

I removed her hand from my chest, planted a delicate kiss on it, and led it to my coin purse. "I'm afraid I'll have to leave you wanting once more, but I have no intention of leaving you empty-handed."

Freya's bright-blue eyes danced with delight as I slipped a silver into her hand.

"I have a proposition for you," I said, "but I need you to fetch me a beer first. Just know that there's plenty more where that came from."

She eased off me with a slow roll of her hips. "I guess I can find it in my heart to forgive you this time. Don't go anywhere. I'll be right back."

While Freya sauntered to the bar, swinging her hips with pride, I took the moment to survey the rest of the room. Although Prince Ander and his guards had a tendency to disguise themselves in street clothing during his nighttime escapades, they were still easy to recognize with my trained eyes.

My smile widened as I spotted one of his guards. He sat next to one of the hallways that led to some of their private rooms.

Despite the burly man's shabby wardrobe, he didn't appear to belong to his clothes. His scruff had yet to see five o'clock, his black hair was far too neat, and the quality of the sword hanging from his waist was much too expensive for a man of his attire. However, the greatest giveaway of all was that he sat at the table by himself. He might as well have hung a sign above him that read, *I'm here for work, not pleasure*.

"So what exactly does your proposition entail?" Freya asked as she slipped back onto my lap.

I couldn't help myself from grimacing when she passed the glass of beer into my hand.

Even though St. Keira had immediately cleaned my wound upon our arrival to Mother Sienna's chambers and applied a special herbal treatment to quicken the healing process and ease the pain, it hadn't dulled it completely.

"Holy shit, Tallis, what happened to your finger?"

I took a swig of the warm, hoppy beer. Part of its foamy head clung to my scruffy mustache, forcing me to lick it clean. "Don't worry about it. My Lord needed it more than I did."

"Oh, you poor thing," she said as she started to play with my curls. "I've always admired your long, strong fingers. Please don't tell me Cuvar has required you to cut anything else off."

A laugh escaped my lips. "As of yet, he has not tried to shorten my endowment, but I feel like we are getting off track. If you look over your left shoulder, there's a man sitting by himself in the back corner of the room. Do you see who I'm talking about?"

Freya peeked over her shoulder. "You must mean the poor bastard who looks even more upset to be here than you usually do?"

"Yes, and did—wait, you think I look upset when I'm here? I was going for an eternal ray of sunshine."

She sucked in a breath. "A little bit, but that's only natural. Any human would feel that way if they constantly deprived themselves of fully enjoying my company for no apparent reason."

No reason? I guessed it would have seemed that way in her eyes. Either that or she thought I despised her profession, which couldn't be further from the truth.

However, I could never explain to her that the only thing that prevented me from paying for her services was the insurmountable debt a deity placed on my head as a child. I didn't have the luxury of spare coins like my fingermates. Every hard-earned coin I stole was either reinvested into the next game or handed over to my Lord.

"If it's any consolation," I said, "my logic disheartens me as much as it does you."

Freya blushed and flipped her hair. "It's a small victory, but I guess I'll have to take it."

"Let's get back to that bastard. He obviously didn't come in here by himself. How many others were with him?"

A mixture of applause and laughter broke out as the bard came to the end of the song.

"You know, I'm not really supposed to share information about our customers, especially the paying ones."

"To be fair," I said as I slipped her another silver, "he's not a customer. He is simply having a horrible time while standing on guard."

The music started up again while she took a split second to pretend to think it over. "You do make a good point. Your friend over there came in tonight with a very wealthy man. In fact, he's so rich that every time he visits, he pays for the entire hall of rooms just to make sure he's not disturbed."

My lips curled into a smile. That was wonderful news. It was far easier to sedate one man than it was to sedate a multitude of them.

"Freya, I need you to listen closely," I whispered, slipping her a third piece of silver. "What I'm about to tell you, you'll need to forget by the time I leave."

She grimaced. "That's going to be a challenge. My mother always said I had the greatest memory she had ever seen."

I handed over yet another piece of silver. "Hopefully, that will help your problem, and I will double the amount I've given you on my way out to compensate for your uncharacteristic memory loss."

"Out with it, then. I don't think I've wanted a man to finish so fast in my entire life," she said with a wink.

"My fathers have sent me here because the lives of that wealthy man and his family are at risk. I need to warn him with such discretion that even his guard doesn't know about it. In order to do that, I will need your help with sedating the guard."

Freya's customary flirtatious expression vanished in an instant as her eyes grew wide.

"Don't worry," I continued. "All you'll have to do is walk me over there. Given his size, this sedative should only knock him out for about twenty to thirty minutes, and this won't take nearly that long."

She nodded, and a faint smile returned to her face.

"After I knock him out," I continued, "you will lead me down the hall as though you're taking me to one of the private rooms. However, you will be actually taking me to the room our rich friend is in."

"He's back there now with Iker and Maite. For an extra silver, I can have them disperse without so much as a fuss."

I couldn't help the smile that crossed my face. She truly knew how to drive a bargain. "You've got yourself a deal. Just keep them close. Knowing him, he'll probably want to resume where they left off after my departure."

After giving Freya her fifth piece of silver and applying a poisoned tack to my bandaged middle finger, we made our way across the room. I swayed and stumbled as she led me toward the hall to imitate a drunkard. It was of paramount importance that Prince Ander's guard saw me as a fool, not a threat.

The guard's sigh was only matched by his look of disappointment as we neared the hall. He pulled his sword partway out of its sheath. "Find yourself another place to fuck this halfwit out of his money. This hall is tak—"

Freya jerked to a stop at his words. I, on the other hand, took the opportunity to "trip" over her, and sent myself flying into his lap.

"Ah!" he yelped as my tack punctured his skin through his pants. "What the fuck?"

I struggled to push myself back to my feet. "S-s-so s-sorry, my friend, but your l-l-lap is not the one I meant to end up in."

The guard shook his head in an attempt to fight the drowsiness that raced to consume him. "Go shove your sorries up..."

When his head wobbled, I knew it wouldn't be much longer.

"Here, rest easy, my friend," I said as I guided his head to the table.

Although it might have been humorous, I didn't want the prick to smack his head when he passed out. By the time his face reached the table, he was sound asleep.

"Now." I paused to hiccup. "Where were we, dear?"

She took me by the hand and led me to the prince's sectioned-off hallway. The hall itself consisted of five doors: two on either side and one at the very end. His Grace's room, of course, was the largest one located at the end.

Freya opened the door without so much as giving a warning to those inside. As a result, we stepped into the room to find Prince Ander on the bed buried beneath his lovers. Maite rode his face while Iker had taken the prince in his mouth.

At the sound of our entrance, Maite turned back to look at us. Relief filled her chestnut eyes as they rolled back in her head. Apparently, His Grace hadn't even learned to do this well during his four decades of existence.

"It looks like we have company," Maite said as she dismounted the heir to the throne.

The prince's brow creased as he stared down at us past his aquiline nose. However, he must have approved of our appearance because his look of confusion was soon replaced by a hungry smile.

"Are you compliments of the Villa, or did Miguel send you as a surprise present?" asked the prince. "Never mind, it does not matter. You"—he pointed to me—"grab the lube and—"

I held up my hand to cut him off. "Apologies, I've been sent to talk to you, not to pleasure you, or anyone else in here for that matter."

"Iker and Maite," Freya said, "our madame would like to have a word with you."

"What the fuck is going on?" demanded the prince as his lovers followed Freya out the door, leaving their clothes behind. "Miguel!"

He shouted for his guard once more as he hopped out of bed and began searching his pile of clothes for a weapon.

"Relax, Prince Ander. If I wanted you dead, then I would never have given you the chance to see me coming."

The prince froze at the sound of his name and looked back over at me.

"I would never have dared to interrupt you if the matter was not so dire," I continued. "I promise that your companions shall return upon my departure, and I will stand guard until Miguel wakes."

The prince's brow furrowed once more. "What have you done with Miguel?"

"I gave him a potent but short-lasting sedative that should wear off within the next thirty minutes. It was the safest way of reaching you without causing a scene."

"And what matter could be so dire for you to go through with all this? Is my life in danger?"

"Yes, Your Grace," I said, taking a step forward. "We have discovered that your sister and the Osigrens are plotting together to overthrow your father at his masquerade, and they are going to frame you for his death. It is also possible that some of the city's clergy are involved as well, but that has yet to be confirmed."

"I don't know whether I should laugh at you or have you arrested for treason for making such an accusation of my beloved Amaya. Do you have any evidence to support such a claim?"

"Does the address 2 Parroco Ugaz mean anything to you?"

Prince Ander let out an annoyed laugh. "I am familiar with the street but not that exact building. How is this relevant?"

"The address belongs to the sculptor you hired to make His Majesty's birthday presents."

He stared at me in silence for a moment with his

eyebrow raised. "Who told you about the sculptures? Whichever member of my guard let this slip is going to have hell to pay."

"Your men have all held their tongues. It was the Osigrens who held me captive in your sculptor's building that didn't realize that my companion is fluent in their language. They were the ones who unwittingly fed this information to me along with the rest of their plan. The moment we escaped, I knew we had to come warn you."

"That sounds like quite the story," he said as he took his seat back on the bed, crossing his legs. "However, your tale left so many questions unanswered. For example, it fails to explain why, or how, my sister is supposedly involved, why you were the one investigating this in the first place, or why I should believe a single word that has come out of your mouth."

I took a deep breath. There were no two ways about it. Prince Ander was not the type of man to be swayed by partial truths, and there was too much at stake to risk crafting a lie.

Due to my lack of options, I sat down beside him, and told him everything from Mother Sienna's death through our escape from the Osigrens. Whether he believed me or not, I couldn't say. It was all in Cuvar's hands now.

18

NEREA

"Is that my miracle child coming to visit me in all black?" my mother asked as I walked into her hospital room. "You do realize I'm not on my deathbed just yet, don't you, Rea?"

Although she wasn't on it yet, it didn't look as though she was far from it either. At least the pain no longer shone in her eyes like the blazing sun. It wasn't much progress, but it was better than nothing.

I eased myself into the seat beside her bed and took her by the hand. The incense that burned on her bedside table sent a pleasant aroma into the air.

"I'm sorry, Mother. I have to go attend Mother Sienna's funeral rites after this."

She scrunched up her face. "Mother Sienna. Wasn't she the one who spoke to us at the temple?"

"The one and the same."

"That's such a shame," she said, giving my hand a squeeze. "She seemed so vibrant when we met her. Then again, who truly knows how death works. All we can do is try to enjoy every moment we have amongst the living. I'm sure she would agree."

Given how the priestess died, I wasn't sure if she would agree with my mother's statement in its entirety. However, I sensed her words were meant to comfort me more about her own life than they were to console me about Mother Sienna's passing.

"Besides that, how has everything else been? What have you been working on? Tell me everything."

Everything? It felt like a tall order. Where in the world was I supposed to begin? The truth was too dangerous for a multitude of reasons.

"It has been like nothing I could ever have expected," I admitted, "but in a good way. They actually have me working on a special project for the king. I'm not allowed to go into details, but it could be beneficial for the entire kingdom."

A smile stretched across her face, sending a wave of wrinkles in its wake. "That's wonderful. I knew their Lord would bring you noble work."

I guessed it wasn't the best time to tell her that after this project, all my other works would be used to help the temple steal from the rich in the name of piety.

"And the people at the temple," she continued, "how do you like them? Is everyone being nice to you? If they are treating you half as well as they are treating me here, then I'm sure you must be loving it."

A tear welled in my eye. She had suffered through too much in her lifetime. If anyone deserved to be treated like royalty, then it would have to be her.

"I've been inducted into the smallest organization within the temple, so I haven't had a chance to talk to everyone. But the ones I have are an oddly delightful bunch. They seem like the type who would be willing to do anything to help me."

That was an understatement given the heroics Dario performed last night to save my life.

"They sound lovely," she said through a yawn. "Maybe you could bring some of them during your next visit, and try to come earlier as well. I am not the nighthawk that I used to be."

"Nothing would make me happier."

"I love you, Rea," she said as she closed her eyes. "Now let this old hen get some rest."

I planted a kiss on her forehead. "I love you too."

As I rose to leave, a woman wearing the pale-blue robes of Potami poked her head into the room. "Hi, I'm sorry to disturb you. I am Sister Jacinta. You must be Sabela's daughter. Could I have a word with you in the hall?"

I nodded and raised a finger to ask her to give me a moment.

Once the priestess vanished back into the hall, I glanced down to discover my mother had fallen asleep with a smile on her face. My heart melted at the sight. When was the last time I had seen her at peace?

"I'll be back soon," I whispered. "I promise."

"I'm so sorry for interrupting your visitation," Sister Jacinta said as I stepped into the hall. "One of our acolytes informed me that you had arrived, and I wanted to catch you before you left."

It was tough for me to gauge the priestess's age. Her lush black hair said she could have been only a few years older than me. However, her practiced smile, and the fact that she had more bags under her gentle green eyes than a street vendor's cart, suggested she had been doing this for quite some time.

"It's okay. What did you want to talk about?"

I cringed internally the moment my question left my lips. *What do you want to talk about?* Of course she had come to speak to me about my mother. It wasn't as though she had rushed to see me to discuss the weather or moral philosophy.

"There's no easy way to say this," said the priestess, "and in my experience, it's best to be frank in these situations."

A lump the size of a boulder formed in my throat.

"Sabela is in the late stages of terminal cancer," she continued. "We've been able to slow the spread, but there's nothing we can do to stop it completely or fix the damage. If we continue the treatments, then we expect that she will last another week, maybe two if the gods will it."

The world shifted beneath my feet. I staggered. If I hadn't caught myself on the wall, then I would have fallen to the floor in a heap.

"I'm so sorry," Sister Jacinta said again as she pulled me into an embrace.

Tears poured down my face like water bursting from a broken dam, soaking the robes of the stranger who held me.

This wasn't supposed to happen. I sacrificed my freedom for her to be healed. How was this fair? I needed to have more time with my mother. I still needed her.

How would the pinky react to this news?

The question made my skin crawl. It shouldn't have been something I had to worry about. All my focus should have been on appreciating what little time I had left with her. Nonetheless, the question ate at me during my walk back to the temple.

"Sorry I'm late," I said when Omar opened the door, allowing me to join the others in Mother Sienna's room.

Omar's stupid grin vanished in a heartbeat. "What happened? Are you all right?"

I shook my head as my tears threatened to unleash themselves once more. "No, I was just visiting my mother at Potami's temple, and the doctors there told me she has a week left to live. Maybe two if we're lucky."

My new family showered me with condolences as Omar gave me a hug. Even through his tunic, I felt his heart thump softly against my cheek.

"I know how important our mission is and how much it means to you all," I said as I pulled out of his embrace, "but I don't know how much more I can give. My mother has moved mountains for me, and I need to be with her at the end. I need to spend every second I can with her."

My hands shook as I awaited their response. As much as my mom had helped me, they had already done so much for me as well in our short time together. Given what was at stake, was I asking too much of them?

Omar gave me a knowing grin. "That's fine. I think we may understand better than most. We have all lost our parents in some form or another, and most of us would do just about anything to spend another moment with them. You do what you have to do."

My jaw dropped as I looked around at the others. They all shared a similar expression and echoed his sentiments.

It was all too much. I couldn't prevent the tears from rolling down my face any longer. My mother had no idea how correct she was when she told me this temple was the place for me.

"Thank you," I said after a moment of silence, "but enough about me. What have I missed? How did the meeting with the prince go?"

Tallis ran his fingers through his thick dark curls. "It's

hard to say. I thought our meeting went well at first, but it looks as though it was all for naught."

I felt my brow furrow. "What do you mean?"

"It has to do with the Osigrens' hideout," Keira explained. "When I got back to it, the whole building was on fire. I joined the others who were trying to put it out, and while inside, I noticed that everything was missing. The statues, the bodies... they were all gone."

Tallis shrugged his shoulders. "That's why I don't know how the prince will react. Even if he believed me, there is now a chance that he'll change his mind because the evidence is gone."

There was that word again, gone. For being such a simple word, it was hard to get both my mind and my mouth around it.

"How can it all be gone?" I asked. "There were at least, *at least*, twenty statues in that place. And they didn't look light by any means. How many men would you need to clear that place out in a matter of hours?"

"It would take a small army," Dario said.

Omar scratched his chin. "So did Princess Amaya take advantage of the city watch, or are there more Osigrens in the city than we ever imagined?"

"I'm not sure if it matters in the end," said the saint. "If they are in cahoots together, then it's essentially one and the same."

Dario's knuckles tightened into fists. "Great, we are back to square one, and there are only two days until the king's masquerade. What are we supposed to do now?"

The question loomed over us like a large cat ready to pounce.

"We do the only thing we can do," Tallis said. "We focus on what we can control."

Although I stopped myself from laughing, I couldn't prevent my eyebrow from arching. "And what exactly is it that we control? No offense, but it doesn't feel as though we have been in control of much this entire time."

To his credit, Tallis didn't miss a beat. "It's looking more and more likely that we will have to intervene at the masquerade. One of the things that is in our control is making sure we are prepared for it. The other thing we can do is keep on looking for evidence with the hopes that we get lucky. Just today, Omar tracked the princess to a meeting with priests at Elbio's Temple. Maybe we will be able to glean new insights from these events."

That was rather unlikely. Given how close we came to unraveling their plans at the studio, I expected that they would try to tighten down on any leads they potentially saw as being at risk. Their moving of the statues and destroying the evidence suggested that would be the case. However, I was not about to fault him for trying.

"What do we need to be ready for the masquerade?" I asked.

"We shouldn't need much more," Keira said, stepping forward. "We have the masks, the weapons, and the sleeping gas. The only other things we will need are our outfits and invitations to the ball."

I scoffed. "You make it sound as easy as spotting the sun on a cloudless day. Although I will be able to finish the last masks in time, how do you expect to sneak all our equipment past the gates, or find invitations for that matter?"

"If you weren't brand new to the order, then I would joke about your lack of faith," St. Keira said with a grin. "All the temple priests are issued invitations for His Majesty's masquerade, and the council has secured me an invitation as well. As the others are aware, I've been considered an expert in forgery since the age of eleven. Making invitations for the rest of you will be a breeze."

Cuvar's greatest thief was also a master forger? Was there any crooked deed that this woman was not capable of performing?

"And," continued the saint, "just as I have snuck in and out of the Hanging Palace these past few days, I will sneak in once more to hide our supplies."

Her points all seemed valid. However, even if getting prepared for the masquerade was as easy as she claimed, I highly doubted what came next would be as simple.

"We're forgetting one thing," Omar said. "If we're all at the masquerade and Nerea is with her mother, then who will we have watching over Ora?"

The room fell silent as we all pondered his question. Was there anyone we could trust?

"I know you have a lot on your hands with your mother, but could you stay with Ora during the masquerade?"

All of their eyes shifted to me. Although I was the only person who wasn't going that they knew they could trust, was it even possible?

"Ora is my family by blood, but the rest of you are my family too. I promised myself that I'd never sit back and do nothing again when my family needed me the most. This is my chance to actually do something, and I need to take it."

My mind went back to our conversation on Ora's bed the other day. He might have grown into quite the handsome man, but there was still a broken boy inside of him dying to make amends.

"I will stay with her," I said.

"Are you sure?" asked Tallis. "I'm positive we can find someone else."

It was sweet of them to want to honor my wishes, but we

all knew there was no one else they could put their full faith in.

"The masquerade doesn't start until after Potami's visitation hours are over anyway. As long as you're not trying to be the first ones to the party, then it shouldn't be an issue."

The church bells rang, signaling that it was time to begin paying our respects to Mother Sienna.

As we filed out of her chambers, I couldn't help but wonder if our plan would cause them to chime again.

19

NEREA

"Savor the slowness, Nerea. Time only quickens with age. A day will come when you'd give the world to slow it down again, but by then it'll be far too late."

My father's warning to me sounded foolish when I was a child. However, the truth of his words was now apparent.

Despite all my pleading to gods I didn't believe in, the next two days passed in a blink of an eye. He was right. I would've traded the world if it would have given me more time with my mother.

Unfortunately, life didn't work that way. After tonight, all I could do was savor every moment I had left with her. All I could do was try to bask in the little time we had left. However, that would have to wait until the morning.

I knocked on the door to Ora's room. "It's me. Open up."

Omar pushed the door open enough to stick his head out. He wore a dark-blue suit with gold trim and clutched something behind his back. "What's the password?"

"Really? You can see that it's me, and that I'm alone."

"No one's above the rules."

"I'm nuts about you," I said through a sigh.

His stupid smirk widened as he slipped on his golden squirrel mask. "You don't say."

I laughed my way past him into the room. "Out of all the masks you could've chosen, why did you pick a squirrel?"

"It's the king's decree. Everyone's outfits are to be inspired by their favorite Arremendian creatures."

"And your favorite creature in all of Arremendia is a squirrel?"

"It makes sense when you think about it," Tallis said from his seat at Ora's desk. "They're adorable and obsessed with their nuts. If that's not a perfect match, then I'm not sure what is."

Although his first point could be debated, his second didn't surprise me. What it did do, however, was make me question the significance of the others' masks.

Dario's mask had a short, curled snout and three antennas branching off it. I had no idea what bizarre insect inspired it, but that was his specialty. Tallis, on the other hand, clutched a river squid mask in his hand. His connection to the creature was the only one that didn't make sense to me.

"Shit," Dario said, grinning from ear to ear, "I wish we had the time to run through my list of jokes at his expense, but we should get going. I mean, we only have a kingdom to save."

"Don't you have to wait for St. Keira?" I asked as they made their way toward the door.

Dario slipped on his bug-inspired mask. "No, she went over early to hide the supplies. We'll meet her in the Hanging Palace."

There was no sense in keeping them waiting. I bid them farewell, slid the lock into place, and began searching Ora's bookshelf for something interesting to read.

That was a more challenging task than I anticipated. With the exception of her bounty of romance novels, all her books seemed to be about the various religions of Yenra, economics, and history. I had just settled on *The Saints of Cuvar* and was about to take a seat when there was a knock at the door.

"I'm nuts about you," said a familiar voice that I couldn't quite place.

Had they come back because they had forgotten something, or was it someone else at the door entirely?

I traded the book for a dagger and made my way over to the peephole. Keira stood on the other side of the door, dressed in all black and carrying a large sack over her shoulder.

"I'm nuts about you," Keira said again, "or did you lie about that, Omar?"

The door squeaked as I pulled it open. "What are you doing here? The others left a few minutes ago."

"Damn," she said as she walked over to Ora's desk and set the sack down. "I'll catch back up to them in a moment."

She took a peek over at me as she started to untie the bag.

"The reason why I came back is I realized there's a chance, albeit a small one, that our plan blows up in our face. I wanted to make sure you had the tools to escape the city, should it be necessary."

Escape the city? How could their plan result in that?

The stupidity of my question became abundantly clear. They might have to use the sleeping gas to knock out people to help secure the king's safety. If the king misinterpreted their actions, then the backlash could be catastrophic.

What would my fleeing the city mean for my mother? I

shuddered at the thought. It was a rabbit hole I could not afford to fall down.

"Go ahead and look through it," she said, waving me over. "Let me know if there's anything you don't know how to use. I'll explain it before I go."

My brow furrowed as I opened the sack. A pair of crossbows sat on the top of the pile. How did she expect me to sneak out of town with one, let alone two, of them?

For a split second, I thought a bug had bitten my shoulder, but then I realized the saint had placed her hand there as she crouched down beside me.

"Don't worry, I'll set it up to give you a quick death. It's the least I can do given how new you are to this corrupt order."

My heart froze in my chest. Had I heard her correctly? One look at her devilish grin erased all doubt.

I tried to run, but the world shifted beneath my feet and sent me careening to the floor.

"Looks like the sedative is kicking in," she said as I crawled toward the door.

Her slow footsteps seemed to echo off the hardwood. "It's okay. This will all be over soon."

As I reached out to claw myself forward, the world faded to black.

~

I awoke unable to breathe or move my limbs. What on Yenra was happening?

My pulse raced as the memory of the saint's betrayal came back to me. I screamed into my gag. The bastard had tied me to Ora's bed and had hung a crossbow above me, pointed straight at my chest.

"Oh good, you're up," Keira said from over by the door, "and just in time."

As she walked back into my line of sight, I noticed she had moved Ora onto the floor. The other crossbow had been hung above her, and there appeared to be a wire attached to its trigger.

Why had she done this? It didn't make any sense. Did this mean she was working with the Osigrens? Were the Osigrens even involved? What was her endgame?

My unaskable questions added to the frustration that tore at my chest. I screamed into my gag once more.

"I understand why you're proper upset, but that screaming won't do you any good," Keira said. I felt the cushion dip as she sat down beside me on the bed. "For starters, no one outside that door can hear you. And even if they could, that would be the last thing you'd want now."

My brow furrowed. What was she talking about? My best chance for survival was for someone out there to hear me and barge in here.

"I'm sure you're aware of this crossbow by now," she continued, "but what you may not have realized is that the wire around its trigger is connected to the door. The moment someone tries to pull it open, they will unwittingly pull the trigger that will seal your and Ora's fate."

A grotesque smile crossed her face as she admired her handiwork. "Although the final results of my contraption is a grim one, I thought you might appreciate the ingenuity behind it given your skill set."

Appreciate the ingenuity? Did she honestly expect me to respect her method of murdering me because it required a small degree of engineering to accomplish? A wave of heat consumed my body as my blood boiled.

"I'm genuinely sorry that you were caught up in all of

this," the saint said as she returned her gaze to mine. "In all my years of planning, you were never accounted for in this moment. Since I can't let you live, it only seems fair that I at least explain to you why you're about to die."

A tear rolled down my face, and I cursed myself for it. The smug bastard probably thought I was stricken by fear, but that couldn't have been further from the truth. It was at that moment that I realized I would never see my mother again. When she left this world, she would now do so either thinking that I had abandoned her or knowing that I had gone before her in death. Either scenario would crush her.

"I'm going to take your gag out," she said. "I have about five minutes until I need to leave for the masquerade. As long as you're quiet, I can answer all of your questions until then. If not, I'll prick you again with the sedative and leave you here to die. Do you understand?"

As much as I wanted to tell her to shove her explanations up her ass, I needed to know how this puzzle fit together. It felt like I had been handed a few edge pieces without any idea of what final image they formed. I did the only thing I could do. I nodded.

Keira pulled the balled-up cloth out of my mouth. "You see, that wasn't too—"

I spat in her face.

Much to my chagrin, she didn't look perturbed as she swiped my phlegm away. "At least you were quiet."

"Fuck you," I whispered. "Why are you doing this?"

"Do you recall the last play you put on for the De La Fuentes Theater Company?"

My eyebrow arched. "It was *The Tragedy of Leojung*, but what does that have to do with any of this?"

She looked at me like a tutor does at an impatient

student. "It was a tragedy indeed. And what exactly was that tragedy about?"

If she only had five minutes, then why was she wasting my time with these stupid questions? Every child over the age of six in Arremendia knew the tale of *The Tragedy of Leojung*. Besides *Zolten's Demise*, it was the only play that the crown was always willing to finance.

"The tragedy is about how the disgraced Emperor of Osigra turned his back on the gods, how Arremendia tried to save his, and how the gods ultimately punished Emperor Leojung for his decision."

Keira laughed maniacally at a joke I failed to see.

"That's a load of propaganda horseshit," she said when her laughter died down. "The gods don't give a bloody crap about us, and they certainly had no hand in murdering my father and the rest of my family."

My father. Those two little words struck me like a bolt of lightning. Had she used that phrase in reference to Emperor Leojung, or was my mind connecting the dots that didn't exist? If so, then wouldn't that make her one of the Osigren princesses who lost her life in the tragedy?

"It is true that when my father chose to lead our people away from the gods and goddesses of old, Arremendia was still our greatest ally," she continued. "It was the cowardly priests of this city that poisoned the young King Kepa's mind against my father. They were terrified that he might turn the kingdom away from the gods as well. The bastards convinced Kepa that if he couldn't get my father to return to religion, then he would have to kill my father in the name of the lords to protect Arremendia."

The pain etched across her face led me to believe she was telling the truth. After all, what was the point in lying to the person she was about to murder? However, there was still one part of her story that didn't make sense.

I tried to adjust my position in the bed, but the ropes around my waist, wrists, and legs were so tight that I could barely move an inch. "If King Kepa had your family murdered at the insistence of the temple priests, then how did you survive, and how did you end up joining Cuvar's temple?"

"The only reason why I'm still alive is because I am a lucky little bugger," Keira admitted. "Fortunately for me, the king's men couldn't justify killing a baby. They gave me to the temple in the city-state of my mother's birth to be raised as an acolyte of Cuvar. What else could one do with such a misfortunate?"

As I stared up at my murderer, a thought came that cut me to the bone. I understood her reasoning. If she wasn't about to kill me, and presumably my friends, then I might have even sympathized with her.

"When did you learn this?" I asked to keep myself from dwelling on the previous thought. "I can't imagine you would've tried to become Cuvar's living saint if you had known about your past."

Keira gazed at the space before her as if the memory was being replayed in front of her eyes. "I didn't know until Cuvar accidentally showed me as my soul was being tethered to him."

"What do you mean he accidentally showed you? Surely you don't mean you can actually communicate to the gods."

"Just because our realities are different, it doesn't make them any less real," Keira said with a laugh. "However, it is tough to explain what it is like to share your mind with a monster of a god who is capable of taking control of you at any given moment."

My brow furrowed. "If Cuvar can take control of you, then why hasn't he tried to stop you? Wouldn't a deity who shares your mind be aware of your plans?"

The saint peered out the window onto the balcony. "It looks as though you've wasted your five minutes arguing with me about the gods. However, I'll answer this last one for you."

She rose from the bed and grabbed her silver eagle's mask off the floor.

"I have to poison myself daily to keep him out. It will kill me in a few years' time, but it's worth it. I would gladly do it all over again if it meant weakening the gods and helping humanity in the war to come."

The black lines that painted her abdomen flashed across my mind. Was that a result of the supposed poison that coursed through her veins?

"What war to come?" I asked, staring at the beak that masked her face.

I winced as she pricked me with the sedative once more.

"It doesn't matter," she said as my world started to fade. "You'll be long gone before the war begins."

20

TALLIS

My stomach lurched as a strong gust blew our elevator into the side of King's Mountain. Our glorified cage reverberated with the impact.

"Is this your first time to the Hanging Palace?" asked the man sitting across from me. His suit, and the outfits of his two companions, were made out of blue and gray feathers meant to imitate a mountain crane.

I smirked. "What gave it away?"

My answer couldn't have been further from the truth. However, I saw no point in telling him that I had ridden the palace lifts on numerous occasions.

"You are clutching the bottom of your seat like a scared newborn does his mother," he said with a laugh.

His assumption of my nerves was correct, but his reasoning was off. Dangling hundreds of feet in the air by a centuries-old chain didn't worry me in the slightest. What had me on edge was the thought of what was at stake tonight. Not only would we be responsible for saving the kingdom, but thwarting the Osigrens' plans was the only way we could avenge Mother Sienna at this point.

"I was worried on my first trip to the Hanging Palace as well," said the feather-dressed girl beside me, "but you will get used to it. Look, we're coming up on the sky cells. It won't be much longer now."

I followed her finger to where it pointed to the wall-less, circular cell. Although dungeon space encompassed the entire lower level of the palace, the sky cells that hung beneath each of the castle's ten turrets were reserved for the most egregious of criminals.

"Those cells used to haunt my dreams," continued the masked beauty. "Any time I stepped out of line as a child, my mother would threaten to send me up there."

We drove Mother Sienna to the brink of issuing similar threats on multiple occasions. The thought brought a smile to my face.

"It was always 'The king owes me a favor, Irene,'" she said, wagging her finger. "'If you don't finish your vegetables, then I'll have him put you in the sky cell.' Or better still, 'If you don't stop picking on your sister, Irene, then I'll have the king put you in a sky cell. He is an old friend, you know.'" Irene laughed gaily at her impersonation.

"It sounds like you were a real handful for her," Omar said with a cheeky grin.

Damiana must have seen where his mind was racing as she elbowed him in his side. Her quick strike garnered more than a few raised eyebrows from our lift companions.

"Apologies," Damiana said as our view of the city below vanished behind a wall of rock. "He's here tonight to court my cousin. Given that we've been friends for over ten years, I know how fast his eyes can wander before he's committed. It was a friendly reminder to stay on track is all."

Irene blushed. "You flatter me, but I'm part of a trio."

Her words soothed the glares from her two male lovers as the lift came to a stop.

"Good luck with the courting," she said to Omar before gesturing to Damiana, "and you keep your elbows sharp."

"Did you really have to throw me under the carriage like that?" Omar asked as the trio stepped off the lift. "It was just a bit of harmless flirting."

I eased myself out of the elevator and onto the Old Bailey with the others close behind me.

"Did I have to?" Damiana shrugged as she pretended to ponder her own question. "No, but I did rather enjoy it."

Although the bailey served as a giant courtyard between the palace and Gorka's Wall, it was also a testament to the kingdom's history. Every ruler who sat on the mountain throne, regardless of how long they ruled, had a statue of them added to the bailey upon their death.

"How do you expect me to fit in if you won't allow me to flirt?" Omar asked as we weaved around the statue of Queen Natalia the Generous.

A smile crossed my face as I realized all the statues had been given an animal mask to fit the theme of tonight's masquerade. "Do what you need to in order to blend in. Dance, make small talk, but our mission needs to remain at the front of your mind. You need to keep your wits about you and your eyes peeled."

"Speaking of which," Damiana said as we followed the crowd up the stairs toward the palace's arched door. "Has anyone spotted Keira?"

In our few minutes on the bailey to that point, I had noticed a few key details. For starters, the only people not wearing masks were the guards, and they seemed preoccupied with funneling everyone through the main entrance. If we found ourselves with a dire need to escape, then we'd have to avoid this route at all costs.

The other topic of note was the sheer amount of valuable targets that were begging to be stolen. It wasn't every day people had an opportunity to impress the king, and judging by the wealth on display, they weren't planning to let this chance slip through their fingers.

On any other occasion, I could have walked out of here with enough gem-laden watches, rings, and necklaces to put a small dent in my debt. However, that wouldn't happen tonight. We were here with one objective in mind, and the person we needed was nowhere to be seen.

Omar shook his head. "I haven't seen our silver eagle anywhere. Wasn't she supposed to meet us on the stairs?"

"There's still time," I said. "We've yet to reach the top of them. If she doesn't join us by the time we get to the door, then we'll be better off looking for her inside." I signed my reasoning. *We don't want to draw any unnecessary attention.*

The others agreed to my plan. As a result, we continued to follow the crowd through the door and into the palace.

Keira's absence sent my mind racing. What did this mean? Had she been taken, or had she simply realized waiting on the stairs could be viewed as suspicious?

Odds were that it was the latter as none of the guards appeared to be overly worried. If they had received word about a woman hiding strange masks and weapons in the palace, then one would think they would be more on edge, wouldn't they?

My worries were soon replaced by itchy fingers as we entered the three-story ballroom. So many priceless works of art adorned the walls that my mouth began to salivate.

"Any sign of her?" Damiana asked as we stopped near the edge of the dance floor.

Omar grabbed us each a flute of champagne from a server's tray. "No, but have you ever wondered what it would look like to see Father Roberto enjoying himself?"

My arched eyebrow brushed against the underside of my mask. How was that a relevant question?

"We've all seen him fail Ora," Damiana said with a laugh. "I think that's the closest we will ever come to witnessing that old bastard experience joy."

One of Omar's troublesome grins crossed his face as he gestured to a point in the room with his head.

Across the dance floor, our stubby middle finger stood out like a sore thumb. It was customary for priests to wear their temple's robes to these types of affairs, which made spotting them a much simpler task. My stomach turned as I watched him drunkenly hit on a woman in a scaled mask and dress that resembled the most appealing salmon I had seen in all my life.

Damiana's mouth hung open for a moment. "Poor girl... I think I'm at a loss for words. Have any of you ever seen him drink before?"

Omar shook his head.

"Only once at that council meeting I was forced to attend," I admitted. "But that was nowhere close to this extent."

Omar laughed softly and raised his glass. "Here's to the first miracle of the night. May it not be the last."

As we clinked our glasses, I couldn't help but dwell on the priest's behavior. Father Roberto's drunken buffoonery was not a miracle. It was him acting distinctly out of character, but what was the cause of it?

Was it a sign of fraying nerves from aiding the enemy, or did he have another unknown stressor weighing on him? Someone had given the Osigrens the correct attire for

Cuvarian priests. If Father Roberto was the one to supply them with the robes, then would he also be aware of tonight's plot? Participating in a coup would explain both the nerves and the drinking.

Glancing around the room, I spotted Prince Ander holding court near one of the balcony rails on the second floor. He wore an intricate pale-golden suit and donned the mask of a mountain lion. The sight of the prowling prince gave me a new idea.

"I haven't seen her yet either," I said, swirling the remainder of my drink in my glass. "Let's split up to find her and meet back here in a half hour. Keep your eyes peeled for anything suspicious. Even the smallest bit of information may make the difference tonight."

With the plan in place, the three of us went our separate ways. While I set my sights on the stairwell across the room, Damiana disappeared into the crowd behind us, and Omar threw himself onto the dance floor.

Due to His Majesty getting up there in years, reaching the prince proved to be no simple task. After all, poachers always flocked to power like maggots to spoiled meat. The maggots had surrounded him in hopes of currying his favor. Only time would tell if Ander would allow them to feast upon his carcass.

"Apologies for my late arrival, Your Grace," I said with a deep bow when I finally got in front of him. "It was not my intention to keep you waiting."

"I didn't realize I was supposed to be expecting a river squid," the prince said before turning to the guard over his left shoulder. "Did you know anything about this, Rafael?"

The crowd laughed as the guard shook his head.

I took a calming breath. Now was the moment of truth. Although I doubted that the prince had Keira seized, if he did, then he'd do the same to me upon revealing myself. It was time to find out if our night had been fucked before it ever began.

"It's hardly fair to expect Rafael to remember something he wasn't there for," I said. "Though I don't expect Miguel to recall our meeting either, as his falling asleep on the job is what led to our conversation in the first place."

A spark flickered in Ander's eyes. Whether it was from anger, disappointment, or shock, it was far too early to tell. The only thing I was confident of was that he now knew exactly who he was addressing.

"If you would be so kind as to grant me a minute of your time in private, then I will be out of your hair for the rest of the night."

Miguel's knuckles had visibly whitened around the shaft of his spear. Not only did he remember me, but he seemed to be none too pleased by my presence.

"Let's get this over with, Master Tallis," said the prince. "Something tells me that I won't be able to get rid of you by ignoring you."

He motioned for me to follow. As his guards created a path for us, I tried to parse his words. What had he meant by get rid of me? If I was following him to my death, then there was nothing I could do about it now. Cuvar would need to intervene if I had any hope of escaping from an escort of six armed guards by myself.

They led us into a private hall, up a flight of stairs, and eventually stopped before a large dark wooden door.

"Alfonso and Pablo, make sure my library is vacant," the prince commanded.

The pair of guards was only gone for a few minutes before they returned to give the all clear.

Ander gestured for Miguel, Rafael, and me to enter the

room. "Unless the king is asking for entry, no one is to disturb us. Do I make myself clear?"

"Do you not want us to check him for weapons?" asked Pablo.

While Prince Ander chastised his guard for asking a logical question, I peered around his personal library. The space was large enough to fit most of the pubs in Arremendia inside of it. Instead of being filled with booze and drunkards, it had been taken over by row upon row of bookshelves and sprawling cushioned seats. If this was only his private library, I couldn't imagine how vast the royal library would be in comparison.

The prince's most recent reads were stacked on a nearby desk. While most of them were historical texts, the one that caught my eye was *Betrothed to Fire*. It also happened to be the only book with a marker left in it.

My eyebrow arched. I had a tough time picturing Prince Ander cozying up in one of his many lounges with his nose deep in a romance novel. Was he actually interested in romance or just the genre's smuttier details? Given his track record at the local brothels, it was probably the latter. But maybe I was selling him short.

The door clicked shut, and my attention jumped back to him.

"What the fuck are you doing here, Tallis? I know we invite the local priests, but I'm confident all the acolytes don't receive an invitation as well."

"Come now, Your Grace," I said with an easy grin. "You and I both know that I'm not your ordinary acolyte."

"Are any of you ordinary?"

I couldn't help but laugh. "I'm in no position to speak for the other temples, but the ordinary never slip into Cuvar's grasp."

A moment of silence fell as he pondered my words.

"So what are you doing here?" he asked. "You don't have another conspiracy for me to chase, do you?"

The C-word made me cringe. "I gave you a lead, Your Grace, not a conspiracy. It's not my fault the Osigrens burned all the evidence."

"No, but it is rather convenient."

Convenient? My blood began to simmer. Why would the destruction of our evidence be convenient for me?

"The reason why I came," I said, "was to find out what you discovered, what was being done about it, and to offer you my assistance should you need it tonight."

Prince Ander cracked his knuckles. "Is that all?"

I nodded.

"As you're aware of the fire, you should know that we didn't find anything."

"But—"

Prince Ander slammed his fist against the desk. "Do not dare cut me off! I am your prince, gods dammit. Do not forget your place nor who you're speaking to, acolyte."

Miguel and Rafael snickered. I guessed they enjoyed the sight of someone other than themselves on the end of one of his tirades.

With my head down, I offered what I hoped would pass for a sincere apology.

The prince straightened his suit jacket. "As I was trying to say, although the evidence doesn't support it, I believe your concern to be a genuine one."

A sigh of relief escaped my lips.

"Not only have we doubled his guards, I even got His Majesty to agree to retire early this evening. It might not sound like much, but his chambers are the most defensible position in the palace. He'll be the safest there."

"Thank you, Your Grace," I said with another bow. "I feared this conversation would not go this well. You have my gratitude."

Ander laughed. "I do not want your gratitude."

His words begged an obvious question.

"Then what do you want?"

"I need you to promise me that you will do nothing," he said, placing his hand on my shoulder. "You've already done enough. Go dance, drink, and be merry. I've got it from here."

"But—"

"No buts. The last thing we need is for you to stick your nose where it doesn't belong and worry our guests in the process."

The prince motioned for his guards to get the door.

"If you can't handle my simple request, then I'll have my men give you a tour of the sky cells for the rest of the night. Now, promise me you won't cause any trouble."

"I promise," I said, keeping the caveat to myself. *So long as nothing happens.*

21

NEREA

How had I not seen this coming?

With death staring me in the face once again, maybe chastising myself wasn't the best use of my remaining time. However, I couldn't help it. My entire life, I had prided myself on my ability to solve puzzles that others couldn't. The clues had been staring me in the face this whole time, and I still hadn't managed to put them together.

Upon the traitor saint's arrival, she immediately convinced us that we couldn't trust anyone in the temple except for her through the use of a forged letter. When we needed someone to watch the Osigrens' hideout, she was more than happy to take the responsibility, and all the evidence conveniently disappeared. If those warning beacons didn't burn bright enough on their own, then there was the added insult to injury of us catching her withholding information from us.

I screamed into my gag.

The signs had been in front of me all along, and I had refused to see them for what they were. Like a rabbit too enticed by the bait, I didn't notice Keira's snare around my neck until it was too late.

The analogy made me sick to my stomach. I was not a helpless hare. I was a daughter of the Binsoro. A thousand generations of survivors coursed through my blood. We were born to survive what others could not, and I would survive this as well. The only question was how?

If my years as an inventor had taught me anything, then it was that there was no such thing as a flawless design. Everything had a weakness. All I had to do was spot the weak link in Keira's death trap and exploit it to my advantage.

After a few minutes of observation, the flaw in her plan became clear. It relied on me being in this exact position when the crossbows fired. If I could get out of the bolt's path, then I could put myself in a position to foil her plan.

From what I could tell, there were only two ways to pull this off. Either I could find a way to loosen the restraints and move my body out of the way, or I could move the bed out of the bolt's path and work on the restraints from there.

Since I could hardly move an inch in any direction, working on the restraints first wasn't a viable option. My only chance at survival would be to move the entire bed out of the way and then try to get someone's attention to free me from this mess.

Based on my limited vantage point, it appeared as though the ropes that dug into my skin were tied to each leg of the bed. If that was the case, then theoretically, I should have been able to transfer my energy to that structure. Assuming I could generate enough kinetic energy, and that was a big assumption, I could slowly jerk the bed out of harm's way.

With a plan in mind, I slid my body to the right as far as

my confines allowed. The rope bit into my skin as I launched myself to the left. I felt the mattress barely shift beneath me before I jerked to a sudden stop.

My heart thumped in my ears like a hammer against a blacksmith's anvil. Had the bed budged at all? It was impossible to tell. If it had moved, then it couldn't have scooted more than a millimeter or two.

How far it shifted didn't really matter. There was too much at stake for me to dwell on the minuscule nature of my progress. I couldn't afford to give up. Not only would it allow Keira to get away with her treachery, but it would also doom the pinky and leave my mother alone on her deathbed.

After a half hour of repeating my process over and over and over again, I needed to catch my breath. I winced at the stinging pain caused from sweat rolling over my freshly earned rope burns.

If it weren't for the gag in my mouth, I would've smiled. My agony wasn't in vain. Through my consistent effort, I had managed to shift the bed over a solid two inches. The bolt's blow would still be fatal in this position, but if I kept moving at this rate, I would be out of its line of fire in an hour's time.

As I slid my body into position to launch it once again, a noise made me freeze. It sounded as though someone had yawned inside the room. How could that have been possible? The only other person in here besides me was... Ora!

Had she woken from her coma? My heart leapt at the possibility as I tried to catch a glimpse of her. Although I couldn't see her where she lay on the floor, my eyes fixated on the spot where Keira's crossbow hung above her. Tears of joy streaked my face as the black-haired beauty pushed herself into a seated position. This changed everything. Ora could cut me free, we could rush to the Hanging Palace, and if we were lucky, we could warn the others before it was too late.

"Ora! Ora!" I screamed her name again and again only for it to be muffled by my gag.

I needed to get her attention. We had no time to waste.

Her eyes widened as they snapped to mine. All my hope vanished as she loosed a scream.

No, no, no! This can't be happening! I pleaded internally as she scrambled to the door.

If she opened it, then all my hard work would have been for nothing.

My body tensed for the blow as Ora's hand gripped the doorknob, but it never came.

"This is my room," Ora whispered to herself. Her fingers traced the engravings on the board that barred her door shut. "This is my room."

A wave of relief washed over me as she stepped away from the door.

My eyes remained glued to her as she surveyed her bedroom. When she realized I was the only one in here and that she was in no immediate danger, she stumbled her way to me and took the gag out of my mouth.

"Who are you, and why are you tied to my bed?" she asked.

From this close, Ora looked like her brother wearing a wig. Not only did the pair have the same brown eyes, upturned nose, and dimpled chin, but they even made the same facial expressions.

"My name is Nerea," I said, my voice coming out hoarse. "I am the newest member of the pinky. I will explain everything as you cut me free, but we need to move fast. Omar and the others will die if we don't get to them in time."

22

TALLIS

"It's about time you showed up," Omar said as I joined the others. "We were starting to wonder if you got taken."

"Sorry I couldn't arrive early like you. I was held up by the prince."

Damiana snickered.

"Don't you dare say it," Omar said, pointing a finger at her. "He was referring to me being punctual, and there's nothing wrong with that."

Damiana's grin nearly stretched the full length of her mask. "I didn't say a word, but if you want to refer to it as 'being punctual,' then that's fine by me."

"It looks like neither of you found Keira either," I said, changing the subject, "but—"

"Apologies for my tardiness," the saint said, her tone as cool as a mountain breeze. "I haven't missed much, have I?"

I jumped at the sound of her voice and whirled on her. With the exception of her silver eagle mask, the saint had disguised herself as a man wearing all black. Her jacket continued the bird theme as its detailed stitching made it appear as though it had been crafted from feathers.

"And where have you been?" asked Damiana.

Saint Keira surveyed the room to ensure no one was listening. "I completed my task much sooner than anticipated, so I decided to leave Nerea some tools in case tonight goes disastrously wrong. I actually wanted to head back over with all of you, but according to our inventor, it sounds as though we just missed each other."

Omar cleared his throat. "If you are all done catching up, I did find something of interest while you were away."

"As did I," Damiana added, "but you can go first."

"While making my rounds, I overheard some guards complaining," Omar said. "It sounds as though the king decided to double his personal guard for tonight, but instead of promoting from within his own ranks, he hired mercenaries for the job."

My heart raced at the implication. "The prince did inform me that they doubled the guard. Do you think the mercenaries could be the Osigrens?"

"They are," Damiana said. Our eyes snapped to her. "Well, at least one of them is. I recognized one of the king's guards as one of the bastards who held us captive in that hideout."

"How is that possible?" asked St. Keira. "I thought we killed all the Osigrens who were there."

"*Who were there* is the key part of that sentence," she said. "This fucker left before you arrived. Trust me, I would recognize that tattoo anywhere. I mean, what kind of moron gets a purple dragon tattooed on their neck?"

Purple dragon? The memory of the purple dragon wings I saw before passing out in the studio flashed before my eyes. Were they part of the tattoo she had referred to?

A trumpet sounded, and the room slowly fell silent. Everyone turned and peered up to the third-floor balcony, where the aging king stood surrounded by his king's guard.

"Holy shit," I murmured to myself. The man with the dragon tattoo stood behind the left shoulder of King Kepa. Even from this distance, I recognized the tattoo. There was no mistaking those ugly-ass wings.

"Hello, my honored guests," said the king, "and welcome to my seventy-eighth name day celebration!"

The partygoers roared their approval.

The king basked in their applause for a moment before waving for silence. "Thank you, friends, thank you. With each passing year, I am reminded more and more of just how honored I am to serve you. On any other night, I would celebrate with you until the sun greeted the palace once more. However, my job as king means my work is never-ending, and there is business that I must attend to. Before I leave to take care of this matter, let us make a toast."

His Majesty raised a glass, and everyone in attendance echoed the gesture.

"Here's to my health," the king continued, "and another year of prosperity in Arremendia."

Cheers erupted from the crowd, along with a cacophony of clinking glasses. However, the noise was soon drowned out by the sound of the music starting up again.

"We need to do something," Omar said as the king left the hall, flanked on all sides by his guards. "He is surrounded by his murderers, and he doesn't even know it."

"No," I said, grabbing his wrist before he could do something stupid. "The prince made it clear to me that he would throw us out if we made a scene. If that happens, then the king will truly be screwed."

Omar stared at me, slack-jawed. "Are you serious? We can't afford to stand here with our thumbs up our asses and do nothing."

"I said nothing of the sort. Prince Ander informed me that they had come up with an excuse for the king to retire to his chambers early. That must be where they're going."

"If that's the case, then we need to go now," St. Keira said. "There's no telling how long the Osigrens will wait to strike once they reach the privacy of his chambers."

Damiana cracked her knuckles. "Take us to our supplies, then. We only have a kingdom to save."

As St. Keira led us out of the ballroom, I had to remind myself to act calm. Although part of me wanted us to rush to our supplies, that would draw far too much attention. No one else was in a hurry tonight, and we needed to blend in.

Once we exited the ballroom, the noise level dropped significantly. Instead of music, the soft chatter of voices filled the air. We weaved our way around groups of friends joking with one another, lovers prepared to consummate on the spot, and even a couple in a heated row over one of their wandering eyes.

After what felt like an eternity of meandering through corridor upon corridor, the saint finally ushered us inside a room. It wasn't just any room. She had led us to Bolivar's Chapel.

Throughout history, the royal family made periodic visits to the city's three temples. However, King Bolivar II notoriously hated how long it took to reach them from the Hanging Palace. His solution was to repurpose one of the rooms in the heart of the keep by transforming it into a miniature chapel.

"Did you really hide our supplies in here," Omar teased

as St. Keira locked the door behind us, "or did you just need to say a quick prayer?"

The saint walked past us to the room's altar. "Why can't both be true? Besides, you also forgot the added benefit of this room."

"And what's that?" asked Damiana.

"Privacy," she said, smiling at the statues of the gods and goddesses, whose placements followed the curved wall of the turret behind them. "People came here for many reasons tonight, but none of them came to find the gods. No one will disturb us here."

A smile stretched across my face. This was one of the reasons why many considered her to be one of the greatest thieves of all time. Her mind was always working a few steps ahead of everyone else.

"Brilliant," I said. "So where are our supplies? We need to get going."

The saint peered back at me over her shoulder. "Patience. I need to say a quick prayer first."

Instead of approaching our Lord or Elbio, the half-ram, half-man God of the Mountains, she stepped up to the statue of Potami, the mermaid Goddess of the River. She leaned forward, whispered a prayer into her ear, and then planted a kiss on her cheek while pulling something behind her head.

That something must've been a hidden lever as a large panel on the floor popped up in front of the altar.

Lifting the cold stone panel all the way open, I looked down to find a ladder, our supplies, and a hallway that disappeared out of sight. "Where does this tunnel lead?"

"There are many secret passageways throughout the Hanging Palace," St. Keira said as she joined me by the opening, "but this is the only one that leads from the king's chambers to the city below."

Omar grabbed a torch and hopped down the ladder. "So are we taking this all the way to his chambers, then? I didn't think that was part of the plan."

"No," the saint said as the rest of us followed down after her. "The door that connects this passage to his chambers can only be opened from inside his room. However, there is another door that leads to the hall in front of his chambers. That is where we'll exit."

St. Keira closed the panel above us as we put on the supplies.

"Wait to the very end to put your gas mask on," Damiana said. "You can see just fine with them on, but you can barely hear or talk worth a damn."

With our supplies ready, we followed the saint up the passage. The little offshoot we had entered connected to the innermost section of the turret. As His Majesty's chambers were on the highest floor of the palace, the spiraling walk to the top was grueling. By the time we reached the end of the stairs, my heart pounded from both excitement and exhaustion, and sweat coated our faces.

While the rest of us caught our breath, the saint wandered over to the secret door and carefully opened the peephole. After a few moments, she shut it silently and crept back over to us.

"All right," St. Keira said, crouching down beside us. "All eighteen of the guards are positioned outside his door. Are you ready?"

Omar shook his head. "Let's recap the plan one more time."

I was on the verge of having all the wind back in my

lungs, so the few additional seconds this bought us was much appreciated.

"That door there opens right next to the turret," the saint explained. "When I push it open, we'll all run out, chuck our glass balls of spavati at the guards, and block off their only means of escape. The sleeping gas is potent and fast-acting enough that none of them should be able to put up a fight. Once they've all passed out, you and Damiana will tie them all up while Tallis and I inform the king of what is happening."

The three of us nodded our understanding.

"You two will then need to protect the door until the guards wake back up," St. Keira continued. "When that happens, let us know, and we'll have the king come out to identify his normal guards. Their release will give us extra help while keeping the Osigrens at bay."

Omar rose to his feet. "Let's do this—"

The rest of his words were unintelligible as he slid his gas mask into place. Damiana's earlier warning turned out to be spot-on.

As we lined up in front of the door, I slipped my gas mask on and tied it shut. The outside noises dampened in an instant. All I could hear was my heavy breathing and the thumping of my heart. I stared down at the gray spavati gas swirling inside the two glass balls in my hand. This was really happening.

Omar nudged my shoulder to get my attention. The saint had been giving us the ready signal, and they were all waiting on me.

Ready, I signed.

St. Keira signed back. *We attack on three. One...*

My heart raced faster than a horse at full gallop.

Two...

This was for more than saving the kingdom or our religion.

Three!

This was for Mother Sienna!

Light flooded the secret passage as St. Keira shoved the door open. The moment we charged into the room, we launched the sleeping gas at them.

They were not ready for us. A few of the guards managed to take a single step as the glass shattered all around them. However, none but a few of them managed to take a second step. Just as the saint had promised, the gas knocked them out almost instantaneously.

I tossed my rope on the ground to give Omar and Damiana more to work with as the last guard collapsed. My face burned against the leather mask as I rushed to the king's door. I tried to turn the handle, only to find that it wouldn't budge. His Majesty had locked himself in for the night.

There was a light tap on my shoulder. I turn to find St. Keira offering me her lockpicks. As I snatched them from her hand, it all felt too surreal.

Not only had we saved the kingdom and our temple's way of life from the Osigrens, but I had gotten to do it alongside my idol. My name would forever be linked to her legacy. If I was lucky, this would also be the start of me becoming her eventual replacement.

The slight reverberation of the pick informed me I had beat the lock. I smiled inside my mask as I pulled the door open.

King Kepa was across the room, staring out over his balcony, when I entered. He turned at the sound of my approach and drew his sword at the sight of me untying my mask.

As I pulled my mask free, I heard a click, followed by the sound of metal sliding against wood.

"I know you're alarmed, Your Majesty," I said with my hands above my head to show I wasn't wielding a weapon, "but we are only here to protect you. Your guards have been infil—"

I never finished the word. Something solid collided with the back of my head, sending my world into darkness.

23

NEREA

Ora stumbled as she pushed open her bedroom door. If it weren't for the hallway wall across from her room, then she would've toppled over on the spot. However, her fortune ran out when we reached the stairs. The awakened acolyte's legs gave out, and she tumbled head over heels down the stairs until the wall brought her to an abrupt stop.

"Shit, shit, shit," I said as I hurried after. "Are you all right?"

She pushed away my offered hand of assistance. "I'll be fine. My legs are worn out from disuse. You need to go to the Hanging Palace without me. I'll only slow you down."

Although I wanted her to come with me to add credibility to my words, maybe dragging her through the temple in her nightgown wasn't the best idea. "The palace? Shouldn't I tell the priests first? Surely they would have a better idea of what to do."

She shook her head. "The priests will all be at the king's name day celebration. You need to find a horse and hurry there."

"But I've never ridden a horse before."

If it weren't for the laughter coming up the stairwell, then the only thing I would've heard was the sound of my own despair. How could I make it to the palace in time if I had to sprint my way there?

I turned to find three acolytes gawking at us. None of the frozen trio could have been older than fifteen.

"That's, that's..." mumbled a boy who had even darker skin than me. "Cuvar's cock, you're Ora, aren't you?"

The freckled redhead beside him gasped. "Oh my Lord, it is her. Are you all right? When did you wake up?"

"Silence," Ora said.

She didn't bother to raise her voice. The sharpness with which she laced the word was enough to command their attention.

"My health is not of importance," she continued. "Right now there are greater things at stake. Can any of you ride a horse?"

The other girl stepped forward. She was small and slender, with long, dark curls so tight that they billowed around her head instead of falling down beside it. "My parents used to race horses. They had me start riding the moment I was able to walk."

"Good," Ora said as she unclasped her gold necklace. "What is your name?"

"I am Liliana Escobar, a server of our Lord and a member of his ring finger."

Ora tossed her necklace to the girl. "Liliana, Cuvar needs you to use that to get a horse and take Nerea to the Hanging Palace as soon as possible. Do you understand?"

"Are you sure you can't come with us?" I asked as the girl nodded eagerly.

"No," Ora said. "I'll only slow you down. You need to

leave. The lives of the pinky and the king rest in your hands."

"I won't let you down," I said to her before turning to the others. "You make sure she gets the help that she needs. Liliana, I need you to lead the way. I am barely familiar with our grounds during the daytime, let alone at night."

We sprinted away to a chorus of blessings. Liliana quickly ushered me from the dorm, through the garden, and out a side gate to the temple that I didn't know existed.

Despite Cuvar's temple only being half a mile away from the base of King's Mountain, the lifts that gave access to the Hanging Palace were about a mile and a half to the east of our temple. We ran for two blocks in that direction before we came across an inn with an attached stable.

"We need to commandeer your fastest horse in the name of Cuvar," Liliana said as she shoved Ora's necklace into the stable boy's hands. "This is for your silence. Will have the horse back before morning."

"A comma-what?" the stable boy asked as he slipped the necklace into his pocket. The greasy teen was somewhere between Liliana's and my age and had already developed quite the impressive gut.

Liliana never broke her stride. She turned and strode into the stable. "It means we're borrowing a horse."

The stable hand's mouth fell open. "Now listen here, you little whore, neither of you are taking sh—"

I kneed the little prick in the balls with all my might when he turned to go after her. He collapsed to the ground with a satisfying thud.

"Speaking like that to a lady is going to cost you," I said as I fished the necklace out of his pocket. "Just consider yourself lucky that we're bringing the horse back at all."

As the little shit continued to writhe in pain on the

cobblestone, Liliana exited the stable on top of a mare so black it practically disappeared into the night sky. With her assistance, I swung onto the horse, and we took off for the palace at full speed.

The city passed by us in a blur. People dove out of the way as we galloped through the streets. However, the chaos proved to be worth it as we arrived at the lift in a matter of minutes.

I hopped from the back of the horse, only to find myself surrounded by three city watchmen. The well-dressed stragglers who were still waiting in line for the party looked at me with a mixture of disgust and curiosity.

"Ma'am, I suggest you hop back on that horse and leave," said one of the blackcoats. "You can't get on any of the lifts without an invitation."

The three men took a step toward me, tightening the circle.

"You don't understand," I said. "The king is in danger. You need to go warn him."

The city watchmen laughed.

"If I had a silver for every time I heard that one," said the blackcoat from before, "then I would be living in one of these villas with servants waiting on me hand and foot."

My heart sank. They didn't believe me. How could I make them believe?

"You don't understand," I pleaded. "The Osigrens have infiltrated his party. They're going to usurp him tonight."

More laughter greeted my pleas. This time even the onlookers took part in the jeering.

I sighed. One could not erode a stone by blowing on it. If I couldn't convince the blackcoats, then I'd have to convince someone else.

There was only one thing left for me to do. I sprinted for the lift.

"The king is under attack!" I yelled as I narrowly avoided the hands of one of the watchmen. "The Osigrens are attacking the king!"

The lift began to rise as I continued my warning. I needed to get on it before it was out of reach.

It was only a couple feet above my head when I leapt. Six masked faces stared down at me as my fingertips clung to the bottom of the lift. I tried to pull myself up, but I didn't have the strength.

"Help," I pleaded as I hung on for dear life. "The king is in danger. We need to warn the palace guards."

The man seated closest to me wore the mask of a bear. "If he's in danger from anyone, then it's from people like you."

Before I could utter another word, the bear stomped on my fingers, and I fell to the ground with a thump.

Fortunately for me, the lift had been a mere twelve feet above the ground. Pain radiated through my body as I pushed myself back to my feet, but at least I wasn't dead. Not yet anyway.

"Seize her!" said one of the watchmen.

I tried to limp away, but I couldn't move fast enough. They were going to arrest me.

Before any of the blackcoats could follow through on the command, the sound of galloping hooves filled the air. I turned to find Liliana racing toward me with her arm outstretched.

"Take my hand!" she shouted above the excitement of the crowd.

My arm felt like it was being ripped from my shoulder as she took hold of my elbow. However, my pain didn't matter.

She had gotten me onto the horse. I didn't want to imagine what would have happened if her attempt didn't work. After all, the blackcoats weren't renowned for their gentle nature.

As we rode away in silence, I tried to convince myself I had done everything in my power. Despite my internal reasoning, I couldn't escape reality.

I failed the kingdom. I failed our temple. Worst of all, I failed the pinky.

24

TALLIS

"Do you know why I'm going to kill you?"

The saint's voice sounded distant.

Another man groaned. "Because you're a lunatic with a death wish?"

His voice, like the rest of the world around me, seemed to be shrouded in a haze. Was I dreaming? As I couldn't sense the rest of my body, it seemed like the most plausible possibility.

St. Keira's laughter cut through my dense mental fog. "That may be true, but if I'm a bloody lunatic, then I am the karmic one that you created."

"Spoken like a foolish child," said the other man. His voice may have been weak, but it carried an edge of defiance. "You can blame me for your problems all you want, but your troubles lie solely on your shoulders."

In the momentary silence that followed, some feeling returned to my body. I felt the softness of the cloud I lay atop and the soothing heat of a fire in the distance.

"Of course you don't know who I am," said St. Keira. "A man like you has enough skeletons in his closet to fill up the whole of this palace. You have too many options to know which demon of your past is sending you to your grave."

Her words snapped me out of my haze. I wasn't dreaming. I was in King Kepa's chambers with Cuvar's living saint. But what was I doing on the floor, and why was my head throbbing?

"Let me make this easier for you," the saint continued. "I am Friyun Werbu, the youngest daughter of Emperor Leojung V, the last true Emperor of Osigra."

My mind whirled at the implication. If what she said was true, then Cuvar's living saint was the rightful heir to his greatest enemy in this realm.

King Kepa scoffed. "That's impossible. I had Emperor Leojung and his entire family assassinated."

"No," said the saint through a snicker. "Your assassins murdered my family, but even they couldn't find it in their hearts to kill an infant. They were unsure of what to do with me, so they sent me away to the Isle of Opara to be raised in Cuvar's temple as one of his acolytes."

As much as I wanted to stand and challenge her, I couldn't move. Her words had me glued to the floor.

"So you are here to exact your revenge," said the king. "That I understand. However, if you expect me to apologize for what I have done, then you shouldn't hold your breath. I did what I had to do to protect my people and our way of life. I warned your—"

A loud smack silenced the king.

"You may lie to yourself all you wish," said St. Keira, "but don't waste your breath lying to me. You sacrificed eleven years of peace between our empires because you caved to the fearmongers who called themselves priests. We did nothing that deserved the wrath you chose to rain upon us."

I couldn't believe my ears. We had always been taught

that the Osigrens had broken the peace. That they wanted to instill their godless ways upon us. Had everything I'd been taught been a lie?

"I did not come here to make you recant for your sins," St. Keira continued. "I came here to make you suffer. You took everything from me, and now you'll die knowing that I've taken everything from you."

The coldness of her voice sent a shiver down my spine.

"Everything?" asked King Kepa. "I am an old man who's lived a full life. Let's face it. My life is the only thing that you can take, and I'm even willing to give you that."

The saint let out a boisterous laugh. Apparently, the king's attempt to taint her satisfaction failed.

"What's so funny?" asked the king.

"You speak with the confidence of a man who doesn't know of the plans already set in motion. Let me be so kind as to disillusion you."

An insufferable silence flooded the room as she let the king dwell on her words.

"The first thing I will take from you is your family," said the saint. "Starting with your precious Amaya."

The king gasped. "You wouldn't dare."

"I don't need to dare when your son will gladly kill her for me."

His Majesty made an unintelligible sound. It was almost as though he was choking on his own words.

"Don't act so surprised," St. Keira continued. "Prince Ander is well aware of your plan to name her as your heir. He was more than willing to assist me in framing her for your death."

The prince's inclusion hit me like a punch to the gut. It explained Keira's knowledge of the tunnel, how she was able to sneak in and out of the palace with ease, and how they were able to get rid of the evidence in the studio so quickly.

"But that's not all I'm going to take," the saint said as the king continued to sputter. "Ander will see to it that your kingdom is destroyed. He won't run it into the ground intentionally, of course. He is a self-centered, egotistical idiot who will have no problem ruining things on his own. Though you are more than aware of this, that's why you are —sorry—*were* going to name Amaya as your heir, was it not?"

"You can't do this," said the king, his voice cracking. "You... you can't."

The saint smiled as she hushed the king.

"Oh, but we haven't even gotten to the best part," said St. Keira. "Do you see that young man over there? The one I knocked out when we entered the room."

My heart stopped as I realized she was referring to me.

"He and his two friends guarding the door are members of Cuvar's temple," he continued. "Just like Amaya, they, too, will be framed for your death."

Her mentioning of how we fit into his fucked-up scheme didn't merely release me from my stupor, it shattered it. I had to do something. Despite the complaints of my aching limbs, I pushed myself off the floor.

"Ander will conduct an investigation that will link their involvement to all the city's temples," she continued. "As a result, he will outlaw religion throughout the entire kingdom to punish them for their involvement in your death."

For the first time since being knocked unconscious, my eyes fell upon the king. St. Keira had beaten him and tied him standing upright with his hands above his head to one of the large wooden vertical beams of his four-poster bed. A mixture of blood and tears trickled down the old king's face and matted in his sculpted white beard.

“You'll do nothing of the sort,” I said, drawing my sword and pointing it at her.

“Well, this is proper awkward,” the saint said as she looked back and forth between the king and me.

A distance of ten yards stood between us. However, I had to tread carefully to close the gap. She had not become Cuvar's living saint through her thieving ability alone.

“It looks as though our time has run out,” St. Keira said to the king. “May the eternity of the afterlife grant you nothing but suffering.”

With speed and grace faster than lightning, the saint grabbed the dagger from her belt and slit the King’s throat.

Covered in King Kepa’s splattered blood, she turned her attention back to me. “So how much of that did you hear?”

I had to physically shake off my disbelief. If I wanted to live, then I needed to focus on the monster before me. It would be dangerous to dwell on what she had just done or who she had been in my life before entering this chamber.

“I heard every word.”

St. Keira tried to wipe the blood from her face but only succeeded in smudging it across her cheek. "Brilliant. I'd hate to have to explain it all over again."

I didn't know what disturbed me more, the nonchalance with which she had killed the king or that she thought I'd still be on her side given everything I had learned.

The saint strode across the room to a large bust of the king, exchanging her dagger for a hatchet from the wall along the way. I followed her from a safe distance and kept my rapier at the ready.

"What the fuck are you doing?" I asked. "Did you honestly think I was going to be okay with all this?"

She delivered a swift blow to the bust with the blunt side of the hatchet. The stone shattered like porcelain, revealing a leather bag hidden inside.

"No," St. Keira said, slipping the bag straps over her shoulders and cinching the strings around her waist, "but no one expects the sacrificial lamb to understand or be pleased by their sacrifice."

My knuckles whitened around the hilt of my rapier. How had I ever idolized her? Why had I ever wanted to be like this woman?

"Though I'll see to it that your good deed doesn't go unrewarded," she continued. "For aiding me in my revenge and, more importantly, giving your life for the betterment of all humanity, I free you of your debt to Cuvar as promised. You won't get to enjoy your freedom for long, but at least that asshole won't own your soul in the afterlife."

The iron bar rattled as someone pounded on the door.

"That must be Prince Halfwit and his guards," St. Keira said, laughing at her own joke. "I must be going. The plan was for me to be gone when they arrived."

She took a step toward the balcony.

"I can't let you do that," I said, hurrying to block her path.

The saint's eyes softened, and her smile dropped from her face. "Please step aside, Tallis. I don't want to kill another person I care about with my own hands ever again, but I will do what must be done."

Another person she cared about? She clearly bore no love for the king. Who else had she killed?

"Mother Sienna," I whispered.

The world shifted beneath my feet at the realization.

"I didn't want to kill her," St. Keira admitted, "but she refused to take part in my plan."

Of course she turned her down. We were her acolytes, her children, not lambs to be slaughtered.

"She left me no other choice. My plan required the use of the pinky."

No other choice? No other choice! How could there be no other choice?

"Open this door now!" Prince Ander bellowed from the hallway. "Ready the ram!"

If I were to die, then I would not do it alone. The saint would either die by my blade or hang alongside me. All I had to do was keep her here long enough to force the prince's hand.

I readied my feet. "You killed my mother. Prepare to die."

All she could offer me in return was a sad smile. "As you wish."

I charged.

As I closed the gap, St. Keira flung the hatchet at me. I dropped to the floor in time for it to soar over my head. However, it forced me to give up the attack and any advantage I had along with it.

Two sounds competed for dominance as I rolled back onto my feet: the splintering of wood at the door and the clattering of steel on stone as the hatchet skidded onto the balcony.

I barely got my sword up in time to meet the blade of St. Keira's rapier.

"It doesn't have to be this way," she said as she drove me back one step at a time.

Another boom rattled the door.

"You left me no other choice," I said, spitting her own words back at him with the venom they deserved.

A smile crossed my face as the cracking of the door

echoed throughout the room. I wouldn't have to hold her off for much longer.

My moment of confidence was short-lived.

When I took a step backward to parry another blow, I tripped on one of the dead king's legs. The saint's blade bit into the shoulder of my sword arm. The searing pain caused me to drop my rapier. Unarmed and off-balance, I awaited her deathblow.

It never came.

As I fell, St. Keira bolted for the balcony. I caught myself on the back of a chair and hobbled after her.

By the time I reached the balcony, she was standing on the railing with her back to the city.

"What the fuck are you doing?" I asked, grimacing as I scooped the hatchet off the ground.

She gave me half a grin. "I said I had to leave, didn't I?"

My eyes widened as I realized what she was going to do. The bastard was going to jump.

"I know you always wanted to be a saint," she continued, stealing a quick peek at the door. "If it's any consolation, you had the skills to make a great one."

What in Potami's murky depths was she trying to get at? There was nothing she could say to amend the pile of shit she decided to drown me in.

"However," she continued, "it gives me peace to know you'll never have to bear the curse of having that monster in your head. Goodbye, Tallis."

"No!" I screamed as she dove backward off the ledge.

The chamber door burst open as I sprinted to the railing. Instead of seeing her body free-falling toward her death, the pale light of the two full moons revealed a large white cloth gently floating toward the city below.

My blood boiled as I realized that it had come from her

bag. The person who had cheated me of so much couldn't be allowed to simply float away. I wouldn't stand for it.

"The king, the king, the king is dead!" I heard the guards yell as they poured into the room.

I would only get one chance, and I had to take it quickly. Pain shot down my arm as I threw the hatchet toward her fabric device.

The steel gleamed in the moonlight as it spun end over end.

"He's on the balcony!" a guard shouted.

"Seize him," commanded Prince Ander, "and take him alive."

I stood frozen in place as the guards' footsteps clattered toward me. Only one thing mattered at that moment, and I kept my attention on it.

Right before the guard tackled me, it happened. St. Keira was still hundreds of feet above the ground when the hatchet cut through her sheet.

As they flung me to the ground, a smile rippled across my face. She had sentenced me to death, but I had sent her to the afterlife first. At least I would be able to die knowing that Mother Sienna had been avenged.

25

NEREA

When I first arrived in Arremendia, the sigil of Cuvar's temple simply represented the giving nature of the church. In the days following my initiation, it came to symbolize the temple's secret practice. However, as I stood before the council, and their moronically large hand-shaped table, I was reminded that those hands could do far more than give and take. They could crush.

Father Roberto stared at Ora and me from his seat at the middle finger like we were two rats who had dared to take a bite of his meal. "Which one of you ladies would like to explain to us why we were interrogated by the prince this morning and now have a standing army surrounding the temple?"

Although his frustration was more than understandable, I couldn't begin to fathom how he could lay any of the responsibility at Ora's feet.

"I will answer any questions you have to the best of my ability," I said. "All I ask is that you don't punish Ora. Not only was she in a coma for all the events that transpired, but the first thing she did upon waking was save my life."

"I'm afraid there's been a misunderstanding," Father Sebastian said as he leaned forward in his seat. "We have not broken our traditions by allowing you to enter this sacred place to punish you. What occurred last night has placed the temple in a precarious situation, and we have no clue as to how it happened."

Father Ignacio cleared his throat. "All we know is the king is dead, and three members of the pinky were found at his chambers. What were they doing there?"

Despite the priests' reassurance, I couldn't shake the feeling of being judged.

"They were there to save King Kepa from an Osigren plot to overthrow him and outlaw religion within our borders," I said, "but it was all a lie. St. Keira tricked us into helping her get her revenge on the king."

Father Roberto's brow creased. "The living saint? Why would she want to get revenge on the king?"

I felt the grit of disbelief that coated his question. Keira had earned her title from being the best thief among thieves, not because she was holier than thou. Did he think I was up here spewing bullshit?

"When Keira's soul was tethered to Cuvar, she discovered her life was a lie," I explained. "Our Lord not only revealed to her that she was the daughter of Emperor Leojung but that the king's assassination of him and her family was spurred by the insistence of Arremendia's priests."

The head of the middle finger crossed his arms as his skin tried to match his crimson robe. How long had Roberto been a priest at this temple? Could he have been one of the people who pushed for Emperor Leojung's death?

"That's why she used us," I continued. "She needed to kill the king in a way that could destroy the temples as well."

Ora gave my shoulder a comforting squeeze as silence filled the room.

Father David stroked his chin with his thumb. "You sound so assured. How do you know all this?"

Truthfully, a part of me wished I knew none of it. The sight of Keira staring down at me with the unnerving assurance of an apex predator haunted me whenever I closed my eyes. In her mind, I was already dead, and only a miracle prevented her from being correct.

"Keira told me I deserved to know why I was going to die," I said, fighting to keep the emotion from leaking into my voice. "She told me all this because she thought I was as good as dead, and if Ora hadn't woken up, I would be."

I cracked. As much as I didn't want to appear weak before the council, I couldn't stop the tears that followed. The trauma of last night was still far too fresh to pretend I didn't notice my festering mental wounds.

"It's okay," Ora said as she pulled me into an embrace. "It's okay. You're doing great."

When we let go, I wiped my face clean as I turned to address the council. "The mechanism she set up to kill us is still in Ora's room. After this interrogation is over, you can examine it for yourselves."

Father Roberto let out an exasperated sigh.

"I'm sorry that we have made this feel like an interrogation for you," Father Sebastian said. "That was not supposed to be the purpose of our meeting. What you shared with us so far will be quite helpful for when we meet with the prince later today. I only have one more question for you, if you don't mind."

"Of course," I said, not buying the "if you mind" comment for a second. It was his attempt at being polite.

"Earlier you said that St. Keira tricked the pinky into helping her. Could you elaborate on that?"

I took a deep breath. Recounting how my would-be murderer managed to con us had been nowhere close to the top of my to-do list.

"When Keira arrived at the temple, she revealed a letter to us from Mother Sienna that was written a couple of days before her death. Although I can't recall it word for word, it essentially said that she feared for her life because she stumbled upon an Osigren plot to overthrow the king with the assistance of Princess Amaya and unknown members of our very temple. The letter also made it clear that the only people the priestess thought she could trust were members of the pinky."

Father Roberto flared his hairy nostrils. "Are you serious? My life is now at stake because you all read one letter and fell knee-deep into this conspiracy?"

I squeezed my hands together to prevent myself from smacking the table. We had all been fooled by Keira. How had he managed to make it all about him?

"I'm sorry to hear that the middle finger thinks so little of you that they wouldn't take you at your word," I said, unable to hold my tongue. "Did the traitor saint take advantage of my fingermates' faith in Mother Sienna? Absolutely, but that was just the beginning of her deception."

I told them everything. I explained how Princess Amaya's meeting with the fake Cuvarian priests led to the discovery of the Osigrens' base. I explained how everything we learned from Tallis's and Dario's capture further cooperated with Keira's original lie. She had tied everything together with such precision that it was impossible for us not to believe her.

When I finally finished, it was Father Sebastian who broke the silence that followed. He ran his fingers through his graying curls as he looked at the other priests. "I have no further questions for her, do you?"

"I have a question for the council," Ora stated when the priest remained silent. "If you don't mind, of course."

Father Ignacio's wheelchair creaked as he straightened in it. "That would only be fair."

"During your meeting with the prince," Ora said before the others could interject, "did he mention what happened or what would happen to our fingermates or St. Keira?"

Father David took the lead. "Nothing about the saint came up with him in our meeting. However, she is believed to be dead. A person fell from the Hanging Palace last night, and according to our birds, their attire matched what St. Keira wore to the masquerade."

"On the off chance that wasn't her body," Father Sebastian added, "we will send word to the other temples of her treachery immediately following this meeting."

"What about my brother?" asked Ora. "What about my friends? Didn't he say anything about them?"

My heart dropped as the priests exchanged looks with one another. There was clearly bad news to be delivered, and none of them wanted to be its bearer.

"Unfortunately," Father Sebastian said, softening his voice even further, "they are to be hanged above the Beltza at dusk in two days' time."

His words robbed me of my breath. It shouldn't have come as a shock. After all, we had unwittingly participated in and enabled the king's assassination. However, the reality of a situation always stung harder than its theoretical likelihood.

"What are you doing about it?" asked Ora.

Father Roberto stared at her without the slightest bit of remorse. "There is nothing to be done. Regardless of their intentions, they did aid in His Majesty's death."

Ora's eyes turned to slits. If looks could kill, then the middle finger would be halfway down the Beltza.

She wasn't alone in her frustration. Although I understood the prince's need to punish them, the priest seemed a little too eager to agree with his sentiment.

"I believe we are done here," Father Ignacio said. "The two of you may retire to your chambers. It would not surprise me if His Grace wished to speak to you, so make sure you are prepared."

An idea struck me as Ora and I turned to leave. Maybe there was something we could still do to save the pinky.

"Excuse me, Father."

Their heads snapped to look at me.

"Would it be possible for us to retire to Mother Sienna's chambers instead?" I asked. "Given what transpired in Ora's chambers last night, neither of us would be comfortable there, and there is nothing for us to do in my room as it is still blank."

"Certainly," Father Ignacio said with a shrug. "It is the least we can do for all the help you have given us today."

Ora arched her eyebrows at me as we turned to leave once more, but she held her tongue. However, her curiosity got the better of her as we started up the stairs.

"Is your room really that bad?" she asked.

I laughed. "It's far worse than you could ever imagine."

"And why is that?"

"Unlike Mother Sienna's room," I said, lowering my

voice to a whisper, “my chambers don't come with an escape tunnel filled with weapons.”

Ora’s smile stretched past her ears. “You're a genius.”

“Let's not get too excited yet. All I’ve done is found our way out, but we still need to discover how we can save them.”

The scarred beauty took my arm in hers. “I'm sure we'll think of something.”

26

TALLIS

"Can you imagine a shittier day to die?" Omar asked as I was marched from my lift to where he and Damiana stood waiting for me.

Based on their tattered clothes and dirty, bruised faces, it appeared as though they had received the same royal treatment I had these past two days in my sky cell: beatings, beatings, and more beatings. At least they hadn't managed to knock his sense of humor out of him.

"What?" said Damiana, feigning a gasp. "I thought that being hanged on a hot, humid, breezeless day had always been your dream scenario."

Omar cracked a smile. "I was striving for a dragon's death. You know, dying of old age while lying atop my piles of gold."

"Please," I teased. "Even if we avoided the noose, you were always bound to be stabbed by a man you cuckold long before you could acquire that much wealth."

Our laughter died on our lips as a group of shadows encircled us.

"Do you dickheads find your own death to be funny?"

asked a burly blackcoat. The apparent leader of Arremendia's "finest" sported a graying, scruffy beard and had a nose that appeared to have been broken more times than he could count.

My common sense begged me to keep my mouth shut, but we were about to die anyway. "Can you be more specific, please? Are you referring to the varying levels of irony that surround our impending doom or the fact that we are being marched to it by the ugliest-looking goatfucker I have ever seen and who probably thinks irony has to do with blacksm—"

The gathering crowd a few blocks away roared with delight as his fist collided with my kidney. Although I saw his strike coming from a mile away, between my hands being tied behind my back and my physical state after days of torture and starvation, there was nothing I could do to stop it.

"Speak that way to me again, smart-ass, and I'll send you to your grave with a belly full of your own teeth." He shifted his gaze to glare at Omar and Damiana. "The same goes for you two."

Pain seared through my body as I struggled back onto my feet.

"As we march you to the gallows," continued Captain Dipshit, "you will be silent, you will keep our pace, and you will remain in a single-file line. If you cannot manage any of those three, then we will lash all of you. Nod if you understand."

I nodded.

"Don't bother trying to escape into the crowd," he said while we lined up. "The noose is a far kinder death than any of you deserve, and it's an absolute blessing compared to what the mob would do to you if you tried to escape through them."

That was an understatement to say the least. It became clear during our march that the guards who formed our path were there to protect us from the people and not the other way around.

Never in my entire life had I experienced pure hatred from any person, let alone the thousands that lined the streets to see us hanged. Not only did the men, women, and children of Arremendia hurl insults at us, they also threw everything they could get their hands on. On our trek to the gallows, I was showered with rocks, rotten food, random debris, and someone even managed to dump their chamber pot on me from an upper-story window.

The worst part wasn't the taste of shit in my mouth or the cutting sting of the lash across my back. It was that I couldn't blame them.

They didn't know the whole truth of the matter. In their eyes, we were the ones who had killed the king and cast their lives into doubt. They had no way of knowing that we had been equally fooled as they were now. We might have reacted the same way if we were in their shoes.

"Hold here," one of the blackcoats said when we reached the gallows steps.

If one wasn't paying attention, then it would be easy to mistake the gallows for the city's first bridge. Located only fifty feet from Erromon's Gate, the gallows had been strategically built over the Beltza so Potami could carry away the dead from the city as quickly as possible.

Not that I was this displeased by the additional seconds of life that our delay granted us, but I peered over the blackcoat's shoulder to see what was causing the holdup. A group of actors had taken advantage of the large audience to put on a performance. It took me a second to realize the battle they depicted was supposed to be Prince Ander defeating us in combat.

“I need to tell you both something,” Damiana said from behind me.

Her trembling voice stood out to me as odd. When was the last time I had heard her sound nervous? I turned around to give her my full attention.

“I didn't think I'd be telling you this under these circumstances,” she continued, “but I can't die as a secret. I can't die as someone I am not.”

Omar arched an eyebrow. “What are you getting at, Damiana?”

“I'm not Damiana. I'm Dario.”

My brow furrowed as I tried to grasp the meaning of her words. Ever since we were teens, Dario had been the name she had taken when she had to disguise herself as a guy for our various games. What had she meant by that?

“Although I was born a girl,” she continued, “I've never truly been one. I've known that I'm a man since before I joined the temple. I wanted to tell you sooner, but I was afraid you wouldn't accept me just as my own family hadn’t.”

Tears streaked through the dirt on Dario's face as Omar rested his forehead on his shoulder to comfort him. “We love you, brother. We will never abandon you, be it in this life or the next.”

Much to my great shame, my first reaction was to feel hurt. Not because of who he was but because he hadn't told me sooner. I ached because I wished I had more time to know him as his true self. However, that was selfish of me. Dario trusted us enough to let us see the real him, and I was going to appreciate every last second we had together.

"I'm glad you told us," I said, "and I'm honored to die alongside both of my brothers."

Dario smiled through the tears as the blackcoat berated us for not facing forward.

With the actors off their deadly stage, I walked up the gallows steps for the second time in my life.

As they tightened the necklace of death around my neck, I couldn't help but think about the last time I wore it. Back then, I was a terrified eight-year-old who was so small they needed to stand me up on a box just to reach the noose.

There had only been a few hundred onlookers on that fateful day. Instead of the orange and purple pastels that tinted today's sky and enhanced the city's beauty, the glare of the midday sun off the river had practically blinded me.

However, the biggest difference was that Mother Sienna wasn't in the market to the left of us. It was there where my birth mother had begged her to do something to spare my life. Maybe her spirit was with us here now. If she was here, then I hoped she had found some peace in knowing that we had avenged her.

The crowd jeered as the executioner read off each one of our crimes.

"Holy shit," Dario said. His voice barely reached my ears over the sound of the boos.

My head snapped to the right, where he stood between Omar and me. Dario's eyes focused on the river as his hands twitched behind his back.

No, I realized. He was attempting to sign a message to us. However, the only signal he successfully managed to create was *boat*.

Boat? What was so significant about a boat?

As I scanned the murky river before us, I couldn't help but wonder what about a boat would make him so excited that he wouldn't risk mentioning it in front of the black-coats. However, it soon became clear.

With trade being done for the day, there weren't many boats left on the Beltza. The last of the traders to leave steered their ships to the edge of the river to make sure they didn't float underneath us. All of them except for one.

The vessel that floated toward us was the strangest I had ever seen. It looked like a wide-set canoe with wooden wings that fell from its sides and dipped into the water. What was even stranger was its lack of an obvious power source. It had no sail to catch the wind, no oars to push it forward, or a river pole to propel it. All it had was the two people aboard it, and even they didn't appear to be doing much.

"Cuvar's cock," I muttered to myself.

The boat was fifty yards away from us when I recognized one of the two figures. Nerea sat at the rear and manned the rudder. My realization prompted two other questions: who was the slender figure that stood at the front of their boat, and what were they going to do?

Unfortunately, I recognized Ora at the same time the executioner pulled the lever.

The rope sank deep into my neck. It not only cut off my breath, but it also created an unbearable pressure in my face. I felt like the head of a dandelion about to be popped off by a child.

Why had Cuvar showed me she was still alive just to take my life instead? I had spent almost my entire life trying to convince myself that I didn't love her, and now I would never get the chance to tell her how I felt. It was beyond cruel.

Hope surged above the pain in my chest as I watched Ora pick up her bow. Working from her left to right, she loosed three shots in quick succession at our respective ropes.

I hardly had time to register Dario's and Omar's fall to the river before my own free fall began.

I managed to take in half a gasp of air before the Beltza's cold water consumed me.

Despite the release of pressure on my neck, there was no time to celebrate. We might have evaded death for now, but we hadn't escaped it completely.

While I was still submerged, I contorted my body to step backwards through my arms. My wrists were still tied together, but at least they were no longer behind my back. All I had to do now was find the boat.

The screams of the crowd disoriented me as I broke the surface. I gulped down breath after breath of air.

Where the fuck were they? Where was I for that matter?

"Tallis, Tallis!" Nerea's voice rose over the panicked crowd. "Over here, Tallis! We're over here!"

Her voice had come from my right. I rolled over in the water to try to locate her.

I finally spotted them as we passed through Erromon's Gate. Omar was already aboard, and Ora was helping Dario climb up the wing. I pointed myself in their direction, rolled onto my back, and kicked with all my might.

Alarm bells rang throughout the city as my head bumped against the wooden wing.

"Grab onto the balance shield and pull yourself up," Ora said. "It has notches carved into it to help you climb."

Once I got my upper body on top of the wing, Ora gripped me under my armpits and dragged me the rest of the way. I rolled into the hull of the boat face-first and collapsed on the floor. We had done it. We had actually done it.

"There's no time to waste," Nerea said. "It's only a matter of time until they send boats and riders after us. Find a seat and get pedaling so Ora can raise the shields."

My brow furrowed. What had she meant by pedaling?

I looked around the hull to see I was lying on the only flat strip in the whole boat. It ran down the center of it and had two sets of sunken seats on either side of it. A few feet in front of each seat was a strange contraption the others were pushing in circles with their feet.

I scooted my way to the front left seat and began to mimic their movement with my feet.

With us all properly seated and the shields connected above our heads, we focused on pedaling our way to safety.

"So where are we going to now?" I asked after a moment of silence.

Ora, who sat across the aisle from me, shrugged. "I have no idea. We honestly didn't have enough time to plan that far ahead."

"Anywhere is fine by me," said Nerea. "Does anyone have any preferences?"

Dario let out a low laugh. "As long as we go somewhere where people don't want to immediately kill us, then I'll be good."

"We need to go to a place with a bunch of rich, self-assured assholes," Omar added. "I've grown accustomed to a certain standard of living, and I can't give it up now."

"What about you, Tallis?" Ora asked.

As I glanced around our escape boat, the answer became abundantly clear. Cuvar had taken so much from us in the span of a little over a week. However, he also made me aware of the greatest gift I possessed.

"It doesn't matter where we go," I said. "Everything I'll ever need is on this boat."

Naturally, a chorus of boos and insults greeted my heartfelt answer.

"That's gross," said Omar. "We don't have a chamber pot in this thing. You can't spend the rest of your life shitting all over us."

A grin crossed Ora's beautifully scarred face. "No, that's what he has you for."

Our boat filled with laughter, and it would continue to do so as we joked and pedaled our way into the dark.

ACKNOWLEDGMENTS

A phrase I often hear in writing circles is that the process of writing a novel is a lonely endeavor. While that may be true during the first draft of the book, it never ceases to amaze me how many people have a hand in helping me finish a story by the time it is published. *Church of Thieves* would not be the same without them, and I'll try my best to thank you all.

The first person I always need to thank is my wonderful wife, Abby. You have been a blessing in my life for a magnitude of reasons. For the sake of not turning this acknowledgement section into its own novel, I'll focus on one of them. I love you for supporting my dreams. Life can be hard and unfair, and it has forced many people to stop pursuing what they truly want. There have been many times when I could have stopped or eased up on my writing dreams. However, your support has been a pillar that has enabled me to keep chasing my dreams.

The next group of people I would like to thank is my beta reading team which included Lucy, TM Ghent, Paige Lobianco (@paigebypagebooks), Monica (@moni.lib), and Kaitlyn Kelly (@katesbookstagram). Your insightful feedback enabled me to see my blindspots and, hopefully, produce the best possible version of this story.

As any of my students would gladly tell you, I like to ramble. As such, I need to next thank the people who helped refine my ramblings into the story you just finished.

They included my editor, Taylor, my proofreader, Irene, and my sensitivity reader, Kelsea Reeves. This story was infinitely better due to your feedback and guidance.

The next person I would like to thank is the myth, the legend, Rachel George. Although that might sound hyperbolic, you have earned those monikers in my eyes. Every time I received an email update for this cover it was like witnessing magic in stop motion. Each image slowly built off the previous one until we had the magnificent cover that graces this book. Thank you for all that you do, and I can't wait to see what you cook up for *Trial of Saints*.

As always, dear reader, the last person I need to thank is you. Sometimes, when I'm at a mental low point, I'll have intrusive thoughts that question why I even bother with writing. On days where my love of storytelling isn't enough to shut up that annoyingly snarky voice, I fall back on the knowledge that this story has reached your hands. That I haven't toiled away hours of my life dumping words into the void. Thank you for taking the time to read and support my art. It truly means the world to me.

Visit
ARREMENDIA
THE PEARL OF THE MOUNTAINS

ABOUT THE AUTHOR

IQ Malcolm is a YA/NA science fiction and fantasy author. Prior to committing to the genre, he dabbled in the realms of psychological thrillers (The Draxler Program) and middle-grade fantasy (The Land of Unlived Dreams).

When he isn't writing, Malcolm keeps himself busy by teaching middle schoolers in the southwest corner of Wisconsin. Outside of work, he enjoys spending time with his lovely wife, playing with their goldendoodle, and daydreaming of Jeff Probst putting an immunity necklace around his neck.

He lives in Platteville, Wisconsin. For more information, you can visit iqmalcolm.com or follow him on social media.

ALSO BY IQ MALCOLM

Made in the USA
Monee, IL
16 May 2023

c08e74e1-5507-4e78-bd1c-1ddccca72529R02